How to
Kill a Guy
in 10 Days

By Kayla Perrin and Brenda Mott

How to Kill a Guy in 10 Days

Also by Kayla Perrin

The Sweet Spot
Gimme an O!
Tell Me You Love Me
Say You Need Me
If You Want Me

How to Kill a Guy in 10 Days

KAYLA PERRIN & BRENDA MOTT

AVON

An Imprint of HarperCollins*Publishers*

HOW TO KILL A GUY IN 10 DAYS. Copyright © 2007 by Kayla Perrin and Brenda Mott. All rights reserved. Printed in the United States of America. No part of this book may be used or reproduced in any manner whatsoever without written permission except in the case of brief quotations embodied in critical articles and reviews. For information address HarperCollins Publishers, 10 East 53rd Street, New York, NY 10022.

HarperCollins books may be purchased for educational, business, or sales promotional use. For information please write: Special Markets Department, HarperCollins Publishers, 10 East 53rd Street, New York, NY 10022.

FIRST EDITION

Interior text designed by Diahann Sturge

Library of Congress Cataloging-in-Publication Data

Perrin, Kayla.
    How to kill a guy in 10 days / by Kayla Perrin and Brenda Mott.—1st ed.
      p. cm.
    ISBN: 978-0-06-088472-7
    ISBN-10: 0-06-088472-X
    1. Female friendship—Fiction.   I. Mott, Brenda.   II. Title.

    PR9199.3. P434H69 2007
    813'.54—dc22   2006036992

07 08 09 10 11 WBC/RRD 10 9 8 7 6 5 4 3 2 1

To Kayla, my "turtle sister," for all the laughs we shared in writing this book. I never had so much fun putting together a synopsis!

And to Lucia Macro and Helen Breitwieser, for seeing our vision through from plot to print.

—Brenda

This book is for my friend, Brenda Mott, with whom I had a blast coming up with this zany story. Thanks for the many, many laughs while plotting and writing this book. We make a great team!

And to girlfriends everywhere—this one's for you! So sit back with a margarita or a latte, read, and enjoy!

—Kayla

Prologue

Hailey

Nothing But Lies.

That's the name of the bookstore I own fifty percent of, a name my business partner and I thought was cute since we sell only fiction. Little did we know it would also fore-shadow events to come, events I hope we never have to experience again.

Lexie Muller is not only my business partner, she's my best friend. The bookstore is a large part of how we re-connected after twelve years, and to say I'm glad we did is an understatement. My name is Hailey McGraw, and now that I've hit the big three-oh, I've come to know what's important in life. Good friends, good books, and the ability to admit when you're wrong.

I was wrong when I married my ex-husband, but that's

another story. First, let me tell you how Lexie and I got to-gether, and how we came to own a bookstore called Noth-ing But Lies. It all began on a day that started with me setting out to shop the pet store for a mate for my turtle, Speedy, and ended with Lexie and me finding a body . . .

Lexie

I've heard that going through divorce is a lot like losing someone who has died. I wouldn't know, since I've never been married. I have lost loved ones, though, and by com-parison I have to say that from where I stand, some di-vorces are not so much like death as they are a rebirth. At least that's the way it seemed for my best friend, Hailey McGraw, when her marriage became a statistic. She was like a butterfly emerging from a cocoon the day her di-vorce became final.

That was a day full of excitement, a day full of hope. A day we decided to celebrate not only her rebirth, but my thirtieth birthday. Hailey had hit that big milestone eight months before me, before we'd met each other again by chance at a Miami bookstore. Who would've thought we'd ever reach the big three-oh, back when we were in high school and full of eternal youth?

Ah, but I digress. What I really want to tell you is how Hailey and I hooked up again after being apart for twelve years, and how we came to discover that "Party till you drop" can have a whole new meaning than the one intended . . .

One

Hailey

GOING OUT OF BUSINESS SALE.
ALL BOOKS 50%–75% OFF.

The sign in the window of Gina's Used Books snagged my attention the minute I pulled my pickup into the strip mall's parking lot. Abandoning my original idea of going to the pet store, I instead headed straight for Gina's. Wind chimes tinkled above the door as I entered, and the smell of cinnamon and coffee wafted across the air-conditioned room. Gina knows how to make her customers feel special, and the thought of her going out of business was enough to put me in a state of panic. I counted on her to provide me with my weekly fix of romance and mystery novels, which I'd purchased by the truckload from her since my high school days. And now that I'd come back to Miami for good, I'd expected to shop at her store once again. Who on earth would support my habit if Gina closed down?

Oh, sure, there was always Barnes & Noble, but there was something about Gina's store with its old-fashioned down-home charm—something that wasn't found on every corner of the busy streets of Miami—that appealed to me. Gina's made me feel like my grandmother had just sat me down in a corner of her country log home with an afghan, a good book, and a cup of café au lait. She couldn't go out of business! Not when I'd just returned to Miami.

My long legs ate up ground as I strode over the mint-colored carpet, straight for the front counter. Desperate times called for desperate measures, and I needed to make Gina see reason. I'd rally the customers around her, float her a loan, do whatever it took to keep her from shutting down my retreat, my solace, this store of my heart. Gina would listen to reason once I pointed out to her the ninety-nine reasons why she must stay open.

But before I could locate her, my gaze fell on a pretty black woman standing near the register as I approached the front counter. She was browsing a shelf of books on the display rack, and something about her profile jiggled my memory. She stood relaxed yet poised, as though she had not a care in the world, and as I drew close, she glanced at me, a polite smile curving her lips. Recognition registered in her expression at the exact moment a grin broke out on my own face.

Alexia Muller, my old high school friend. We'd become best buddies in eleventh grade, after she'd rescued me—the new kid from Sage Bend, Montana—from a group of bullies, and we'd grown closer as the years passed. But I hadn't seen her since I'd left Miami.

"Lexie?"

"Hailey!"

We leapt at each other at the same time, only Lexie's move was more of a glide. Unlike me, she's graceful, which I can only claim to be on the back of a horse. She's so damned pretty it's hard for strangers to see how down to earth she is at first glance. Lexie's one of those women you want to hate, but can't help liking within five minutes of striking up a conversation with her. Me, I always admired her looks in a way that I hoped wasn't green-eyed monsterish. Hey, if you've got it, flaunt it, and Lexie had it going on. I'd always loved hanging with her. She attracted men like ants to a picnic. And me—I had enough "cute" in my mirror to keep at least some of them sitting on my side of the picnic blanket. Or so Lexie had always told me.

"Girlfriend, what are you doing here?" She held me at arm's length, her five-foot-eight-inch frame balanced on a pair of cute melon-colored heels that brought her up to eye level to my five-ten.

"I can't believe it's really you!" I squeezed her in a bear hug, not wanting to let go. God, it had been a long time. Too long. No one should ever give up their girlfriends for a man—another lesson I'd learned the hard way when my

5

ex had dragged me back to battle the wilds of Montana just days after our city hall wedding.

"Are you living here again, or just on vacation?"

"I moved back six days ago," I said. My voice dropped to a serious tone. "Dad died."

Genuine sympathy creased Lexie's brow. "Oh, hon, I'm so sorry." She knew I'd lost Mom years ago when we were seniors. Mom's death was what made me give in to Travis when he'd driven all the way to Miami to be with me for the funeral, then convinced me to marry him and go back to Montana. I hadn't had much in the way of family, and now it was just me and my sister, Bailey, and her three darling children from hell.

"Thanks." I shrugged. "It was unexpected. He found out he had cancer and three weeks later he was gone."

"Oh." Lexie wrapped her arms around me and gave me a good long hug.

"But I'm okay," I insisted, pulling apart from her. "And the last thing I want to do is get all weepy and emotional, so why don't we grab a cup of coffee and catch up?"

Lexie smiled and pointed one neatly manicured fingernail at me. "You're on, girl."

I still wanted to talk to Gina, but that would have to wait. It wasn't every day you ran into your former best friend. And God, was it ever good to see Lexie again after all this time. I felt ashamed to have lost touch with her in the first place. But life has a way of interfering with your intentions, and these things happen.

Linking arms, we strolled to the corner of the shop

6

where Gina had a little coffee stand set up, complete with an old-fashioned counter and six cushioned stools. You could order coffee in every flavor imaginable. Customers got one free refill, but here's the really amazing part: the complimentary fresh-baked cookies. Yes, Gina baked them herself. So you could cozy up with a book or a friend, drink specialty coffee, *and* eat free cookies. That perk alone kept people coming back to the store. Believe me, I'd gotten a few extra pounds on my thighs because of it—pounds I'd managed to lose riding my horse. I'd left my trusty little mare in Sage Bend with friends, and now I missed her. But finding Lexie again had me feeling certain I'd made the right choice in coming back to Florida.

I spotted Gina chatting with a customer nearby and gave her a little wave as Lexie and I sat at the end of the counter. A girl who looked barely old enough to cross the street without her mother took our order. Then we settled in like old times, as if only twelve days rather than twelve years had passed between us.

"So, what are you doing back here?" Lexie asked without preamble. "I thought you and your cowboy were riding the happy trails of Montana together."

I grimaced. "He didn't turn out to be much of a cowboy, and the trails weren't so happy."

"Oh?" Lexie arched one eyebrow and flicked her long, straight, cinnamon-colored hair over her shoulder.

"He was more of a wannabe cowboy. I could outride him with my eyes closed!"

Lexie laughed. "No doubt, cowgirl."

"And his ranch turned out to be a run-down double-wide in the middle of nowhere. We barely had electricity, and that wasn't the worst of it . . ." I went on to fill her in on the woes of my almost-twelve-year marriage to Travis Hillerman, whom I'd met in my sophomore year of high school back in Sage Bend. Our whirlwind relationship began with too many tequilas snuck from the liquor cabinet of an unsuspecting parent of one of Travis's friends. One look into his eyes, the color of dark chocolate, fringed by lashes that would've been better justified on a woman, and I was a goner.

Then Mom got a job promotion that led to a transfer, and she'd happily uprooted me, Dad, and Bailey to move to Miami. Travis and I had pined for each other, racking up long-distance bills and writing sappy love letters—since the Internet hadn't quite yet made its way to small-town Montana. Then Mom had died, Travis had come to her funeral, and before I knew it, I'd found myself turning my back on all my friends, including Lexie. I'd simply gotten hitched and left without so much as a second thought.

Something I'd lived to regret.

Thank God there were no innocent children involved, which had been something Travis and I had fought over as well. I'd wanted them, he hadn't. Now I was grateful that no young lives were flung into upheaval over our divorce, though a part of me ached deep inside as my proverbial biological clock ticked at what seemed to be warp speed most of the time.

"My divorce became final on Wednesday," I finished.

Today was Friday. I'd been a free woman, reborn, recapturing my maiden name for an entire forty-eight hours. I wondered if Eddie Murphy would be interested in starring in the movie version.

Lexie clinked her coffee mug against mine in toast. "Here, here. I never did like Travis what's-his-name, anyway. Here's to being free of him."

We sipped our lattes. Lexie hadn't known Travis all that well, and I could only suspect that her real dislike for my ex had come from the fact that he'd not only taken me away, but he'd essentially taken my friendship away from her when I'd married him.

Gina hurried over a moment later, her eyes narrowing as she looked at me. "Hailey McGraw? Is that really you?"

I beamed. "Yes, ma'am."

"Good Lord, I thought my eyes were playing tricks on me." She wrapped her arms around me and squeezed me hard. "What are you doing back in town?"

"Trying to find myself." Briefly, I filled her in on Dad's death and my divorce.

She patted my hand. "I'm sorry to hear you've had such a run of hard luck. But it sure is good to see you again, regardless of why you're back in town. And it's good to see you too, Lexie, as always." She gave us both a warm smile. "You girls let me know if you need a refill."

Gina hustled away to take care of another customer. I still wanted to talk to her about the bookstore, but I supposed it would have to wait.

"So, what are you doing these days?" Lexie asked. "Jobwise, I mean."

"Nothing. Dad left me a pretty decent nest egg," I said sadly. "I'd like to do something meaningful with it. I just haven't decided what yet."

Concern streaked across her face. "Any kids?"

"No!" I exclaimed.

"Don't sound so startled. You're definitely the mothering type."

"One day . . . hopefully." For now, I had Speedy to give lots of love.

"With the right man," Lexie offered. Her warm expression made me feel better about the whole prospect. She was right.

"And you? I'm sure you've got a hot man, but I want to hear about your fabulous career. Because I know you've got one. Are you an actress, like you always wanted to be?"

"Well," Lexie began. "Sort of."

"You *are* an actress!" I exclaimed, but tamped down on my excitement when I saw her wary expression. "What's the matter? You should be proud. Unless you're doing something crazy like . . ." I giggled at the thought suddenly floating in my mind. When she didn't smile, my eyebrows shot up. Oh, God, no. "Unless . . . Lexie, you're not—I mean, you *wouldn't*—"

"Do anything crazy like work in the porn business?" she supplied in a lowered voice.

She didn't even blink, and my heart stopped. "Lexie!"

"Hush, girl! I'm not that insane. Nor that desperate to be a 'star.' It's just that I'm not exactly doing the kind of work I want or can be proud of. I guess you could call me the commercial queen."

She mimed twirling something in her hand, and instantly a lightbulb went off in my brain. "Ohmygod!" I stared at her. "You're the Twirly-Brush Girl! Every time I saw that commercial, I *thought* she looked like you!"

She chuckled wryly. "Yeah, well, I'm her. And the Tidy Toilet Woman. *And* the Zippy Zipper Bag Mom." She shrugged. "It pays pretty well, which is nice, but it's not exactly my ideal career. Either I get calls for all these bimbo roles, which I *don't* want to do, or it's commercials. At least commercials pay residuals."

"I got ya." I heard the frustration in her voice, but still I was impressed. My friend—the commercial queen. How cool was that?

"And what about that hot man?" I asked a moment later.

Lexie held up her left hand and wiggled her fingers. "No ring."

"That doesn't mean—"

"Yes, it does."

Well, that was shocking. With her looks, how could she not have a man? Contemplating just that, I reached for my latte on the counter. From the corner of my eye, I noticed a woman approaching the coffee bar. A *big* woman, and I don't mean fat! She was at least six feet tall, not counting her four-inch, ruby-red stiletto heels. And she filled out the dress she wore with as much pizzazz as Marilyn Monroe. It was short and sassy, and also red, flowing around the knees to add a delicate flavor to the definite sex appeal. My eyes went lower, taking in a set of legs that I couldn't help but envy. The woman was definitely stunning. Her long red hair was thick and beautiful, and went well with her pretty blue eyes and amazingly long eyelashes.

As the woman slid onto a stool a few seats away, she caught me staring and gave me a little wink. Embarrassed, I offered a quick smile and turned back to Lexie. "Oh, God. I think she thought I was checking her out," I whispered. "But I couldn't help staring. It's not often I see a woman taller than me. Do you think she's a model?"

"No." Lexie smirked as she leaned in close. "But you'll never guess who it is," she added in a singsong voice.

"Some movie star?" I asked. I wouldn't be surprised. I preferred old movies to contemporary ones, and didn't know many of today's young stars.

"Remember Gina's nephew? Joey?"

"Joey Coletti? Oh, yeah." I chuckled at the memory of the kid who'd had a huge crush on both of us when we were in high school. "He used to follow us around like a lovesick puppy. What was he, about thirteen when we graduated?"

"About that."

I looked blankly at her. "So, what? Is that his wife or something?" Unobtrusively, I nodded toward the redhead. "You're not telling me that Joey married some big star!"

Lexie pursed her lips, smothering a giggle. "Honey, you've been away from Miami far too long. *That*," she said, also nodding in the redhead's direction, "is Josephine. AKA Joey."

I nearly got whiplash spinning my head around for a second look. Again, Joey/Josephine caught my eye and winked. My face flamed. I gave him/her a weak smile and hurriedly sipped my latte.

I took a moment to let the truth settle over me, then said in an excited hush, "You have got to be kidding!"

"Nope."

"I don't believe it."

Lexie arched a brow and kept her voice low as she said, "I hear he likes to swing both ways, if you know what I mean."

I nearly choked on my drink. "Good Lord!" I *had* been in Montana too long.

"Yeah, times have changed," Lexie went on. "But this is Miami, where crazy shit happens."

"A far cry from Sage Bend!"

We both laughed.

"I hear he's even dating a hot Cuban stripper."

I blinked. "You said 'he.' So, what . . . is Joey a cross-dresser or a transsexual?"

Lexie leaned closer. "He's sort of midprocedure. Actually, Josephine prefers to be referred to as 'she.' She's had the breast implants but not the, shall we say, big one—if you know what I mean."

I cringed and held up one hand. "TMI, girlfriend."

Joey was now a woman and was dating a stripper. *Holy honkin' horny toads!*

I studied Josephine from the corner of my eye. She and Gina spoke for a moment, then Gina handed her a sack of cookies and a large latte to go. Josephine sauntered past us, a Fendi purse on one arm, the bag of cookies tucked under the other. Her fingernails curled around the large paper cup, long and polished to match her dress and shoes.

"Ladies," she purred as she passed us by. "Been a long time."

Not long enough! "Yeah." My voice came out as a croak, so I cleared my throat. "Nice to see you, Joe—Josephine."

She winked at me again, then strutted her stuff out the door like she was on the catwalk.

The moment Josephine disappeared from the bookstore, Lexie bent over in a silent fit of giggles.

"Shut up," I said. "It's not funny."

"I think he . . . she . . . still has the hots for you. Woo, girl!"

I couldn't help but laugh with her. "What can I say? I've still got it, even if I'm not twenty-something anymore." I raised my latte in a self-toast, and Lexie shot me a grin that I remembered all too well. One that had often led us into trouble.

"You know, I hate to admit this, but I'm about to hit the big three-oh myself." She lowered her voice so as not to spread the news for the entire coffee counter to hear. "On

Monday. And I was thinking I ought to go out and have a little fun this weekend to celebrate."

"That's right. Your birthday. I'm so bad at remembering dates." I leaned forward and squeezed her hand. "Happy early birthday, babe."

"Ah! You still do that!"

"Do what?" I asked.

"That thing with your nose. The bunny look."

"Oh, you." I lightly swatted Lexie's knee. She always liked to tease me about my upturned nose. Said that when I wrinkled it, it made me look like a little bunny. What could I say? Upturned noses run in my family.

"It's still cute," Lexie assured me.

"Thanks," I said wryly.

"So what do you say?" Lexie asked. "Want to celebrate?"

"My nose?"

"No, silly." Lexie shook her head. "My birthday. You only hit the big three-oh once. Not that it's necessarily celebratory, but there's also your news. You're a free woman now. I say we par-tay!"

"I say you're on!" Lexie's excitement was contagious, and I grinned. Turtle-shopping would have to wait for another day. "So what do we do? Pick up a couple of wild men and hit the clubs? Are you sure you're not dating anyone?" I asked, narrowing my eyes suspiciously. "Even casually?" It was just so hard to believe.

"I'm *always* dating casually," Lexie said. She blew onto

15

her fingernails in a boastful gesture, then polished the nails on her shirt. Then she laughed. "But who needs a man on the scene when we can have a whole parade of them?" She wriggled her brows suggestively.

"Are you thinking . . ." I chuckled. My mind was certainly in the gutter today, but that was the vibe I was getting. I leaned forward and whispered, "A strip club?"

"Why not? Seeing Josephine made me remember that it's been too long." She bit her bottom lip in a motion that said we deserved eye candy. "Can you think of a better way to celebrate than naked men strutting their stuff at eye level?"

"Not one thing," I confirmed. I covered my mouth and blushed when I realized I'd spoken with such enthusiasm. "But you mean near-naked men, don't you?" I think my voice rose on a hopeful note. It had been a while since I'd seen anyone without clothes on. The only naked creature in my house these days was Speedy, my Red-Eared Slider, and even he never left home without his shell.

There was that mischievous look again. "Well, officially, yes. But I know a club in North Miami Beach—Fantasies—where the men get a little wild sometimes. Girl, they take it *all* off!"

"Ohmygod, please tell me you didn't hear about it from Joey."

She laughed. "None other. Actually, seeing him is what gave me the idea."

A strip club? One recommended by Joey? "But are the men—"

"Gorgeous and hot-blooded? Oh, yeah!"

"What the hell?" I downed my latte as though it were a shot of tequila, no longer caring who might hear our lewd conversation. I needed this. I *deserved* this. "What time do they open and what are we gonna wear?"

Two

Lexie

I've seen some fine men in my time, and a lot of them have been naked, but the brother strutting his stuff in front of me made me feel like I was a virgin again.

One eager to be deflowered.

"Oh, my word. That can't possibly be his . . . I mean, it's got to be stuffed. How could it be so . . ."

"Huge?" I supplied, chuckling at Hailey's wide-eyed stare.

"*Huge?* It's as big as the state of Florida!"

"That it is." As I sighed with pleasure, my gaze wandered back to the hottie on stage. He put the *f* in fine, and that was no joke. I couldn't help wondering how it would feel to be naked with him, those strong arms wrapped

18

around my body, his lethal weapon pressed against my thighs . . .

"Ooh, baby!" I howled.

He looked at me and winked, then ripped the fire-red G-string off in one strong pull. I gripped Hailey's hand and squealed.

"Oh, Lord," Hailey said, fanning herself. "He can put his boots under my bed anytime!"

"I think I've died and gone to heaven."

We watched in awe as Mr. Too Fine gyrated his body in the most suggestive of manners, then did push-ups against the floor as if he were making love. It was all very arousing, reminding me that it had been at least six weeks since I'd last made love.

Too soon the act ended, and the stripper exited the stage. Hailey stuck her fingers in her mouth and whistled. I clapped until my hands were sore.

"I'm so glad you suggested this, Lex." Hailey pulled a leg onto the booth's seat as she faced me. She was dressed in jeans and a halter top and the cowboy boots I saw her in earlier today. "I haven't had this much fun in . . . in forever!"

I chuckled as I looked at her. She seemed totally happy and carefree. Yeah, she needed this. We both did.

I can't tell you how glad I was that fate put us together again. Not to get sappy, but I loved Hailey like a sister. I missed her terribly when she was gone.

But she was back now, and it was just like old times.

"Cheers," I said, lifting my cosmopolitan.

"Cheers!" Hailey tapped her beer bottle against my glass.

I took a good long sip as the emcee announced the next act. Then I lowered my glass, clinking it loudly on the table.

Shaking her head, Hailey raised an eyebrow at me.

"What?" I asked. "I'm not drunk."

"That's not what I was thinking."

"Then why are you looking at me like that, with one eye narrowed?"

"I'm wondering why you don't have a boyfriend."

"Oh," I said, rolling my eyes. "Not that again."

"I can't understand it," Hailey continued. "Look at you. You're so beautiful. You make a simple black dress look like it's a million bucks. I figured guys would be tripping over themselves to get to you."

"Why commit when there are so many to play with?" I glanced at the new stripper and watched him take off his blindfold. He was dressed like Don Quixote, a hot look if you ask me.

"You sure that's it? No one's broken your heart?"

"Honey, *I* break the hearts." In fact, it's a policy of mine—not to get too attached. My mother had been that way with my daddy—too attached—and when he left her for someone half her age in New York, she'd had a meltdown. No way—that's not gonna happen to me. So I play with men, enjoy them, and dump them before things can go stale. It's worked for me, so why fix what ain't broke?

20

Frenzied cries pierced the air, and Hailey and I looked to the stage. Don Quixote had just ripped off his shirt, exposing a wall of hard muscles. *Mmm*, I thought, instantly perking up. This hot Hispanic man was the best kind of eye candy.

He trailed both hands over his delectable chest, then slipped his thumbs beneath the waist of his pants. In one smooth movement, he ripped them off. I got so hot, I would have melted if I were a stick of butter.

Unable to stop myself, I made a funnel around my mouth with my hands and yelled, "Take it *all* off, baby!"

"Lexie!" Hailey smacked me on the arm. "Let him do his little dance first. I like the whole dance routine."

"Oh, my God."

"What—I can't enjoy the dancing? I happen to think—"

"That's not what I'm talking about," I said.

"Then what?"

I leaned in close and whispered, "What if we're getting all hot for this guy and he's . . . he's Joey's boyfriend?"

Hailey gasped. "You think so?"

I shrugged. "Could be. He *does* work here."

Hailey stared at the dancer, her nose upturned as she thought about my words. Then she shook her head vehemently and said, "No way. He's too hot."

"*Much* too hot," I quickly agreed.

"And look at those abs."

"You know he got them working out—on a woman."

"Wom*en*," Hailey corrected.

"The dog!" I joked. Thank God we'd salvaged the

fantasy. "But I don't care about his sexual conquests, he can strut his stiff for me all he wants. It's all about the eye candy, and he's as sweet as they come."

"Here here!" Hailey agreed. She lifted her beer bottle before taking a long swig.

"And speaking of which . . ." I dug a bill out of my purse and waved it over Hailey's head.

"Lexie! N-no!" But Hailey's protest died on a fit of giggles as the Latin hottie strutted toward her.

"Take a good look, honey," I told her. "It's all about the eye candy, remember. And forgetting that Travis what's-his-face ever existed."

"Travis who?"

Grinning, I lifted my cosmopolitan. "That's what I'm talking about."

After I took a sip, my eyes settled on the dancer. I have a thing for Latin men, and this one didn't fail to turn me on. He was Don Quixote, after all—hot, conquering stud.

Wearing a sexy smile, Don danced before us like he was sin and seduction rolled into one. He moved his hands over his stomach, then lower, to the scrap of material that hung over his erection. His fingers lingered on the leather thong, and I practically salivated, knowing he wasn't going to disappoint.

Off went the G-string. Hailey screamed.

I couldn't help laughing. Even the Latin lover chuckled as he lowered himself before us and stroked Hailey's cheek.

Hailey slumped in her chair as the stripper walked away. "Oh. My. God."

"You can say that again."

"Travis always told me the average guy's penis is five and half inches."

"Maybe the average guy's, but that was no average guy." I glanced at the stage, taking in a delicious view of the Latin lover's butt. I sighed. It'd be nice to take him home.

Hey, a woman can fantasize.

Not that I hadn't actually taken a stripper home before. Well, two—if I'm completely honest. But that's another story.

Hailey fluffed her hair, the way one might post-sex. "Good Lord, I've been missing out."

"That's what you get for marrying the first guy to sweep you off your feet. Now do you see why I play the field? Variety is the spice of life."

"Waiter!" Hailey snapped her fingers as a beefcake wearing a bow tie and spandex shorts strolled by our table. "Can we get another round of tequila shooters? Actually, make it a double round."

He flashed a charming smile before stepping away from our table, and I realized why I enjoyed going to a strip club on occasion. The guys here are always smiling, like their only desire is to satisfy you. Yeah, I know—that's the fantasy they sell—but given that in my life the fantasy hasn't lasted longer than three months, it's nice to buy into it every now and then.

Even if I don't believe in long-term relationships.

I laid my head back against the softness of the leather booth seat. "Are you having a good time?" I asked Hailey.

"Are you kidding? This is exactly what I needed. I can't think of a better way to celebrate my divorce."

Maybe it was the alcohol, but I suddenly got wistful. My eyes actually misted. "You believe in fate?"

"I can't say I do."

"Well, I didn't—until right now. You don't know how I've missed having you in my life, Hailey. There were so many times I could have used your levelheaded advice over the years."

"And there were many times I could have used a dose of your wild side."

The waiter returned with the shots, and we both downed them, then grimaced. We'd take a cab if we had to, but to-night was a night for catching up and celebrating.

"I should eat something," I told Hailey. "A cosmopolitan and tequila . . . could be a lethal combination if I don't get something in me."

"Something like that Latin lover?"

I roared with laughter. "I think you're the one who needs a palate-cleanser. You know, to wash away the memory of Travis."

Hailey's gaze wandered to the stage. As she watched the next stripper, her expression grew thoughtful.

"Hmm," I said hopefully. "So you're considering it?"

"It'd be nice," Hailey admitted.

"I won't tell anyone if you take a stripper home."

The Latin lover strolled by, and Hailey eyed him dreamily. Once the guys were finished onstage, they made the rounds on the floor, looking for women who wanted a private dance.

"I'd settle for a private dance from Don Quixote," Hailey said. "He's just too gorgeous."

"You're on," I told her.

I was out of my chair in a flash and all but ran after the guy. Brushing my fingers across his arm, I got his attention. He turned, smiling at me as he did.

He had the most amazing chocolate-brown eyes. In fact, they caught me off guard up close, leaving me speechless for a moment.

I cleared my throat. "Hey, sweetheart. My friend and I would love a private dance."

"No problem, sugar."

This was fantasyland, so I boldly took his hand as if he were my lover. I led him to the booth where Hailey still sat.

"This is Hailey," I announced. "And I'm Lexie."

"And I am Rafael."

His voice had a distinctive Spanish lilt, the kind that would definitely turn me on in the bedroom.

"Do your thing, Rafael. And don't hold back. Hailey's getting over a bad marriage."

For an entire song, Rafael entertained. On the floor, they don't take off their G-strings. Which wasn't a problem. He was sweet enough to look at regardless. Sweet enough to caress with innocent strokes on those rock-hard abs.

25

"Thank you, darling," Hailey said when Rafael was done. "I needed that." She passed him a twenty.

"Anytime."

Both Hailey and I sighed as the hottie strolled away.

For the next hour, we enjoyed an array of strippers, but I was starting to get light-headed and knew I needed some food. The strip joint served appetizers, but I wasn't in the mood to eat there. Besides, the cigarette smoke and stale air from the club were getting to me, and I needed a change of scenery.

I downed the last of my drink, then turned to Hailey and said, "What do you say we get something to eat? There's an all-night pancake joint right across the street."

"Sounds like a plan. I've had my fill of candy. Now I need something solid in my stomach."

We settled our bill, and minutes later we were outside. The fresh air was a welcome change from inside the club. It was sobering, but still I wobbled a little on my three-inch heels as Hailey and I walked arm in arm toward the parking lot.

"We driving?" Hailey asked.

"Noddachance." My words came out as one long slurred one. I pointed to the pancake house across the street. "That's the restaurant. Right there."

"Ah, good."

"That was fun, wasn't it?" I asked as we started across the parking lot. "All those hard, sweating bodies. All those men wanting to please—"

I stopped talking, abruptly halting.

"What?" Hailey asked.

"Oh, hell." I squeezed my legs tightly together. "I've gotta pee."

"Yeah, okay. The restaurant's not that far."

"Maybe not . . . but I gotta pee *now*."

"Girl," Hailey said, "you can't wait?"

"That's the thing with drinking alcohol. One minute you're fine, the next you gotta go *right now*." I did a little dance on the spot and Hailey started to giggle. "Stop laughing and stand guard!"

I took a deep breath to get my bladder under control as best I could. Then I darted for an area of the parking lot bordered by shrubs. I hoisted my dress up and pulled my panties out of the way, hoping I wouldn't splash my three-hundred-dollar Gucci stilettos. Hailey was laughing her head off as she stood guard between two cars. I couldn't help chuckling too.

"Whoo, what a relief," I proclaimed when I was finished—a little too loudly, given my inebriated state. Standing, I righted my clothes. That's when I noticed something peeking out of the bushes. I knew I'd had one too many tequilas, but what I saw looked like . . .

Like a foot.

"Lexie?" Hailey asked, her tone wary.

"I think I see something," I said.

"You're durnk—I mean drunk." She hiccupped. "That's what happens when you have too many cosmos. And tequilas. Damn those tequilas . . ."

"No, I definitely see something."

Hailey took a step forward and angled her head, like she was afraid that something might jump out at her without warning. "What?"

"It's a shoe!" I cried.

Hailey screamed and jumped backward. Then she calmed down, saying, "A shoe?" Her relief was palpable. "Geez, girl. I thought you were talking about something worse."

"I am." Two words, but they filled me with panic. "That's not just a shoe. There's a leg attached to it." My heart beat rapidly as a sick feeling swept over me.

"A . . ." Hailey appeared at my side. "A leg? Like a leg leg?"

"What other kind of leg is there?" I asked.

"I don't know. A frog's leg. Or a dog's leg. Or a hog's."

I looked at her, and she frowned, as though her own words didn't make sense to her. "A hog's leg?" I asked disbelievingly.

"Yeah."

We both started laughing.

I gripped her hand, getting serious again. "Hailey, this isn't funny. I think this is a man's leg." I pointed. "Look."

She gasped. "That's a man's leg, all right."

"So someone's under the bushes?" I asked in a frightened whisper.

"Passed out, right? I mean, he's got to be. Unless he's a rapist hiding out waiting for women who can't hold their bladders—"

"Shh!" I instructed Hailey. I needed to think. Whether

this guy was a passed-out drunk or a psycho, I had to find out. Summoning courage—mostly liquid—I moved forward and pushed the bushes aside.

And then I screamed. "Hailey!"

"Oh, Jesus in heaven." Hailey clamped her hand on my arm.

There was a body in the bushes, all right. And not just any body.

It was the fully clad body of our Latin lover, his striking brown eyes lifeless as they stared toward the night sky.

Three

Hailey

"Ohmygod, ohmygod!" I covered my mouth with my hand, my stomach whirling. Suddenly I wasn't so hungry anymore. "I think I'm going to be sick."

Gagging, the beer and tequila shooters I'd consumed earlier mixing wildly inside my stomach, I staggered away from the body of Don Quixote and retched near the edge of the bushes.

Nervously, Lexie patted my back, her brown eyes round and horrified, reflecting my own disbelief as she glanced back at the dead stripper. Like rubberneckers at the scene of an accident, neither of us could tear our gaze away. "You okay?" Lexie asked.

"Me, I'm fine. Him, I'm not so sure of." I nodded in the direction of the bushes as I fished a tissue from my pocketbook to wipe my mouth. Then panic seized me and I dug my fingers into Lexie's arm. "Oh, shit, Lexie. A body!" I gestured wildly. "And you peed and I puked and our DNA is all over the place! Don't you watch *CSI: Miami*? Oh, shit. Horatio is going to be coming around the corner any minute. They'll arrest us. Come on, we've got to get out of here!"

"Calm down," Lexie said, gripping my arm as well. "We can't just leave him here."

"Oh, yes, we can." My head throbbed and the parking lot tilted dangerously. Swaying on my feet, I steadied myself, using Lexie for balance. "I had that guy do a private dance for me—*you* had him do a private dance for me. Ohmygod, we're both going to jail!"

"Hailey," Lexie said firmly. "Stop." She took hold of both my arms this time, giving me a little shake.

I blinked stupidly at her, my heart racing in time with my swirling stomach. I fought the urge to look back at the body in the bushes. "What are we going to do?" But before Lexie could answer, headlights appeared, and a moment later a spotlight shone in our direction. My breath left my lungs. And my heart stopped beating altogether—I swear.

A Miami Beach cruiser pulled up close, its spotlight blinding as one of two officers raked the damned thing over us. I felt like we were onstage in a really bad play. Never mind *Arsenic and Old Lace*. How about *Two Drunks and a Dead Stripper*?

"We saw you from the road," the cop on the driver's

side said. I couldn't make out his face for the glare of the light. "You ladies all right?"

I raised my hand to shield my eyes, and my throat closed up so tight I couldn't answer.

"We're fine, Officer," Lexie said, smiling sweetly.

That's it, babe. Charm him. Lexie's wiles always worked. She could wrap any man around her little finger.

But the officers didn't drive off. Instead, they angled the spotlight on the bushes. It came to rest on Don Quixote's feet, sticking out of the foliage.

Damn!

Now the cruiser's doors were flying open, and both cops leapt out of the car. They approached us with purpose. All I could do was stand there looking stupid. Panic had a tight grip on my throat, preventing any speech. Lexie and I were doomed. We were headed for prison, sure as anything. I knew she'd look good even in jailhouse orange, but the thought was little comfort.

Get a hold of yourself! my inner voice scolded.

Lexie came to the rescue. "Thank God you showed up, Officers." She clutched her perfectly manicured hand to her D-cup breasts. "We might be fine, but he's not." She pointed to the corpse, stating the obvious.

"What happened here?" The first officer, whose badge I could finally see read SCHAEFER, glanced at Lexie, eyes narrowed.

"I have no idea." Lexie's own eyes widened in exaggerated innocence. And damn it, I almost started laughing.

We *were* innocent, and trying to make that point, so

naturally she should look that way. But for some reason, I felt near hysteria as the same sort of laughter that can plague you at an inappropriate moment—say in the middle of a church sermon or a finals exam—bubbled up inside of me and threatened to surface. Lexie reached over and subtly pinched my arm, bringing me under control.

"You know this guy?" the second officer—Montoya—asked.

"No," I said.

"Yes," Lexie admitted, at the same time.

Schaefer raised his eyebrows and surveyed us skeptically.

"I—I mean, no, we don't *really* know him," I stuttered. "We got a little cozy inside the club with him, but nothing that would make us bosom buddies or anything."

"We just met him tonight," Lexie pointed out. "In the strip club." She pointed to the bar we'd left several minutes earlier. Minutes that felt like hours. "He's a dancer. That's what my friend means by cozy." She glanced my way.

"Yes, all that dim lighting and those leather sofas everywhere. It has a cozy living-room feel. Except with naked guys dancing around. I mean, guys with G-strings," I quickly amended, wondering if it was legal for the guys to take it all off. I looked to Lexie as I rambled. "Of course, they're not totally naked . . ." *Right?* I added with my eyes, hoping Lexie would help me out with this one.

She elbowed me.

"Hmmm." I couldn't detect from Schaefer's tone what

he was thinking, but the suspicious way he continued to look at us told me a lot. "Don't go anywhere, ladies." He scowled at us again, then spoke into the radio attached to the shoulder of his shirt. He rattled off a couple of official-sounding codes and requested backup.

Great. Just. Great.

Montoya poked his nightstick among the bushes, now shining his flashlight on poor dead Don Quixote. I couldn't resist a quick peek of my own, and I noted that Quixote was wearing black pants, a white shirt open at the chest, and black shoes. His equally black hair, thick and wavy, lay plastered against his skin as though he'd been sweating. The Florida humidity hung thick in the night as usual, but he looked like he'd been sweating beyond the norm. What on earth had happened to him?

I didn't see any blood or bruises, no sign of violence or a struggle. But his eyes—open yet seeing nothing—told a haunting tale.

Montoya turned off his flashlight and faced us once more beneath the fluorescent glow of the parking lot lights. He flipped open a notebook and took a pen from his pocket, then gestured at me. "I need you to step over here for a moment."

I gulped, pointing at myself. Suddenly I couldn't speak again.

"Yeah, I'm talking to you." He spoke as though I were dense. "Please don't tell me you're hearing-impaired."

"Her, hearing-impaired?" Lexie laughed airily. "Not a chance. Why, she . . . she's in shock!"

Schaefer, who appeared to be in his early thirties, looked Lexie up and down. But even his obvious appreciation of her good looks didn't stop him from speaking to her in a firm tone of voice. "You—you're gonna stay right here with me. I need to ask you a few questions."

Divide and conquer. Lexie and I exchanged nervous glances, then I numbly followed Montoya over to a place just out of earshot from Lexie.

"Okay," he said, pen poised. "Tell me what happened."

I cleared my throat, wishing for some water. "Whoa, where do I start?" And thank the Lord, I had my voice back.

"The beginning," Montoya instructed me.

I gave him a recap of our evening as best I could remember. My brain was gradually beginning to unfog—probably as a result of the shock that had jolted me damn near into sobriety. Yet my head still felt funny, like it was stuffed full of cotton candy.

"When was the last time you saw this guy—Quixote?" Montoya's scowl said he was sure I was hiding something.

Which I was. I was hiding the fact that I still felt like puking. "You mean alive?"

His scowl deepened. "That's exactly what I mean. Unless you saw him dead before now."

"No!" I wondered vaguely if Lexie and I would share the same jail cell, and if we'd have cellmates named Bertha and Helga. "We—we saw him dance, and that was it. He left the stage and another dancer took his place." I shrugged, purposely leaving out the part about getting a private dance from the guy. "We left a couple hours later, came out, and Lexie had to pee. Like immediately. She had no choice but to run for the bushes. That's when she noticed the body. You showed up right after that."

Montoya took some notes, asked a few more questions, and even wanted to see my ID. Then, with a nod of his head in Lexie and Schaefer's direction, he invited me to head back over there.

I immediately took Lexie's hand. The two cops spoke to one another in low tones. Then Montoya addressed me once more.

"What did you say this guy's name is?"

"Um . . ." I gulped. "Don Quixote?"

"*You* said his name was Rafael," Schaefer accused Lexie.

She and I exchanged glances. "It is," we said in unison.

"Quixote is just his stage name," I added.

"I thought you said you didn't know him."

"We don't," Lexie and I spoke in unison again.

I wondered if Schaefer and Montoya were planning to run us in, stick us underneath a row of bright lights, and feed us stale coffee until we confessed. Suddenly I longed for Sage Bend, with its one sheriff and two deputies, where everyone knew everybody.

About that time, an ambulance arrived—a pretty futile addition to the chaos, if you ask me. Then three more squad cars pulled up, lights flashing, and surrounded the area. Schaefer and Montoya went over to fill them in, and things got even crazier as the CSI unit arrived.

I know my face went completely pale when I saw their van, because Lexie took me by the arm.

"Hailey, are you okay, sweetie?"

"I think I'm gonna faint."

"No, you're not." She braced me up by crooking my hand through her elbow. "Do you think they'll notice if we leave?" she continued in a conspiratorial whisper.

As though reading our thoughts, Schaefer strode over to talk to us again. "I think we've got enough information from you ladies for the moment." I half expected him to warn us not to leave town. "If we need you to answer further questions, we'll be in touch." He handed us each his business card. "If you think of anything else that might be helpful, give us a call."

"Thanks." Lexie flashed him a brilliant smile, then tugged me by the arm. "Come on." She lowered her voice. "Let's get out of here."

Our appetites gone, we headed for the street. Lexie pulled her cell phone from her purse to call a cab, but I spotted one passing by and flagged it down. The driver had big round eyes like a beetle—and I'm not talking John or Ringo.

"Where can I take you ladies?" His gaze locked on Lexie's hemline and I shot him a firm stare that had him rethinking his attitude.

Lexie looked at me. "Where are we going?"

I sure didn't relish the thought of going home alone

after what had happened. "Want to go to my place?" I asked. I needed to go home and feed my turtle. Hopefully Speedy would forgive the fact that I'd gotten sidetracked that day and hadn't ended up buying him a mate. Of course, Speedy probably wouldn't understand any talk of dead bodies and running into old friends.

Lexie shrugged. "Sure. You have to tell me what that cop asked you."

"Lexie . . . not here." I gestured toward the cabdriver, who was eavesdropping, watching us in the rearview mirror as though wondering if Lexie and I had a thing going. Hoping, probably—the slime. I glared at his reflection and he averted his eyes to stare out the windshield. I gave him my address and he sped down the street.

A short while later, as we were cruising south on Collins, I tapped Lexie on the shoulder. "Hey, look." I pointed. "There's a light on in Gina's bookstore."

The driver stopped at a light, and Lexie leaned forward to peer through the window. "What in the world is she doing there at this hour?"

"She *wouldn't* be there at this hour. The store closes at seven."

My already overactive imagination—fueled by what had just happened to Rafael/Quixote—went into overdrive. This *was* Miami, after all, and there were plenty of creeps on the streets.

"Pull over!" I shouted to the cabdriver. "Now!"

Four

Lexie

"Hailey . . ." I stared at her, wondering what she was thinking. "You don't really think—"

"Something's wrong," she blurted. "Maybe someone broke into Gina's. Oh, God. What if they've hurt her?"

I stared out the window, and wouldn't you know it, there was a full moon. "We're both shaken up right now—"

"It's two in the morning. Since when did Gina start opening all hours? Or have things changed since I've been away?"

The light turned green. The driver asked, "What do you want me to do?"

"Turn around, please. And pull us into that strip mall in front of the store with the light on. The bookstore. Thanks."

The cabdriver did a U-turn, drove a short distance, then turned left into the parking area of the small strip mall. As he came to a stop in front of Gina's store, Hailey already had her hand on the door handle.

"Wait one second, Sherlock." I took her by the arm. "Shouldn't we call the police? If someone *is* in there—"

"Are you kidding? After what we just went through with Starsky and Hutch? I don't think so."

And then Hailey was out of the car, hunkering down in a semi-crouch as she slunk toward the bookstore window.

I passed the cabdriver some money. "My friend . . . she doesn't get out much," I explained. "And she reads all these crime novels, it's like she thinks she's some kind of detective." I didn't want this guy thinking we were up to no good.

"You want me to wait?" he asked, his disgusting gaze crawling over my skin.

"No. We'll be fine."

He winked at me as he drove off. At least he didn't insist on sticking around.

"Come on!" Hailey called to me in an urgent whisper. Keeping to one side near the window's edge, she peered around through the glass. "Oh, my God."

"What?" I crept toward Hailey. "Please, no more bodies!"

"No, it's Gina. She's packing!"

I glanced into the store. There stood Gina amid boxes of books, packing up the shelves. I knew she was selling the store, but how odd for her to be packing in the middle of the night.

Hailey's eyes flew to mine. "I had no idea she was going out of business *that* fast." Hailey stepped in front of the window and rapped on the glass with her knuckles.

Gina whirled to face us, eyes wide. She clamped one hand to her breast and briefly closed her eyes, then, muttering something under her breath, came to the door and opened it.

"Lordy, you scared the tar out of me, Hailey! What on earth are you doing here at this hour?" Her gaze fell on me. "Lex, you too?" Gina gestured. "Come in, come in."

We hustled inside and Gina relocked the door behind us.

"We saw your lights and thought something was wrong," I said. "Gina, you're *packing*."

"Yeah." She nodded as though to emphasize the obvious, then gestured around her at the markdown signs. "That's why I've been holding a going-out-of-business sale."

"But you're already packing," I said, still puzzled. "Like you're ready to leave right now or something."

Gina shrugged. "I'm not clearing out completely for another week. I just thought I'd organize a few things . . . take inventory and decide what I might want to keep for personal use."

"A week!" I exclaimed. "Gina, I had no idea you were even closing the store until I walked in today. What's going on that this is all so rushed?"

Gina sank onto a stool at the coffee counter. "I can't

deal with it all anymore," she said, looking more worn and tired than I'd ever seen her look. The Gina I knew was always chipper and very Pollyannaish.

I covered her hand with mine. "Is something wrong?"

"Everything." She sighed deeply. "You two want a latte? It's on the house."

My stomach growled, reminding me that Hailey and I had been on our way to get some food when we'd found Rafael dead in the bushes. "I'd love one."

"Me too," Hailey echoed. "And some water, please." She made a face that said she still had a bad taste in her mouth.

Gina whipped up three of the frothy drinks, then re-joined us. Handing a bottle of water to Hailey, she leaned on the counter across from us while we sat.

"So, what's going on?" Hailey coaxed in her soft, sweet voice. She had a way of making you feel that she'd under-stand any problems you cared to lay on her strong shoul-ders. It wasn't like her to panic the way she had when we'd found Quixote in the bushes.

"Like I said, everything." Gina slumped once more, stirring her latte with a wooden stick. "My mom is sick, my brother is an irresponsible idiot, and then there's my ex, who's been dogging me for money. I just can't take it anymore."

"What's wrong with your mother?" I asked.

"Heart problems. She's always had a weak ticker. She needs a new one, but I don't think she's going to make it long enough for her name to come up on the donor list."

"I didn't know that," I said, genuinely sad to hear of Gina's hard luck. She was such a caring person and deserved only happiness. "I'm so sorry."

She shrugged, looking older than her years, which I suspected to be somewhere in the early-fifty area. "I'm sending my mother all the money I can, which has been a strain, but at least she's getting good health care." Gina sighed. "I could probably deal with everything that's going on if it weren't for my ex-husband. He's got it in his head that we should get back together, and he's been calling and harassing me. Showing up at the store sometimes."

"Oh, no," Hailey said.

"Yeah, the jerk's scaring me something good these days. I think it's best if I head off as soon as possible. Be there for my mother when she needs me most, and keep away from Walt."

I shook my head with dismay. "Of course."

"So, what will happen now?" Hailey asked.

"As you see, I'm putting the store up for sale," Gina said. "I figured I'd clear out my inventory, then sell the building. At least I own it free and clear, so that'll help. I'm going to put whatever money I can toward helping Mom with her medical expenses."

"I hate to hear this," Hailey said.

"So do I." I pursed my lips. "Things won't be the same around here without your bookstore, Gina."

Gina let out a tired sigh. "It feels alien to me too. I've been here for what seems like forever." She looked sadly around her. "I thought about selling the store and inventory together, but I hate the thought of putting my baby into some stranger's hands—someone who would do things differently. Maybe not treat my customers the way they're used to being treated." She grimaced. "I know it's stupid, but I'm a little possessive of them, and—well—I don't want anyone spoiling the memories I've got or the ones I've given to people who have spent time in my store."

"I completely understand," Hailey said, patting her arm. "Why, just today I was thinking how this store had been a mainstay in my life for as long as I can remember. I've really missed shopping here."

"Same here," I added, leaning my chin on my hand. I sipped my latte, then suddenly an idea hit me. "Gina, what if you didn't turn your store over to some stranger? What if you sold it to someone you know, someone who would run it the same way you did? Who would treat your customers in the manner to which they've become accustomed, with top-notch service and home-baked cookies . . . the whole nine yards."

Though Gina smiled, her eyes were sad. "That'd be perfect. But I don't exactly have anyone busting down my doors to step up to the plate here. Not with Barnes & Noble six blocks down the street."

"You don't need anyone to bust down your doors," I said with triumph. I leaned back and gave Hailey a look I knew she'd understand.

"Lexie . . ." she began, reading me all right.

"We could," I insisted. "You said you wanted to do

something positive with the nest egg your dad left you. And I've got quite a bit saved up."

"What?" Gina looked from Hailey to me and back again. "What are you saying? That you two . . ."

"Why not?" I grinned and I winked at Hailey. "After all, girlfriend, you're ready for a fresh new start now that what's-his-name is out of your life, right?"

"Well, yeah, but—"

"And you love books and you love this store, and so do I."

"Yeah."

"And we're great together." I hooked my elbow through hers. "We're a team, babe! Not even twelve years can change that."

We would later blame this rash decision on the tequila shooters and the stress of finding a dead stripper in the bushes, which I'd nearly forgotten all about in my excitement.

My enthusiasm rubbed off on Hailey. "Yeah," she said, a thoughtful expression on her face. "I can totally picture the two of us running this bookstore together." She smiled. "We'd be partners, just like we were back in high school."

"And I could still do auditions—for meaningful roles. Oh, Hailey. This will be *perfect*."

"I think you're right."

I reached across the counter and extended a hand to Gina. "Gina, darling—I think you've just sold your bookstore."

Five

Hailey

I woke up with my head pounding. It felt like I was wearing a football helmet jammed full of rocks. And I was pretty sure the Roto-Rooter man's boots smelled better than the taste in my mouth. Groaning, I rolled over and squinted one eye at the clock on my nightstand. Almost noon! Lexie and I had stayed at Gina's until nearly four A.M., talking, planning. Excited about the prospect of taking over the bookstore.

Now I wondered if it really was such a good idea. At the moment, the only good idea in my mind was heading for the bathroom. I brushed my teeth twice, then headed for the kitchen to start a pot of coffee. I got a breakfast of fresh lettuce for Speedy as the pot brewed, and with my pet taken care of, I headed for my apartment door. I had the *Miami Herald* delivered daily, and liked to peruse it with my morning coffee.

I poured myself a large cup of black coffee—loaded with sugar—then sat at my small kitchen table. A story on the front page caught my attention, just below the headline news of a bank heist. THREE TEENS DEAD AFTER ECSTASY OVERDOSE. My heart broke as I read about three young lives thrown away by kids who'd taken some bad Ecstasy while at a rave in a club on South Beach. One had died at the rave, one was en route to the hospital, and the other was pronounced dead within minutes of arriving at the ER.

Too sad.

I flipped to page three to finish the story, but the headline there made me forget all about the teens and my hangover. EXOTIC DANCER FOUND DEAD—POLICE INVESTI-GATE.

My heart leapt as I scanned the news story, and I gasped when I spotted my name and Lexie's. "Ohmygod." Forcing my eyes to focus, I read the article.

The body of exotic dancer Rafael Martinez was found early this morning in the back parking lot of Fantasies by clubgoers Hailey McGraw and Lexie Muller. Police arriving on the scene discovered Martinez's body lying in the bushes. McGraw and Muller were questioned and released. Cause of death has not yet been determined . . .

Questioned and released? Clubgoers? The story made me and Lexie sound like a couple of party animals on the lam. The article went on to tell a bit about Rafael, and a color photo of him dressed in his black mask and tight pants accompanied the piece. It also stated that he'd been the live-in lover of Josephine Coletti.

So Quixote *had* been Josephine's man!

I reached for the phone.

"What?" Lexie's voice came across the line, a sleepy grumble.

"Lex, have you seen the paper?"

"Paper? Hell, Hailey, I'm asleep. Call me back in . . . five— ten—hours."

"Lexie, listen. There's a story in this morning's paper about Don Quixote's death. And our names are in it!"

"What?" This time she sounded more awake. She groaned, and I could picture her sitting up in bed, clutching her head.

I hurried to give her details. "Here, wait. I'll read it to you." I did, then took a gulp of coffee. "I can't believe this! I've never seen a dead guy before. At least, not one lying in the bushes." I shivered.

"I can't believe they printed our names!" Lexie sounded appalled. "What if my agent sees the article? No one wants a Zippy Zipper Bag Mom who hangs out at a strip club!"

"No, but a Tidy Toilet Girl who cleans up dead bodies might sell."

"Very funny."

"Hey, are you up for coffee and a bite to eat? We never

did get our pancakes, and I think we need to talk things over some more. About Don Quixote, and about Gina's bookstore."

Lexie groaned. "I just want to forget about that stripper."

"Yeah. Me too." But deep down, I was curious about what had happened to poor Rafael.

"I do need coffee," Lexie said, "and a shower."

"Wanna meet at Starbucks? Say in about an hour?"

"Sure. But hey, which one? Where are you living again?"

"Alton Road and Nineteenth. There's one three blocks from me."

"Sounds good to me. I'll meet you there."

I hung up, my thoughts whirling. Maybe a hot shower would help clear my mind—and make my head stop pounding.

An hour later I dressed in jeans, Rockport sandals, and my favorite comfy T-shirt that pictured a barrel racer on the front. I headed outside to my pickup, and the humidity hit me like a wet electric blanket. Whew! I'd forgotten how thick it could get in Miami in the summertime. If not for the heat, I would have walked. But I wanted air-conditioned comfort. Thank God, after our visit with Gina, Lexie and I had had the foresight to take a cab back to the club and pick up our cars.

In my Ford Ranger, I put on my sunglasses, turned up my Rascal Flatts CD, then headed south on Alton Road.

The one thing about Miami—it made you conscious of your car. In Montana, I'd always been comfortable in my pickup. On South Beach, I felt out of place next to all the convertibles and sleek sports cars.

Though Alton Road was blocks away from the main strip, it was bustling with people nonetheless. Women in bikinis and sarongs strolled leisurely outside of the shops. Guys who looked like underwear models passed me in hot cars. Tourists snapped pictures of Art Deco buildings. No matter the time of day, there was always action on South Beach.

Even if the action was murder.

I found a spot on the street in front of Starbucks and parallel-parked into it. Lexie was waiting in front of the shop beneath the shade of a leafy palm tree. She looked pretty put together for someone with a hangover. She wore a peach-colored tank, a matching skirt, and cute high-heeled sandals. And like me, she had on sunglasses—armor against the brain-piercing sunlight.

"Hey, girl," she said. "It's about time you got here. If I don't get a latte this minute, my head's gonna explode."

"I think I need something more like a double espresso. Come on."

Inside, we ordered, then made our way to a corner table with our drinks and a couple of slices of lemon pound cake. *Ambrosia!* I bit into mine and practically quivered. But my pleasure was short-lived as I remembered the newspaper article. "So, did you take a look at the newspaper for yourself?"

Lexie nodded. "God, I can't believe Rafael was Joey's lover! And here we were joking about the possibility."

She shivered, and so did I. I couldn't help remembering how seductively Quixote had danced for us. We'd had so much fun.

And now he was dead. It was so hard to believe.

"I thought it was sort of weird that nothing was mentioned about a murder," I said. "I mean, all the story said was that the cause of death was undetermined."

"I thought the same thing." Lexie took a bite of her pound cake. "If he wasn't murdered, then why was he wedged into the bushes? It's not as if he had a heart attack and decided that might be a good place to die. I wonder—" The muffled ring of her cell phone cut her short. Lexie pulled it from her purse. "Hello? . . . Hey, Monty . . . Yes, it's true." She rolled her eyes at me. "Uh-huh . . . I was as shocked as anybody, believe me. I don't know any more about it than what was in the paper . . . No."

I could hear the buzz of a man's voice on the other end. *Wa-wah-wa-wa-wa-wah.* Lexie chatted another minute, then hung up. "That was my agent. He saw the article."

"Ah. Guess we're local celebrities."

She shoved the phone back into her purse. "Believe me, that's the sort of publicity I don't need."

"So, what do you suppose happened last night with Rafael?" I asked, keeping my voice low. I glanced around, making sure no one was listening. In spite of the seriousness of the situation, I felt a little Nancy Drew type of thrill. "I mean, one minute he's dancing . . . the next he's dead."

"I've no idea."

Of course she didn't. Last night, I'd been so shaken up I

had only wanted to forget about what had happened. But now, with our names in the paper and everything, my curiosity was taking over.

The sound of a ringing cell came again, this time mine. I answered, and immediately my sister's voice assailed my ear. "Hailey, for God's sake! Have you seen the paper?"

I groaned, then said, "I assume you're talking about the article regarding the dead stripper." Now it was my turn to roll my eyes in Lexie's direction.

"I can't believe you!" Bailey shrilled.

"Hey, it's not like we killed him," I shot back defensively—in case she was having any doubts about that. My headache was back with a vengeance. Bailey had a way of bringing out the worst in me.

"What on earth were you doing at a *strip club*? For God's sake, Hailey! Mom and Dad must be rolling over in their graves, God bless their souls."

So in my sister's eyes, the real crime was having gone to a strip club—dead Don Quixote be damned. "Come on, Bailey. It's not like I committed a crime. And it's not my fault Lexie and I stumbled on a dead body." Though the police seemed to have thought otherwise, at least for a minute or two.

"You know Mom would've had a fit if she knew you hung out in a place like that. My neighbors are going to read that story . . . and my mother-in-law . . . shit! What's gotten into you anyway? Your marriage fell apart and now you're having some sort of breakdown?"

I had to wonder if my sister wasn't one taco short of a

combination platter. I wanted to scream, *Hello! What about the dead guy?* Instead I said, "Gee, thanks for your concern, Bailey. The next time I run across a dead man, I'll try to make sure it's at someplace more suitable."

"Don't you sass me, Hailey Winona McGraw. I'm still your older sister, and—"

A sudden shriek on Bailey's end of the line overrode her voice. Thank God. I heard the muffled sound of a hand covering the phone's mouthpiece, then Bailey was shouting at her kids. A moment later, she was back. "Listen, we'll talk more about this later. I've got to go. Corey just put Connie's running shoes in the toilet, and Cody's about to flush!" With that, she hung up.

Lord help me! I shoved my cell back into my purse. It was bad enough that Mom and Dad—Tina and Todd—had thought it cute to name us girls Hailey and Bailey. But Bailey had taken the family tradition too far, with the whole Cody-Corey-Connie thing.

"That was my sister," I said, rolling my eyes again. "Be glad you're an only child. Trust me—"

Lexie's phone rang again, cutting me off.

"Geez!" We spoke in unison.

It was Lexie's mom this time—with a thousand questions. Lexie did her best to cut the call short, then quirked her mouth at me. "I can't believe my mother heard the news—in *Orlando*. One of her old friends from here must have seen the article and called her right away." Lexie shook her head. "The big shocker would be if my daddy called next."

"You think he might?"

"Honey, I haven't heard from him in thirteen years—ever since he left us to live with that stripper in New York. You remember—the one he'd met while she was vacationing on Miami Beach?"

"Oh, that's right!" I'd completely forgotten about that episode in Lexie's life, one of the events that had helped us bond as teenagers. It had been shortly after she'd rescued me from two high school bullies, and as much as she'd acted all tough and strong, I knew it bothered her that her father, a hotel bellman, had been tempted by some whore he'd met who'd been staying at the hotel where he worked. Right after that, we started hanging out a lot on Miami Beach, sneaking into clubs we were too young to legally get into. Maybe the fondness of that time was what had us both choosing to live here, years later, instead of the Kendall neighborhood where we grew up.

Lexie's lips twisted. "Looks like we're not going to get much peace and quiet until this whole thing dies down."

"I guess not." I frowned. "Hey, if *we're* getting this much commotion over that newspaper article, can you imagine what Joey—I mean Josephine—is going through?"

"Poor thing." Lexie shook her head. "I always liked Joey, even though he was a little pest."

"Yeah. He had it bad for both of us, didn't he?" I still didn't understand how hot-blooded Joey had become sexy Josephine. But hey, whatever floats your boat.

"He sure did." Lexie's wistful smile faded. "I'll bet

Josephine's truly heartbroken now. Maybe we ought to swing by and check on her."

"You know where she lives?"

"Uh-huh. Coconut Grove. Close to where Sylvester Stallone used to live." Lexie sipped her latte. "She's got a gorgeous piece of waterfront property, and a house that is *unbelievable*."

Sly Stallone—I could only imagine. "Wow! Guess Joey's come a long way."

"And how." Lexie chuckled, and I couldn't help but join her. "I hear she makes pretty good money as a female impersonator."

"Well, let's go!" I downed the rest of my espresso. "I can't wait to see the house."

Outside, Lexie paused near her sleek silver-blue Lexus convertible. "You want to take my car?"

"I don't know if I should leave my truck here on the street. I don't want a ticket." I frowned.

"Tell you what," Lexie said. "We have to head south anyway, so follow me to my place. It's not far. We can park your truck there, then ride together."

"All right."

I followed Lexie, but when she went south of Fifth Street, I perked up. We were quickly running out of land. And yet she kept zipping past the low-rise apartments, and I couldn't help wondering if she possibly lived in the gorgeous peach-colored high-rise at the end of the strip. It was an enviable South Beach address, and striking with its color combination of peach and ocean blue.

My mouth fell open as I followed Lexie to that exact building. I was still in awe as she got me access to the building so I could park.

"Lex, you live here?" I asked as I sat in the passenger seat beside her.

Smiling, she nodded. "But I'm not on the top floor or anything. Only the ninth floor, but still the view of the ocean is amazing."

"Wow."

"I know." She sighed as she headed back toward Fifth, and I detected a story in what she *didn't* say.

"What?" I asked.

"I feel a little guilty about this place sometimes. Would you believe it was a gift?"

"Get out!"

"Yeah. A guy I was seeing. I didn't know he was married. I guess I should have—considering all the lavish gifts he gave me. I found out when his wife accosted me outside of my car one day. I broke up with him right away, and would have given this back, except it was in my name already." She shrugged. "What do you do?"

I had no clue. Travis had given me my ring on our wedding day, but pretty much nothing else after that. Except heartache and grief.

"Who was the guy?" I couldn't help asking.

"It doesn't matter anymore," Lexie told me, effectively ending any conversation on the subject. I was curious, but if she didn't want to talk about it, I wasn't going to press her.

A couple minutes later, we were cruising on the causeway with the convertible's top down. My hair blew wildly around my face, making me feel like Lexie and I could've been Romy and Michele, if only we'd had "Footloose" playing on the radio.

Or maybe Thelma and Louise, the way things were going.

Lex in a Lexus. I grinned to myself. *Too cool.*

We passed the monstrous cruise ships in the Port of Miami, and finally exited the MacArthur Causeway onto I-95. Ten more minutes, and we were turning left off of U.S. 1 into Coconut Grove. It had been years since I'd seen the area, and with the sprawling oaks and large palm trees, it still maintained its touch of old charm.

Lexie finally slowed as we neared the large gates of an exclusive-looking, upscale area. In the distance, I could see the shimmering waters of Biscayne Bay between two mammoth houses.

"How will we get in?" I asked.

Lexie lowered her sunglasses and wriggled her eyebrows. "Just watch." She pulled up beside the guard hut. "Hi, Dewayne. How's it hanging?" Coyly, she tucked the tip of one earpiece on her sunglasses between her parted lips.

Dewayne—an attractive black man who was clearly too short for Lexie—practically melted into a puddle. "Hey, Lexie." He stepped out of the guard hut and leaned his elbows on the car door. "How about you meet me here at seven and I'll show you?" He glanced my way. "You can bring your friend too."

"Thanks, but we've got plans." She stroked her fingers on his arm. "Right now we're here to see a friend. Josephine—"

"Coletti. Of course. You haven't been to see her in a while."

"I've been busy."

Dewayne raised one thick eyebrow. "You shouldn't be a stranger."

"I know. I'll be better in the future. I promise."

Reluctantly, Dewayne straightened and stepped back a little. "Go on in, Lexie. But if you change your mind about later . . ." He grinned.

"I'll let you know." Slipping her sunglasses back on, Lexie gave him a little wave, then pulled on through the wrought-iron gates.

"Wow! Teach me how to do that," I teased.

"It's a gift," Lexie said, giggling.

She drove slowly through the neighborhood. The branches of the picturesque oak trees reached well into the road from both sides of the street, providing lots of shade. I couldn't help gawking at the stately homes—the houses here were large enough to fit my apartment into five times over.

When we came to a corner, Lexie turned left. Unlike the first street, which had been tranquil and unpopulated, this one had cars lining the block up one side and down the other, with people everywhere.

I looked down the street, craning my neck to get a better view. "Geez, what's going on?"

As we got closer to the crowd, the smell of barbecued chicken floated through the air, and on the lawns of at least two houses, I spotted kegs of beer. Reggae music blared from a stereo somewhere; some of the people were dancing in the street. This wasn't exactly a scene I pictured when I thought of gated communities and majestic old homes.

"Looks like a block party," Lexie said, squeezing the convertible into a barely-big-enough space between two other cars. She frowned. "And I'd say the majority of the crowd is at Josephine's." She pointed. "That house there."

The place was breathtaking, all right—and easily the tallest and largest one in the area. Surrounded by a manicured lawn with rows of neatly trimmed shrubbery, the house sprawled over what I'd guess was at least a two-acre lot. There were sizable oak trees near the road, and graceful palm trees lined the circular driveway. The house itself was a two-story stucco building, painted pale beige, with rose-colored California shingles covering the roof. And it had enough windows to make a person hope the neighbors' kids weren't into pitching baseballs.

"Come on," Lexie said. "Let's see what's up."

She didn't have to ask me twice.

Close on Lexie's heels, I elbowed my way through the crowd. There was a mix of people here—white, black, Hispanic. Being tall, it was pretty easy for me to see over everyone else's heads, except for some of the guys.

"Do you see Josephine?" Lexie asked me.

"No." And with that long red hair of hers, she shouldn't have been hard to spot.

"I don't either. Let's see if she's inside."

Lexie led the way across the lawn to the front of the house. The exterior front entrance was impressive with large columns, but my breath snagged in my throat when I walked through the door. The ceiling in the foyer was at least twenty feet high, made only more impressive by a giant crystal chandelier. The floors were black marble, and the walls a bright white with abstract art pieces that had to cost a fortune.

"Excuse me—have you seen Josephine?" Lexie asked a dark-haired woman in short shorts and a tank top, with breasts so large they would surely keep her afloat in the Atlantic for days. Her back pressed to the wall, she had a joint in her fingers.

"Josephine?" the woman repeated slowly, then a smile spread on her face. "Yeah, what a party!" She took another hit of the weed.

Lexie rolled her eyes. "Come on. Let's go."

There was no one else in the immediate area, except a couple at the top of the spiral staircase engaged in a serious lip-lock. My eyes bulged. Was the tall woman really a man?

I shuddered as Lexie grabbed my arm. "Come on, Hailey. I want to find out what's going on here. How can Josephine be having a party when her lover was just murdered?"

That thought brought me back to reality, and the reason we were there. Lexie led me to the right, and into a living room so large, I began to gawk again. It had to be at least eighty feet wide, with a series of glass doors that led to the patio. No wonder the house was so tall—the ceiling in here was at least twelve feet high, and there was still a second floor. The view of the glistening water and boats floating in the distance was simply spectacular. But what really got my attention was the throng of people gathered around the pool, staring upward.

"What the hell?" Lexie asked, voicing my opinion.

She moved faster, hustling to the closest set of doors that led to the back patio.

"Excuse me. Coming through." I continued to press through the crowd behind her when we stepped outside, but stopped abruptly when a short, chubby guy in a Hawaiian shirt elbowed me in the ribs.

"Oh, my God." Lexie gasped. "It's Josephine!"

I glared at the chubby guy, who didn't have the decency to apologize, then moved up beside Lexie. My breath caught in my throat when I looked up to the roof.

Josephine stood high on the California shingles over one end of the pool, sobbing hysterically. Dressed in a bright purple cat suit with matching spiked heels. I couldn't understand her choice of outfit on such a hot day—unless that was her version of a spa wrap to drop a quick five pounds.

Her red hair was a wild mess. Mascara ran down her cheeks, and she looked as if her world had ended.

"Josephine!" Lexie called, rushing forward and flailing her arms. "Honey, come down from there right now!"

"Stay back!" Josephine shouted. "I don't want anyone else to get hurt."

"We don't want *you* to get hurt," Lexie shot back. "Now come down from there before you fall."

Where Josephine stood, she was positioned over the shallow end of the pool. I had no doubt that she would plunge at full speed into the pool and surely break her neck.

"I *want* to fall!" Josephine turned her long-lashed eyes on us. "The man I loved is dead. I'm going to be with him."

"No, wait!" I stepped forward, holding out my hand. "Joey—Josephine. It's me, Hailey. Remember me?"

"Of course I do." She sniffed. "You've got no business being here, Hailey. This is none of your concern."

"It damned sure is." I tried the angry tactic. "I've known you since you were nothing but a scrawny little tadpole." One hand on my hip, I gestured with the other. "Now come down off the roof and have a beer with me. We'll catch up on old times."

"I don't want to catch up on old times. I don't even want to be here anymore!" Josephine wailed. "Rafael is gone! I have nothing to live for."

"Don't say that," Lexie said, taking a more gentle approach. "Honey, you've got everything to live for." She took a couple of steps closer through the crowd. "Hailey's right. It's been a long time since the three of us have hung out together. Come on down and have a drink with us, girlfriend."

Just the thought of a drink had my head floating off my shoulders all over again. But the thought of watching

Joey plunge off the roof was even worse. I cast a look at the pool below—in which some morons obliviously splashed around in the deep end. One wrong move, and the pool party would be over.

"No man is worth dying for," I told Joey. "And I oughta know. Come on down and I'll tell you all about it."

"No!"

Lexie threw a concerned gaze at me. "We have to do something," she said.

"How do we get to the roof?" I asked, glancing around.

And then I saw it. The ladder leading from a second-floor bedroom to the roof. Joey must have climbed up there, though God only knows how in those killer heels.

"Upstairs," I said to Lexie urgently, pointing to the balcony.

She nodded, then took off for the house. Inside, she kicked off her shoes, scooped them up, then raced for a staircase off the back of the kitchen.

Every step of the way upstairs, I prayed Joey wouldn't take a dive—or an accidental tumble—off the roof. But so far, I didn't hear any frenzied screaming, so I figured we still had time to get to her.

"That balcony's off Josephine's master bedroom," Lexie explained as she led the way down the second-floor hallway. "The one with the double doors."

Lexie and I burst through the doors at the same time. The pulsing sound of house music wafted through the open windows. You'd think someone would have the good sense to turn the music off. I wondered if all the guests were wasted and stoned.

Lexie tossed her shoes onto the floor before stepping onto the balcony. She wasted no time starting up the ladder. As she ascended, the crowd erupted in applause. At first I thought it was because we were doing what none of them had had the presence of mind to do—until the catcalls and loud whistling started. I glanced up then, and saw that Lexie's ass was totally visible beneath her short skirt—and my good friend appeared to be only wearing a thong.

"Oh, shit, Lexie." There was no way I could cover her. And there were more pressing matters—like Josephine, who was moving closer to the roof's edge.

I climbed the ladder and gingerly stepped onto the roof.

"Stand back!" Josephine shouted, her eyes widening. "Or I'll jump! I swear I will!"

I felt like Lexie and I had been cast in some B movie. First a dead stripper, and now a suicidal cross-dresser. Maybe I should've stayed in Montana.

"You don't mean that," I said, moving closer.

"Yes, I do!" Josephine took a step closer to the edge, teetering precariously. "I mean it, Hailey! Get back."

Lexie hopped uncomfortably from one foot to the other. "My God, this roof is hot." She looked over her shoulder at me. "Maybe this is a bad idea."

"We have to get to her," I told her, moving quickly now, past Lexie.

"Maybe you shouldn't get any closer," she told me, her tone low. "Just keep her busy talking, and I'll head back down to her room and call 911."

"I don't think you should do that," I advised.

"Why not?"

"Until that crowd clears, you're better off on the roof."

Lexie shot me a quizzical gaze. "Huh?"

"Your skirt!" I said in an urgent whisper. "On that ladder, you're mooning everyone—if you get my drift."

Her eyes widened in brief alarm. Then she said, "We have to do something. We can't just let Josephine kill herself."

Looking to the crowd below, I mimed holding a phone to my ear, hoping someone would catch my drift and call the cops. I didn't want to alarm Josephine by suggesting it out loud.

"I just called the cops," someone yelled. Narrowing my eyes on the crowd, I saw that the person speaking was the guy in the Hawaiian shirt. "They're on their way."

"No! No police!" Panic etched Josephine's voice, which was entirely too masculine for her appearance. "I don't want to face anyone," she went on. "I just want to end it all and be with Rafael!"

I shot Mr. Big Mouth a glare, then started again for Joey, negotiating the shingled slope as best I could. I had no choice. Josephine had moved dangerously close to the edge and had her hands clasped reverently in front of her. Maybe a segment of her female impersonation show featured a walk across the tightrope. Because I just didn't get how she could balance so well in those purple heels.

"Hold on, Joey," I told her. "I'm coming."

Joey spread her legs and flung out her arms like wings. I screamed when she teetered—and so did the crowd.

Dear God, she's going to do it!

Either I would leap for her, struggle with her, and the two of us would tumble off the roof, or I had to figure out a way to keep her from jumping to an ugly death in such a stunning pool. I couldn't take the sight of one more dead body.

"Lexie and I were there last night!" I cried. "Don't you want to know what the police told us?" They hadn't told us anything, but I was desperate.

Josephine hesitated—long enough for me to reach her side.

"You talked to the cops?" she asked, her eyes hopeful yet still desperate. "What did they say? Do they know who killed my sugar-love?"

I glanced over my shoulder at Lexie, who was still doing the hot-potato hop. She nodded, urging me on.

I turned back to Josephine. "Come with me and Lexie, and we'll talk about it." I reached out to take her by the arm, but she shrugged away. Yeah, she had to have mastered the tightrope. On high heels.

"You're lying," she accused. "You just want to trick me into not jumping."

I sighed. I'd never been very good at not telling the truth. "Okay, so the cops didn't tell us much. But we were the

ones who found Rafael, and I am so, so sorry for your loss."
I put my hands together in a pleading motion. "So, please,
Josephine. Come on down and let us help you through this,
hon."

"No." She shook her head. "You can't help. No one
can."

She raised her hands high, and I knew she was going
to lunge. I didn't think, just moved. I leapt for her, shooting my arms out, catching Josephine around the waist.
Momentum was on my side, and because I caught her off
guard, I was able to throw her backward—toward a part
of the roof that came out in an L-shape. Thank God it was
there, or we would both have gone flying—minus the
wings necessary to save us.

I didn't think Josephine really expected me to grab on
to her. With a surprised little cry, she stumbled backward.
But I didn't count on this—she rolled. Toward the roof's
edge. And I rolled with her.

"Hailey!" Lexie screamed. A collective gasp sounded
in the crowd.

I scrambled to gain control, trying to brace my feet
against the eaves trough. Somehow, Josephine had stopped
above me, and my fingers now gripped the shoulders of
her cat suit. How had we not flown over the edge?

"My shoe," Josephine moaned. "It's stuck."

Thank God! A positive use for those damn purple
heels.

Josephine and I were now face-to-face. Up close like this,
she looked like a clown—all that red hair and exaggerated

makeup. And there was something else in her eyes that disturbed me—hopelessness, maybe?

"Hailey. You have to let me *go*."

My eyes locked on hers. "Now, there's no reason to go crazy. I don't know about you, but I'm more than ready for that beer. We can—" The words caught in my throat as my right foot stumbled. Suddenly I felt nothing but air beneath that foot.

"Hailey, look out!" Lexie screamed.

I gulped and held on tighter to Josephine.

Josephine blew out a nervous breath. "Hailey, if you don't let me go, we're both going to fall. And I—I don't want to die," she whimpered.

You couldn't have decided that before you looked like you were ready to dive off the roof?

My heart beating out of control, I carefully glanced over my shoulder, already knowing what I'd see. I wondered fleetingly if my skull would crack against the concrete, or split in two at the bottom of the pool.

One of Josephine's shoes rolled off the roof, punctuating the seriousness of this situation.

"I told you not to get involved," Josephine went on, her voice full of fear.

Damn! If I didn't let go of Josephine, my weight would no doubt drag her down. And if I *did* let her go, I wouldn't be able to hang on to the roof.

Either way you sliced it, I was screwed.

Six

Lexie

My heart leapt into my throat as first one of Hailey's feet slipped over the edge of the roof, then the other. "Good God, somebody help!" I screamed at the top of my lungs. "Get a mattress! Form a human shield! Do *something*! And for God's sake, turn off the music!" The upbeat salsa was getting on my last nerve.

Someone was listening, because the music went off. But instead of gathering close the way teens do in a mosh pit to prepare for Hailey's fall, the crowd separated and moved backward. Two even fell into the pool in their haste to move away. The damn idiots below probably didn't want to break a nail or ruin their hair.

"Morons," I muttered. Despite the roof's scorching temperature, I forged ahead in my bare feet, moving quickly toward Josephine and Hailey. Josephine was crying and repeating, "I'm so sorry, I'm so sorry."

I knelt on the roof in front of Hailey, ignoring the pain to my knees. "Josephine, get a grip," I told her firmly. "We can both do this if we work together. I'm gonna grab one of Hailey's arms, and you grab the other—okay?"

"Okay," Josephine said shakily.

"You're gonna be all right, Hailey," I told her. Her eyes were round and full of fear, but at least she wasn't panicking. Panic had a way of leading people to certain tragedy.

Behind her, I saw the crowd staring up at us. What the hell was wrong with all those people, standing around gawking like Josephine's attempted suicide was a spectator sport? With Hailey as the sideshow. And the perk of seeing my ass made it an R-rated event.

Forgetting the crowd, I wrapped both hands around one of Hailey's arms, and Josephine did the same to the other one. "It's okay, sweetie. Let go of Josephine's clothes. I've got you. You're not gonna die on me yet."

"You sure?" she asked, her voice a bare croak.

"Yes, I'm sure. Remember that day when Rebecca Forster and Donna McEnroe had you cornered and wanted to beat your face in with that bat? Well, I knew then when I charged in to save you that not even one hair on your head would be hurt. Same as I know now. Trust me, sweetie."

Slowly, Hailey loosened her fingers. She didn't fall.

"See?" I said. "Easy as pie." Thank God I sounded cool,

because inside, I was freaking out. "Now, Josephine, on three, we're gonna pull her up. Got it? Nice and slow. One, two, three . . ."

I heaved, and with the help of Josephine, pulled Hailey forward. After a few seconds, Hailey let out a sob of relief as her feet hit the roof.

"That's it, sweetie. We got you."

"Oh, my God," Hailey finally said, getting to her knees and starting to crawl to higher ground. "I swear, Lexie, for a minute there—"

"Don't even say it, okay? Let's just get off this roof."

"I'm sorry," Josephine sobbed. "So sorry." She looked pale, and genuine remorse filled her eyes. "I never meant for you to get hurt, Hailey."

"It's okay, Josephine," I said. "Now come on. Let's get to the ladder. Because I'll be damned if, after all of this, you still take that dive."

"No, no, I won't. Thank you. I mean it, you two. You saved my life." Josephine pulled her foot from the shoe that was wedged between two shingles, then got to her feet. Looking below, she raised her hands triumphantly in the air—giving me a scare for a moment because I thought she was about to leap. Instead, she tossed the shoe—then waved and blew kisses.

Below, the crowd erupted in applause and cheers. I shot them a look I hoped would peel their sunburns. *Hypocrites!* "Yeah, thanks for all y'all's help!" I snapped. I took Hailey by the arm and walked with her toward the ladder.

"I really am sorry," Josephine repeated.

"I'm fine," Hailey told her. But she didn't look fine. She looked shaken, and somewhat embarrassed. "Guess I went from rescuer to rescuee." She frowned. "Is that a word?"

The music started again, and everyone below went right back to partying, swigging plastic cups of keg beer as though nothing out of the ordinary had just happened.

"I feel so bad," Josephine sniffed as Hailey started down the ladder. She dabbed at her eyes with a lilac-colored lace handkerchief she'd produced from her bosom. "You nearly fell, and it's all my fault."

"Are *you* okay?" Hailey asked, pausing on the ladder.

"Not really."

Josephine pressed her fingers to her forehead, and I noted her nails were painted lilac as well. Leave it to Josephine to dress up in her finest to take the big leap. I couldn't help but wonder if she'd done it simply to get some attention. But as soon as the thought hit me, I felt bad for thinking it. How would I feel if my significant other had been murdered?

"I do feel a little faint," Josephine went on. "I guess we could all three use a drink."

"Can we talk about this in your room?" I asked. "My feet are burning up here."

"Right," Hailey said, and continued down the ladder.

When I started down, I felt the wind on my ass just before I heard frenzied applause again. What a bunch of perverts! Had they never seen a woman's ass before? As I stepped onto the balcony, I turned to them and took a bow. What the hell. This had already become some freaky sideshow.

I hurried into Josephine's bedroom and gave Hailey a long hug. We were starting to pull apart when Josephine said, "Group hug," and wrapped her long arms around us.

"How about some cosmopolitans?" Josephine asked when the hug ended. "I make the best ones in South Florida."

"I'll have a double," Hailey said.

"You're on," Josephine told her.

I scooped up my shoes and followed Hailey and Josephine down the back stairs to the kitchen. As they both chatted, Hailey rubbed Josephine's back, offering her comfort. Hailey was the one who'd nearly fallen, yet her concern continued to be for Josephine. Some things hadn't changed over the years. Hailey was the same caring person she'd been in high school, always looking out for others before herself.

In the kitchen, Josephine pressed a hand to a portion of the marble wall, and it magically opened. "This is my private bar," she announced. "Off limits to anyone except my closest friends. We can avoid the crowd in here."

Hailey and I entered the room, staring around in awe. This room was a smaller version of the living room, but still very large. And it was painted dark, with spotlights in the ceiling. It took me a moment to realize it was a theater room with a giant plasma TV and stereo on the left wall. There was a row of comfy recliners about ten feet away from the television, but behind that, there were semicircle-shaped leopard-print sofas surrounding a round table. Three sets of those, to be exact.

The room didn't exactly have a private, cozy feel. I could easily imagine Josephine entertaining fifty people in there. But then, considering the amount of people at the party outside, maybe she figured fifty of them were her closest friends.

Not that'd I'd seen any of those "close" friends outside trying to save her.

On the far wall of the room, there was a massive L-shaped bar. I'd been in her house just once, when she'd had a housewarming party and Gina had invited me to tag along. At the time, I hadn't seen this room.

"Sit back, Josephine," Hailey said, gently pressing her down onto one of the leopard-print sofas.

"But the cosmos—"

"I can make them," I offered.

"If you insist," Josephine said.

Hailey plumped a trio of silk-covered throw pillows, and Josephine leaned back, eating up the attention with a spoon. I strolled to the bar, then jumped with fright when something leapt at me, barking. It was a tiny black chihuahua, which I'd probably woken up. Whining, it pranced past me and hopped onto the sofa and onto Josephine's lap. It licked at her mistress's face.

"Bling-Bling," Josephine cooed to the little dog. "There's

Mommy's baby girl." She smacked kisses against Bling-Bling's muzzle.

"Which way to the nearest bathroom?" Hailey asked.

"That way, sugar." Josephine pointed. "That door to the left of the bar."

Hailey disappeared, and I reached for the bottle of vodka. Less than a minute later, Hailey came out of the bathroom holding a washcloth. I finished making the drinks and brought two to the glass-topped coffee table in front of the couch, then went back for the third one. As I sank onto one end of the plush sofa, Hailey gave me an odd look I couldn't quite read. Then she laid the cool cloth on Josephine's forehead and put a drink in her hand before reaching for her own cosmopolitan.

"So, are you feeling better?" I asked Josephine. I really was worried about her. I'd never known the grief of losing someone, and I couldn't begin to imagine being so distraught that you would want to kill yourself.

"Not really, but this does help." She indicated the drink and the washcloth. "And it's quite yummy, Lexie. Maybe even better than mine." She sipped the drink, then sighed. "Thanks, ladies. For everything."

"No problem." Hailey patted her wrist. "That's what friends are for. Now tell us what the hell you were thinking, getting up on the roof that way!" She gave Josephine's hand a little push of reprimand, and Bling-Bling growled defensively. Hailey eyed the little dog, drawing back, but continued to scold Josephine. "Honey, no man is worth jumping for. My God, what were you thinking?"

"I don't know. I guess I had a nervous breakdown. I'm devastated about Rafael. He was my everything." Josephine honked delicately into the lilac hanky.

"We truly are sorry about what happened," I said. I shivered, remembering the look of Rafael's lifeless eyes. "I have to tell you, it was a little shocking when we . . . found him."

"I read that in the paper," Josephine said, her eyes widening. "I couldn't believe the coincidence." She clutched her hand to her ample breast and rose partway up off the pillows. "How bizarre is that?"

"Tell me about it." Hailey took a gulp of her drink.

"We thought we'd check out Fantasies," I explained. "Seeing you at Gina's, it prompted my memory about the club. And I'd just run into Hailey again. We wanted to go out and celebrate. I knew your lover worked there, but didn't know his name or what he looked like. Only after seeing that article did Hailey and I learn that he was your man."

Josephine went teary-eyed again. "He was more than my man. He was my soul mate. I never thought I'd find someone to love who loved me back the way Rafael did. And now he's dead." She started to bawl. "Oh, maybe I *should've* jumped."

"Oh, hon." Hailey squeezed Josephine's hand. "Is there anything we can do to help you get through this? I hate the thought of you staying in this big house all alone." She looked around, not bothering to hide the awe in her expression.

76

"Maybe you could use some company for a while," I suggested. Hailey was right. Even though I'd mostly lost touch with Josephine over the years, I did feel sorry for her. And I wouldn't mind spending a few days in the lap of luxury. "Hailey and I could stay for a day or two if you'd like, couldn't we, Hailey?"

"Thanks for the offer, girls," Josephine said. "But I'm not alone. I've got Bling-Bling, and my housekeeper. And my friends keep calling, of course. Really, I think I just need some quiet time."

"Well, if you're sure," Hailey said. Then she looked at me and briefly widened her eyes in a little look that told me something was up. But what, I had no clue.

"I'll be okay," Josephine assured us. "From now on, I promise to stay *off* my roof." She chuckled hoarsely. "Really, you two don't have to put yourselves out by staying with me. I've put you both through enough trouble as it is. I'm *so* embarrassed."

"No worries," I told her. "Given what you're going through, it's completely understandable."

"What I don't understand, though," Hailey began cautiously, "is the party. I admit, I'm confused. All this after Rafael's death . . ."

"I know." Josephine sniffled. "This was planned weeks ago—a huge block party with a bunch of my neighbors. We throw them once a month in the summer. But with the shocking news of my Rafael's death, I totally forgot about it. Then people started showing up. And my party planner. I figured I'd just stay in my room, let my friends have fun. But then it all became too much . . . and you know the rest."

"Ah," I chimed, understanding. It was hard to see Josephine like this, so utterly devastated. "You know, sweetie," I went on, "maybe it'll lift your spirits to go out and join your neighbors. If only for a little while."

"Just promise us you won't get anywhere near the roof," Hailey said.

Now it was my turn to give her the look. The last thing Josephine needed was a reminder of her crazy stunt. Despite the crowd, she'd planned a public suicide. Who was to say she wouldn't do so again?

Maybe going back out to the block party wasn't such a great idea.

"I have a better idea," I suddenly said. "Have you had lunch?" It was nearly two-thirty.

Josephine shook her head. "I can't eat."

"You need to eat something to keep your strength up. At least let Hailey and I fix you a snack tray. You can take it up to your room and settle in with a good book, and then take a nap. I really think you need some sleep, babe."

"Good idea," Hailey agreed, casting a look around the room. She reached for a paperback mystery lying on a nearby end table. "Nothing like chocolate and a good book to relax you."

As Hailey grabbed the paperback, Josephine's bookmark fell out onto the marble floor. I reached to retrieve it. A picture of a naked man graced the front of it. A very well-endowed naked man, wearing a pink-feathered boa and a come-hither look.

I gulped and stuck the marker back inside the book. "Come on. Up with you, now."

In spite of her protests, Josephine seemed to continue to relish the attention Hailey and I gave her. She told us where her chocolates were, and her favorite cookies. I helped her upstairs while Hailey arranged the comfort food and a Diet Coke on a small silver tray.

Pretty soon we had Josephine all tucked away with her chihuahua in her heart-shaped, king-sized bed, pink satin sheets tucked around her waist. I pulled the blinds down most of the way to darken the room but leave a little light so it wouldn't be too depressing.

"If you need anything," I said, "you call us right away. We're gonna write our numbers on this pad of paper on your desk, okay?"

Hailey snitched a chocolate off of Josephine's tray. "Promise us you'll call, even if you just need to talk."

"I promise." Josephine crossed her chest with an X gesture, then settled back against a pile of pillows. "One more thing, if you don't mind? I could use a Xanax before you go. To help me sleep." She fed Bling-Bling a cube of cheddar cheese.

"Where are they?" Hailey asked.

Josephine indicated the adjoining bathroom. "In the cabinet above the vanity, sugar. I keep them on hand for emergencies. You know?"

"Should you really mix them with booze?" I frowned.

"I only had one cosmo," Josephine said. She popped a chocolate into her mouth, chewing delicately.

Hailey gave me that weird look again. Shrugging, I raised my eyebrows at her. What could we do? Josephine was a grown woman. Well, sort of.

I sat on the edge of Josephine's bed while Hailey went to fetch the pills. Moments later, she returned with a peach-colored pill, which Josephine downed with a sip of Diet Coke. Sighing, she wriggled into a more comfortable position beneath the covers. "Thanks, sweeties. You two are such dolls. Love you."

We gave her a little wave and departed.

Outside, we moved past the partying crowd to my car. There, I faced Hailey. "So, what gives?"

She knew immediately what I was talking about. She glanced over her shoulder, as though making sure no one was listening. Given the thumping bass of the current hip-hop tune, I doubted they could hear a thing if they tried.

"When we were downstairs in that private bar and I got the wet washcloth for Josephine, I found a syringe in her bathroom!"

"A syringe? You mean, like a needle and syringe?"

"Yes! There was a syringe with a needle, and it really alarmed me. What if Josephine is shooting up, and that's why she ended up on her roof trying to fly?"

I pondered that as I climbed behind the wheel of my Lexus. "Or, she could be diabetic."

"But if she's diabetic, she shouldn't be drinking. Right?"

I slipped on my sunglasses, then started the car. "I honestly don't know."

"And she had Xanax."

"A lot of people take Xanax," I said, waving my hand in dismissal. "Doesn't mean anything."

"Well, maybe not." Hailey settled back in the passenger seat as I started to drive. "I just don't want her mixing the wrong combo of things. What if she passes out and never wakes up?"

"Then that'd be a better way to go than falling off the roof into the shallow end."

"Lexie!"

"Relax," I told her, staring at her from my seat. "I'm only kidding."

"I'm worried," Hailey went on. "Maybe we should have stayed with Josephine." She paused. "Then again, maybe not."

"Yes, my little Montana cowgirl," I teased. "You wouldn't want to sleep over on the chance that you might wake up to find Josephine and her friends shooting up and doing X."

"Hey, don't make fun of me. I'm hip." She frowned. "What's X?"

I laughed. "Ecstasy. The 'it' drug these days."

Hailey's eyes bulged. "There's such a thing as an 'it' drug?"

"Well, I can't say for sure—and no, I haven't ever tried it. But I know Ecstasy is really popular with the kids. I saw in yesterday's paper that three teens overdosed at some rave and died."

"Yeah, I saw that too. Shit, maybe we need to go back and check on Josephine."

"As far as I know, X is in pill form, so her syringe could certainly be medically related. When we see Gina, let's ask her if Josephine is diabetic."

"Okay." Hailey nodded. "That's a good idea."

We drove for a while in silence. But as I turned onto U.S. 1, Hailey said, "Did you get a load of that house? Man! And I think her chihuahua was wearing a real diamond collar."

"With a name like Bling-Bling, I wouldn't doubt it. I told you the house was something."

"Yeah, but I didn't expect it to be *that* big. Guess you're right that Josephine makes some pretty good money in the entertainment business."

"Mmm-hmm. That, plus she was dating a wealthy Texas oilman a few years back. When he died, he left her a nice chunk of cash."

"Get out of here!" Hailey grinned. "You're serious?"

"Absolutely."

"Sheesh. Maybe I need to get a few dating tips from her. I meet all the wrong men."

"Hey, me too." We giggled. Just then my cell phone rang. It took me a moment to figure out where it was, and then I remembered that I'd stuffed my clutch bag under my seat before heading into Josephine's house. Now I held the steering wheel with one hand and dug my clutch out with the other. A skill I'd honed over the years. A moment later I answered it, speaking my greeting a little too gruffly.

"Hey there, gorgeous." I was pleasantly surprised to hear a sexy male voice on the other end of my line. "We still on for tonight, or now that your name's all over the paper, are you too famous to make time for me?"

Tyrone Bradford. One of the half dozen guys I'd dated over the last few months. I really liked him. He was tall, with pecan-brown skin and a face so fine he looked good enough to eat with a spoon. He also had a nice ass—and I should know, since I'd seen it bare a time or two.

"Oh, I might be able to squeeze you in," I teased. Actually, in all the excitement, I'd forgotten Tyrone was taking me out to Mango's tonight—one of the hottest nightclubs on South Beach. I eyed Hailey, grinning mischievously. "But only if you've got a friend for my friend."

Hailey's eyes widened, and she immediately began shaking her head, waving her hand, and mouthing the word *No* at me.

I ignored her, loving the way Tyrone's sexy voice tickled my ear. "Of course she's hot. Would I lie to you, baby?" I gave him a throaty chuckle. Hailey smacked at my arm, but I shrugged her off, nearly running a red light. "Eight-thirty is perfect," I purred. "We'll meet you there."

As a general rule, I preferred driving myself to meet a date. That way I could always leave if things went sour.

I slipped my cell back into my Louis Vuitton clutch as Hailey exclaimed, "Lexie! What did you just do?"

"Relax," I told her. "I fixed you up with a friend of a friend for tonight. It'll be fun."

Beside me, Hailey sulked. "I'm not ready to date yet. It's too soon."

"Honey, it's never too soon to enjoy a good-looking man. Who knows? Maybe you'll even get laid."

"Lexie!"

"Why not? Great sex will put some balm on your Travis wounds."

"You're terrible!" But Hailey laughed. "So, where are we going?"

"Mango's." I grinned. "Wait till you see it. Things get pretty wild there."

"Oh, great," Hailey said dryly. "Let's just hope we don't run across any more dead strippers."

I laughed heartily and accelerated through the green light. "It's not a strip joint. It's a nightclub and restaurant on South Beach. And girl, the people there know how to par-tay! You're gonna love it."

"Who's your date, and what's his friend like?"

"My date is Tyrone Bradford. He's a cruise director for Caribbean Dreams, and he mentioned that his friend Cedric should be free for the night."

"Cedric? You fixed me up with a guy named *Cedric*?"

"Hey, Tyrone says he's cool."

"Cool. Hmm." Hailey folded her arms. "Is that guy-speak for the same thing we women mean when we say she's got a great personality?"

I chuckled. "Actually, I've seen Cedric. He *is* cute, sweetie. He's got sandy blond hair, greenish blue eyes . . ."

"Yeah? How tall is he?" She hooked one thumb toward her chest. "With five-foot-ten of cowgirl, he needs to be at least six feet."

"He's that for sure. Maybe around six-one."

"Hmm. That'll do, I guess." She slipped on her sunglasses. "But if he turns out to be a loser, I'm switching with you."

"Uh-uh, girl. Tyrone is one fine brother, and he's mine-all-mine. At least for this month."

Hailey quirked her mouth. "Your current flavor, huh?"

"You bet." I veered right onto the ramp to head north on I-95. I sent the Lexus flying around the curve, giving my hair a toss. "Why own the ice-cream parlor when you can sample the cones?"

"Cones?" Hailey asked. "Or cojones?"

"See?" I said. "I think you're ready to get laid!"

We hooted as I picked up the pace on I-95, heading back toward South Beach.

Seven

Hailey

The excitement of the day and the previous night had me bushed, so when I got home, I went right to my bedroom to lie down for a little nap. We weren't meeting the guys for a few hours yet, which gave me time to hopefully sleep off the remainder of my hangover before getting a fresh start on drinking tonight. It was like I was a teen-ager again, the way I was partying, but my body felt every bit a thirty-year-old woman.

As I stripped out of my jeans, my stomach danced with nerves. I hoped tonight went well. I wasn't really ready to start dating yet, much less with some guy named Cedric.

Flopping down on the bed in my underwear, I fell into a dead sleep that eased into a dream about me and Johnny Depp. He was a sexy pirate, and he offered me a drink of rum from a flask, only when he handed it over the flask was filled with cosmopolitan mix. And a little maraschino cherry stem stuck out of the flask's opening. Surprised, I looked up to find that my sexy pirate was no longer wearing a black outfit. Instead, he wore a purple cat suit, and his fingernails were long and painted. He took my hand and offered to buy a diamond collar for my chihuahua.

I was startled from the midst of the dream-turned-nightmare by the blaring chirp of my phone. Half asleep, I picked it up. "What?"

"Hailey, it's Bailey."

"You'd better have a good reason for waking me from a dream about Johnny Depp," I growled. She didn't have to know he'd been wearing a purple cat suit.

"I've been thinking," she said. "About your little trip to that strip joint."

"Bailey, please. Not this again. I'm a grown woman. I can do what I want."

"Please don't treat me like I'm the enemy. At least hear me out."

I rolled my eyes as I sat up. "Fine. What were you going to say?"

"I was going to say that I . . . I understand."

"You do?"

"Yes. Oh, Hailey. Why didn't you tell me? You could have come over for tea and cried on my shoulder. No wonder you wanted to lose yourself in a raunchy place like a strip club. I can't believe Travis. What a slime!"

"Okay, Bailey. You're gonna have to help me out here. What are you talking about?"

There was a pause. Then Bailey said, "You don't know?"

"No, I'm pretty much in the dark here." Literally and figuratively.

"Oh, my Lord. I thought for sure you would have heard already."

"Bailey, please."

"Travis got remarried yesterday! To Missy Black!"

"What?" Now I was fully awake. "No way." Missy Black was one of five daughters of a wealthy quarterhorse rancher outside of Billings. The guy owned a bunch of stock—both the four-legged kind and the kind you kept in a bank vault. In fact, he owned a bank, and who knew what else. His daughters were spoiled rotten and got everything their little hearts desired. I'd hated Missy Black—the youngest— from the moment I'd laid eyes on her petite, five-foot- nothing, maybe-a-hundred-pounds-wet little body.

"Yes, *way*." Bailey seemed to take glee in my shock. "They had a *huge*, blowout wedding, and they're off to hon- eymoon in the Caribbean—near where Kenny Chesney vacations, from what I understand."

Chesney was Travis's favorite country singer and idol. Travis had mimicked everything the guy did, right down to a cowboy hat pulled low over his forehead and a puka- shell necklace.

"Oh, my God," Bailey went on. "I thought you knew!"

No, I didn't, thank you very much. But how did you know all this?

"I thought for sure that's why you went out last night to drown your sorrows."

"I wasn't drowning my sorrows. I was ogling hot men. And how did you—" I began, but before I could finish asking the question, Bailey shouted, nearly blowing out my eardrum.

"*Connie!* Let go of your brother's hair! Corey, you put down that spray paint!"

I held the phone a safe distance from my ear, but still I wondered if I'd suffered some hearing loss.

"I've gotta go." Inches away, Bailey's voice still came clearly over the line. "Talk to you later. I meant what I said, though. Anytime you want to come over and cry on my shoulder . . . Oh, crud!"

With that, she hung up. I sat with the phone's receiver in my hand, staring at it and feeling sort of shell-shocked.

Travis was remarried?

The ink was barely dry on our divorce papers. How could he be married already?

Obviously he was, because if there was one thing my sister was good at, it was finding out information. Before anyone else. With her skills, she should be a spy for the government.

The reality of my sister's news settled over me like hot tar. So, Travis had just had a blowout wedding and was now off to the Caribbean to honeymoon. Probably at some ultra-exclusive resort with a private staff of chefs and housekeepers. All paid for by his new father-in-law, of course.

That kind of wedding took time to plan, which meant Travis had obviously been seeing Missy behind my back while we were still married. And to think that just last week, as I'd gotten in my pickup and headed south, I'd felt bad, wondering if I hadn't given Travis and our marriage a fair chance.

The scumbag!

I slammed down the phone and bounced out of bed. That did it. I was more than ready to go out on a date now, and I didn't care if the guy's name was Cedric, Francis, or Tweedle-Dee. I took a fresh shower, my hangover pretty well gone. Enough so that a little "hair of the dog that bit me" ought to take care of whatever remained.

I blow-dried my hair, curled the ends, then sprayed it and poufed it. Not southern-Texas-big-hair poufy, but enough to look sexy. Carefully, I applied my makeup and dressed in my best jean skirt, high-heeled cowboy boots, and a frilly little blouse that showed off my tummy. A tummy that was still pretty flat, *thank you very much, Mr. Travis Cheat 'Em High.*

I surveyed myself in the mirror. Not bad, but the outfit needed something else to brighten it up. Hmm. I opened my closet and dug out the pink cowboy hat I'd purchased on a whim at the mall. Not something an honest-to-goodness cowgirl would be caught dead in, but it seemed to fit the Miami definition of western wear. Carefully, I pushed it down on top of my poufy-do. I looked like a rodeo queen. Perfect.

Smiling, I gathered my purse and went downstairs, where Lexie was due to pick me up in her convertible in five minutes. But when she pulled up to the curb in front of my apartment building and got out of her car, I groaned. Suddenly I felt more like a rodeo clown than a rodeo queen.

Lexie looked even better than she had when we went to Fantasies. In her sexy little white strapless number, she could easily be a supermodel. No wonder some guy had bought her a condo. I made a mental note to ask her about that later, maybe when she was well and liquored up.

"Hey, girl!" She threw herself at me and wrapped me in a hug. "That's some hat."

As we pulled apart and slid into the convertible, I noted that her makeup and jewelry were absolute perfection, right down to her aqua-painted toenails and the dainty-looking toe rings that made her feet look pretty and elegant in multicolored heels that must have cost a fortune.

I wanted to yank my hat off my head. But I couldn't. It had stuck to my barely dried hairspray, and if I removed it now, I'd have "hat hair." Poufy hat hair, which is arguably worse than poufy Texas hair.

"I feel like a fool," I said.

"Why?" Lexie's look held genuine puzzlement.

"Isn't it obvious?" I gestured at my outfit. "Look at me compared to you. Let's face it. I've got no fashion sense."

"You look fine, sweetie." She waved away my worries as she pulled into traffic. "That outfit is *so* you."

"It's great for Hicksville, Montana, but not Big City Miami."

"If you want, I'll take you shopping soon," Lexie offered.

"That might be a good idea." But still, I pouted. I wanted toe rings. And a professional pedicure.

"Hailey," Lexie reprimanded, knowing me all too well. "You look cute. Now stop pouting. We're going to have a blast tonight. You hear me?"

"You're right." I sat up straighter in my seat as I remembered the phone call from Bailey. "Especially since I have even more reason to drink my past away." I filled Lexie in on the phone call.

"That pig!" Her pretty eyes flashed fire. "I'd like to find Travis and turn him from a bull into a steer."

We both laughed, and I began to relax. Once we turned onto Ocean Drive, however, my nerves stood on edge again. The strip was crowded with people, mostly tourists, no doubt, and they were all decked out in skimpy, sexy clothes. I was going to stand out like a pair of Payless shoes in a Gucci store.

And truth be told, I was also a bit apprehensive of meeting Cedric. My first date in twelve years! Despite wanting to go out, my confidence began to waver.

Lexie lucked out and snagged a meter parking spot as someone was pulling out in a Mercedes SUV. The sound of energetic salsa music drifted down the street, putting me in the mood to dance. I inhaled the ocean air deeply, thinking that it had been too long since I'd taken a dip in the ocean.

Lexie turned off the car and grabbed her clutch bag. "Let's go."

I smoothed my skirt as I got out of the car. Across the street, I saw the neon sign advertising Mango's, and a throng of people standing outside the door.

"Are you sure I look okay?" I asked.

"Of course you do. Hey, there's Tyrone right now!"

Lexie started to trot, and I fell into step beside her as we crossed the street. A guy who reminded me a lot of Will Smith broke into a grin when he saw us coming.

Lordy, was *that* Tyrone?

Lexie threw herself at him, and he held her tightly. I noticed that his hands went low—onto her butt. Lexie didn't seem to protest. She beamed at him like he was the only man on earth.

He was positively delicious-looking. No wonder Lexie wasn't willing to swap dates. In a loose-fitting black shirt and gray slacks, he had this sexy-casual look that had me getting warm.

"Hailey, this is Tyrone. Tyrone, this is my friend Hailey." Lexie held on to Tyrone's hand like they were lovers. I was sure they had been. And they certainly looked cute together.

Now Lexie gestured to the man standing next to Tyrone. "And this is Cedric."

I offered Cedric my hand, smiling politely. "Hello."

"Hailey." His eyes roamed over me from head to toe. "It is so nice to meet you. God, you're gorgeous! I *love* cowgirls."

"Yeah?" Boy, was I the height of clever conversation or what?

Cedric wasn't bad. He was exactly what Lexie had described—about six feet with sandy blond hair, and he had really nice eyes that were indeed a greenish blue.

And speaking of eyes, Tyrone's were clearly for Lexie. After a polite hello to me, he fixed on her like a bear on a honeycomb. It was Cedric who made me forget I was dressed in a silly pink hat. He looked at me in a way I hadn't been looked at by a man since Travis had sweet-talked his way into my Levi's.

"You look hot in pink," Cedric told me, tucking my arm through his elbow. "And I love that perfume you're wearing. What is it?"

"Um . . . Pink Sugar."

"Get out of here!" He laughed, and the sound filled me with little tingles. He had a nice laugh.

"No, really, it is." I smiled, trying not to show my nervousness. I needed a drink.

Though there was a lineup outside, Lexie waltzed over to a bouncer, whispered something in his ear, and then he motioned for our group to enter. Inside, the four of us made our way to the bar through a crowd that was already near standing-room only. I took in my surroundings, awed by the atmosphere of Mango's—and the shirtless guys dancing on the center bar. I wondered if they would strip down to G-strings. Probably not, but they helped perk up my mood nonetheless. Yeah, tonight would be a blast!

"What do you want to drink?" Cedric asked me, speaking loudly so I would hear him above the club's music.

"I was thinking about a beer," I told him.

"No." Lexie spoke into my ear. "This isn't Montana, baby. Try a Midori Margarita. It's made with melon liquor."

"Okay," I told Cedric. "I'll try that."

A couple minutes later, I was sipping the drink, which was absolutely scrumptious. The bartender—a total hottie who gave me a lingering look—served it up in a pretty glass with a lime slice, cherry, and a little paper umbrella. It was the kind of drink that made me think of the islands and white sandy beaches.

Which made me think of Travis and Missy and the fact that they were probably rolling around in the sand right about now.

"I hope the sand fleas give you malaria," I muttered.

"What?" Cedric asked, leaning his ear close to my mouth.

"Uh, I said thank you. This is just what I needed." I smiled sweetly at him, remembering exactly why I was here—to put Travis out of my mind.

"Your drink looks cool," I told Lexie. It was a lame thing to say, but I was shy about talking to Cedric. It's not easy to get back into the rhythm of dating when you've been off the market for twelve years.

"This is a Banana Cabana," Lexie explained of her drink, garnished with an orange slice, cherry, and sugarcane stick.

"Cheers!" I clinked my glass against hers. "To having a blast and forgetting the past!"

"And to getting laid," she whispered in a singsong voice.

I threw my head back and laughed. *Eat your heart out, Travis.*

Instead of a tropical beach, I pictured him in some rundown Montana honky-tonk, drinking watery draft beer from a chipped mason jar. Ha!

I turned and purred at Cedric. "I'm so glad we're out. This is going to be a waaay fun night!"

Cedric leaned in close, and for a minute, I thought he was going to try to kiss me. Instead, he did something worse.

He sprayed spittle as he talked.

"You have no idea, sweet thing."

Holy moly, his breath smelled like he'd eaten a skunk's butt for dinner. I jerked back, and managed a weak smile.

Terrific. So much for the possibility of getting laid.

Sipping my drink, I turned to Lexie. "This place is awesome!"

"Isn't it?" Her pretty lips curved. "This is my favorite club on the strip. I try to come here at least every other weekend. Hey, we can make it a girls' night out. Me and you. A couple hotties . . ."

"Sounds like a plan." Only next time, we'd leave Cedric at home.

"So, do you want to dance?" Cedric shouted over the noise of the crowd.

I looked at him . . . and thought of Travis. And Missy. And wondered just how long they'd been seeing each other behind my back.

Forget Travis!

"Why not?" I smiled brightly at Cedric. Maybe it would help pass the time. Slugging down about half of my drink, I reminded myself that I was here to have fun. I let Cedric take my hand as the band struck up a catchy reggae number, and the party kicked into high gear.

So did Cedric's hips.

As we reached the dance floor, he was already wiggling and shaking all over the place. He pranced around me like a parade pony, still holding my hand, whirling and shaking. I wasn't quite sure if he was dancing or if he had to go to the bathroom. I hoped no one I knew was watching. Unobtrusively, I eased my hand out of his and did a little dance step of my own. I still had it. Getting into the beat of the music, I cut loose.

"Nice moves!" Lexie teased, dancing up beside me. Across from her, Tyrone looked hot and cool all at the same time, dancing like he'd been born to it.

"Are you sure you don't want to switch partners?" I said directly into Lexie's ear.

"No way." She gave me an evil grin, then boogied merrily away.

The night wore on, and several Midori Margaritas later, Cedric began to dance much better. Or at least from my drunken perspective he did. But everything else just got worse.

Cedric hung on to me like a leech, breathing skunk/beer fumes into my face. I knew I had to escape him, at least for a little while.

I braced my hands on his shoulders and leaned in close to him. "I've got to head to the little girls' room."

"I'll go with you."

"No . . . I think I can find it by myself."

"All right. I'll be waiting for you."

As I walked away from him, Cedric continued to dance like a wild man on the dance floor. Sheesh—did he *ever* get tired?

I sidestepped people as I made my way down a long corridor, figuring this had to be the way to the restrooms. It was, and with the goal line in sight, it was suddenly hard to hold my bladder. Now I shimmied around like Cedric's dance moves had rubbed off on me, dutifully waiting my place in line. I couldn't help remembering Lexie the night outside of the strip club, but thankfully I made it into a stall before my bladder burst.

Oh, the relief.

I was barely out of the restroom and starting down the hall when I felt a hand on my arm. Someone was grabbing me, making me halt. I whipped my gaze around to see who had a hold of me.

A black man with a long, pointy beard stared into my eyes. "Hey, pretty lady. Want some X?"

X? Oh, my God—X!

I yanked my arm free. "No, I don't want Ecstasy!"

My heart pounding, I hurried back toward the dance

floor, wanting to share what had just happened with Lexie. But as I neared it, I suddenly had second thoughts. Lexie would probably laugh her head off if I ran to her and told her some guy had tried to sell me X. She'd remind me I wasn't in Montana anymore.

And I wasn't. No big deal.

"Hey, you." Before I could search for Lexie, Cedric took my hand in his, not missing a beat in his offbeat dance. "Have I told you how gorgeous you are?"

"Yeah, you did." *About a million times.*

"And did I tell you how much I *love* cowgirls?"

"I think so." Where was Lexie?

I scanned the room in desperation. I'd lost sight of her about five dance numbers ago. As my gaze snagged on the door, I saw her. She was leaving! Her arm tucked through Tyrone's elbow, she leaned close to him and said something that made him laugh. Then they were gone. Just like that, leaving me alone with Cedric.

"I got you another drink," Cedric announced, reaching behind me to a wooden ledge.

"Oh," I said glumly. "Well, thank you. But I'm not sure I can drink any more. What are Lexie and Tyrone doing?"

Cedric shrugged. "Maybe hitting another club."

Another club! It could take me all night to find her with the amount of clubs on the strip, not to mention the number of people.

"Hey, you want to get out of here?" he asked, as if reading my mind.

And how! "Actually, I do. I think I'm ready for some sleep."

"Already?"

"Yes. I've got a terrible headache." It was only a half lie.

"I was kinda hoping we could go someplace a little more quiet." Cedric sprayed spittle. "And get to know one another better."

In your dreams.

"Maybe another time," I said. Then I remembered I didn't have a ride home. "You know, we should hurry out and try to find Lexie and Tyrone. She's my ride." Maybe they'd only gone outside for a breath of fresh air, but I doubted it from the way they'd been looking at each other all night.

Cedric set his half-finished beer down on the ledge. "No worry. I can drive you home."

Oh, brother. "Oh, that's okay. I don't want to put you out of your way."

"Out of my way?" He snaked his arm around my waist. "Baby, I promise you it won't be out of my way."

I peeled his hands off of me. "Cedric . . . be good."

"Oh, I can be good, honey. Let me show you."

"No, seriously. I'm just getting over a bad marriage. Right now I'm only interested in making new friends. Nothing more."

"All right." Cedric's lips twisted in a slight scowl. "I'll be good. I'll drive you home and nothing more."

Thank God, he was getting the picture. But did I really

want this guy to know where I lived? Did I really have a choice?

Maybe I could have him drop me off a few blocks away from my apartment, and from there I could walk the rest of the way home. Even in these boots that were already killing my feet.

I plastered on a saccharine smile. "All right, Cedric. You can drive me home."

He placed his hand on the small of my back as we weaved our way out of Mango's. Outside, he led me to a purple Kia Optima parked about fifty yards south of the club. Ever the gentleman, at least in *his* eyes, Cedric held the door for me as I climbed inside. The car smelled like cheap cologne, but not cigarettes, thank goodness. I buckled up and away we went. I gave him directions to my neighborhood and sat back while he talked.

And talked. And talked.

Did the guy never shut up? By the end of the fifteen-minute drive, I knew more about him, his dog, and his family than I cared to. My eyes searched for a likely place to pull over. "Here we are," I lied, as we neared an apartment building located three blocks from mine. I unbuckled my seatbelt, and to my horror, Cedric did the same.

"Aren't you going to invite me up for a nightcap?" he asked. He practically licked his lips.

"Not tonight. My headache has gotten worse. Too many of those drinks." I gave a weak smile. "Maybe another time."

"All right, Pink Sugar. I'm gonna hold you to that."

I tried not to roll my eyes. The guy thought he was too cute.

I was about to try to make my escape when Cedric leaned over and grasped me by the shoulders. He pulled me into a wet, sloppy kiss that had me trying not to gag. I pushed away from him and discreetly wiped my mouth with the back of my hand.

"Oh, my." I tried the coy, country-cowgirl attitude. "I'd better go. Good night." Hastily, I made my exit, climbing the steps to the apartment building's front entrance. I pretended to fumble with my keys, hoping he wasn't going to wait and see if I got safely inside.

He was.

Shit!

Then luck turned my way. A little old lady with white hair came walking up the steps, wearing a brightly colored kimono. On a leash, she led an ancient-looking pug that eyeballed me warily. More importantly, in her hand dangled a set of keys. She bent to pick up Pugsy, cradling him in her arms.

"Oh, what a cute little doggie," I cooed. "Here, let me help you inside."

"Why, thank you, honey," she said, turning over her key without further thought. She really ought to be more careful, but I wasn't complaining. I unlocked the door and followed her inside, turning to wave good-bye to Cedric. Then I lurked in the entryway near the mailboxes, peering through the glass to make sure he was gone.

Ms. Kimono and Pugsy were also gone, already safely

inside an apartment a few doors down the hallway. Cautiously, I headed back outside, hoping Cedric didn't decide to circle the block and come back for another try. But to my relief, he was nowhere in sight. I walked the three blocks to my place as quickly as my sore feet would allow. I hadn't danced so much in ages. In spite of my not-so-hot date, I'd still had a good time at Mango's. Even if Lexie had abandoned me.

I'll bet *she* didn't try to shake Tyrone by having him drop her blocks from her apartment. I could only imagine how they were entertaining each other right now.

Inside my apartment, I deadbolted the door, then slumped against it for a moment, glad the evening was over. I checked on Speedy, gave him some fresh water and some shredded carrot, and promised to buy him a mate first thing tomorrow morning.

I'd been promising to do that since forever, and it was time I got around to it.

After all, I knew what it was like to be alone.

Eight

Lexie

The week after Hailey and I went to Mango's sped by at warp speed. We were still in the talking-things-over phase with Gina in regards to the bookstore. The price was still up in the air, and we needed to make a definite decision soon. Meanwhile, we kept an eye on the paper, and on the local news broadcasts, to see if anything further came to light regarding Rafael's death. But it seemed like the police were doing little or nothing to investigate. The only news that seemed to make the headlines was in regards to the three teens killed by taking the overdose of bad Ecstasy.

Both Hailey and I had checked on Josephine a few times, and she was despondent over the lack of investigation by the police. So when another week passed and there was still no concrete news, Hailey and I decided to do something about it. Both of us hated to see Josephine in such bad shape, and if the situation were reversed, I'd want someone checking things out for me.

On Wednesday afternoon, Hailey picked me up in her little red pickup, and we headed for Fantasies to question the owner of the club. I'd met Sidney Wolfe a time or two, and knew that he'd owned the club for a number of years. Maybe he could shed a little light on the situation.

The place was already buzzing with an afternoon crowd by the time Hailey and I arrived. The people who say that Vegas is the city that never sleeps have never been to Miami.

"Hey, sugar," I said to a passing waiter. "Can you tell me where Sid's office is?"

"Anything for you, gorgeous."

I smiled bashfully and followed the hunk down a hallway that led to a back corridor. He gestured me to the right and a door that was open.

"Thank you, darling."

He winked and strolled away.

Sidney was behind his desk scowling at his computer when I rapped on the open door. He stood as Hailey and I entered the room.

"Lexie Muller." His lips grew wide in a sexy grin. "Come in, come in. What can I do you for, gorgeous?"

Sid was the ultimate definition of beefcake. Probably in his late thirties, he had to be at least six-foot-three, and his tanned biceps bulged beneath the sleeves of a black T-shirt. His teeth were near-perfect—though one had a tiny chip that lent charm to his smile. His eyes were a genuine shade of deep green that really set off all that thick, dark hair he wore in a neat cut. And that Aussie accent of his—I could only imagine what a turn-on it would be in the bedroom.

Mmm-mmm-mmm.

For a moment, I forgot why we'd come.

Hailey touched my arm, bringing me back to the moment. She gave me a look—reproof, or curiosity?—then spoke. "We were wondering if we could have a few minutes of your time, Mr. Wolfe," she said, ever Ms. Sherlock Holmes. "We'd like to ask you a few questions."

"Please, call me Sid." He motioned us to a pair of leather chairs opposite his desk, then perched on the edge of it. "And that sounds very official. Are you a cop?"

"Hailey?" I chuckled. "God, no."

"We have a few questions about what happened to Rafael Martinez," Hailey went on.

"What kind of questions?" Sid asked.

"We hate to be nosy," I said, opting for a subtle approach. "But his significant other is a good friend of ours, and the police don't seem to be doing much to find out what happened to him."

"Ah." Sid nodded, folding his delicious arms across his brawny chest. "You're talking about Josephine."

"Yes," Hailey said. "She's quite shaken up, as you can imagine."

"Well, I don't know how much help I can be." Sid shrugged casually. "The police have already asked a bunch of questions. They searched Rafael's dressing room, his car. The whole nine yards, you know? What more can I tell you?"

"They searched his dressing room?" Hailey squinted in an eager, Nancy Drew sort of way.

"Yep. But they didn't seem to find anything, at least not that I saw."

"Do you mind if we mosey on back and take a look?" Hailey asked.

Sid frowned. "I don't know if that's such a good idea. It might be considered a crime scene or something, you know?"

"Did the police tape it off?" I shifted in the chair and crossed my legs beneath my butter-yellow skirt, so that Sid got a good view of them.

Bingo. Sid's eyes zeroed in on them, then ventured back up to meet mine. "Tape it off?"

"Yeah. With yellow crime scene tape?"

"Oh. Naw, they didn't do that. But they had some of that stuff wrapped around those bushes out back for a while." He jerked his thumb in a gesture toward the window that overlooked the rear parking lot. A location I'd not soon forget.

"Well, then his dressing room is not an official crime scene," I said, giving Sid my sweetest smile. "So, maybe Hailey and I could take a little peek?"

She smiled too and gave him a little wink, and Sid melted into a big beefcake heap of testosterone-laden mush.

"When you put it that way . . . I guess there's no harm in looking." He slid from the edge of his desk and showed us the way down the hall. "Third door on your left, ladies," he said. "Just close it up again when you're done lookin'.'"

"Thank you, Sid, honey." Hailey flashed him a sugary smile.

I hid a grin. The girl was catching on.

Inside Rafael's dressing room, the two of us gazed around. I know I felt a bit anxious being in the room of a man who'd so recently died, and I assumed Hailey had to feel the same.

The room was painted dark green, a dismal color if you ask me, but the lights in the ceiling and on the vanity provided ample illumination. It was small, though, surprising me. I guess I'd expected a big, glamorous dressing room.

Turning, I faced Hailey. "Not exactly what I expected," I commented.

"Yeah." She wrinkled her nose. "It's sorta cramped, isn't it? Lord, you couldn't spin a pig sideways in here." She moved about the room, checking out the modest vanity table that stood beneath a round, lighted mirror. Several items lay scattered on top of it—an array of men's colognes, hair gel, and even a stack of eight-by-ten glossies of Rafael as Don Quixote.

I looked around as well, peering into a tiny closet on the wall opposite the vanity. Some costumes were draped on wooden hangers, and an array of leather shoes and boots lined the floor.

"Hey, look here," Hailey said.

"What?" My heart racing, I turned away from the

closet. Hailey's girl-detective syndrome was rubbing off on me. "Did you find something?"

"Yep. Chocolate!" Triumphantly, she held up a box of chocolate Turtles she'd extracted from beneath the pile of publicity photographs on the vanity, then opened the lid. "Look, the box is still half full." Hailey bit her lip. "Oooo, I *love* Turtles!" She took one from the box and bit into it, moaning with pleasure.

"Hailey, I don't think you should be eating those."

"Why not?" she asked around a mouthful of pecan and caramel. "They're too good to let them go to waste. It's not like Rafael will be eating them." She popped the rest of the candy piece into her mouth and started to reach for another.

"Hailey! You're eating the chocolates of a *dead* man." I shot her a look of reprimand.

"Oh." She paused midchew, then swallowed the candy with a little gulp. "Ew." She wrinkled her bunny nose. "You're right." With a faux-shiver, she closed the lid and set the chocolates back on the vanity. "So, do you see anything else?" She licked chocolate from her fingers. "Anything interesting in the closet?"

"Just costumes and shoes."

"Hmm." Hailey opened the drawers on the vanity and rummaged through them. A laugh sputtered from between her lips as she held up a cinnamon-flavored bottle of massage oil. "Lord have mercy! Guess Josephine likes things sweet and spicy."

"Too much information!" I giggled, then clamped my

lips together. "We should be serious, Hailey. A guy is dead."

"You're right. I'm sorry." Hailey sobered and put the lubricant back in the drawer.

We poked around a little more, but there wasn't anything of interest—other than a complete set of G-strings in every color and fabric imaginable, including blue suede. Remembering the way Don Quixote had strutted his stuff for us, I felt a little sad. He had really been a gentleman, a class act. Why did the good ones always die young?

"No wonder the police didn't find anything." Disappointment laced Hailey's tone. "There's nothing here to find."

"I guess not, unless they took it with them." I sighed. I wanted to help Josephine. "Maybe we can pry some more information out of Sidney. Come on."

"Ladies," he said, when we he saw us strolling toward his office. "Find anything useful?"

"Nope." Hailey shook her head. "Are you sure you don't know anything else that might help the police find out what happened to Rafael?"

Sid shrugged. "He died in the bushes. End of story. My guess is a heart attack. Or maybe drugs. Who knows?"

"Did he have any family?" I asked.

"Yeah. His parents live here in Miami. He seemed pretty close to them, always talking so highly of them. Apparently they used to live in New York, but after he got out of prison, they moved back here."

I stood a little straighter, and beside me, so did Hailey.

"Prison?" we asked simultaneously.

"Yeah. He did a little time for passing some drugs on the street. Nothing big—just some weed, you know?"

"Sure," I said, wanting Sid to trust us. "No biggie. Who doesn't get high off a little weed now and then?"

Hailey threw me a sidelong glance, but I didn't meet her gaze.

"I know, mate. That's what I thought too, you know? I didn't care about that when I hired him. Rafael was a good guy and a great performer. I'm gonna miss him."

"So, where exactly do his parents hang their hats?" Hailey asked.

"Hang their hats?" Sid looked amused.

"Where do they live?" she reiterated.

Sid pursed his lips. "Now, that I can't tell you. It being private information and all that, you know?"

"Oh, come on, Sid," I pouted. I stepped a little closer, and I swear Sid's nostrils flared as he inhaled my Chanel Allure perfume. I ran one fingernail along the edge of his T-shirt sleeve. His muscles were rock-hard, and for a minute I almost forgot that *I* was trying to tempt *him*. "Hailey and I just want to help. Like I said, Josephine is a good friend. She's devastated. You know?" I added his pet phrase.

He looked down, checking out my cleavage, and I was glad I'd worn my lacy Victoria's Secret push-up bra. A tiny bit of the frilly white edge showed—which had to be driving him nuts.

Sid swallowed. "Yeah, well, I guess I can understand that."

"So, can you tell us where they live?" I gave him a coy look.

He melted again. "Oh, what the hell?"

As he reached over and flipped through a Rolodex, I let my hand linger on his back. Sure, it was part of my seduce-information-out-of-him act, but it felt damn good.

Sid scratched an address on a scrap of paper. "They live in Little Havana," he said. "Rosa and Enrique Martinez. They're good people."

"Thanks," I purred, taking the paper from him. I gave him a lingering peck on the cheek. "See you later, handsome."

He wrapped an arm around my waist and whispered, "Lex, you're killing me."

"The feeling's mutual, babe."

"Maybe we can get together again soon. One-on-one. A nice dinner, some wine. You know?"

I did know, and it was a tempting offer. "I'll call you," I told him, and stepped backward to join Hailey.

"'Bye, Sid, honey." Hailey gave him a flirty little wave of her fingers.

Sid grinned from ear to ear as his attention fixed on her. "You ladies don't be strangers, now, you hear?"

"You'll definitely see us again," I told him. I found myself wondering if I'd take him up on his offer for dinner . . . and something else.

"Hey, hold up a sec." Sid held up one finger. He fumbled through the mess on his desk and came up with a couple of neon-green business cards. "These are good for a free drink. Maybe you can make the show this weekend, you know?"

"You bet your boots," Hailey said.

"Thanks, Sid. We'd love to." I tucked the card into my purse and said in a singsong voice, "Buh-bye."

Outside, Hailey shuddered despite the Miami heat. "I don't know if I can stand to watch a strip show here for a while."

"Yeah, I know what you mean. But at least we've got a lead." I held up the scrap of paper with the Martinezes' address on it.

"Good job, Watson!" Hailey grinned at me. "And that was fun. I thought poor Sid was going to die from pleasure when you kissed him on the cheek."

I climbed into her pickup, saying, "He is a hottie."

Hailey shot me a look as she started the truck. "But you've never . . . you know . . . with him . . . ?"

"Had sex?" I supplied, chuckling.

"Yeah, that."

"Hailey, Hailey. I think you do need to get laid. What thirty-year-old refers to sex as 'you know'—except, perhaps, for Sid." We both smiled at that.

"Well?" Hailey prompted.

"No," I told her. "Not that he isn't tempting—and scrumptious-looking. Hey—he could be a perfect palate-cleanser for you!"

"Oh, no—no more setting me up. Not after Cedric, thank you very much."

We both shared a laugh, then headed for Little Havana,

113

and were able to find the address Sid had given us without too much trouble. Rosa and Enrique lived in a cute little house made partially of pale pink frame and partially of shell-pink rock. Square rock pillars held a tiny awning over an equally small porch. Hailey parked, we got out of the truck, then climbed the three steps and knocked on the door.

A middle-aged Latino man with salt-and-pepper hair and a thick mustache answered the door. He had kind eyes. "Yes?" he said, pronouncing it *jes*. "May I help you?"

Suddenly I wasn't sure what to say. Hailey and I hadn't thought to rehearse our conversation as we'd raced over here.

"Are you Enrique Martinez?" I smiled politely.

"*Sí*. I am."

"Hello, Mr. Martinez. My name is Lexie Muller, and this is my friend Hailey McGraw. We're here to offer our condolences in regards to Rafael." I put on a serious, sympathetic look, feeling a little stupid. Sure, I was sorry Mr. Martinez had lost his son. But I really didn't know Rafael.

"*Quien es?*" a woman's voice called from the living room. "Who is it, Enrique?"

Enrique looked over his shoulder as a short round woman with long black hair and equally dark eyes came into view. A second later, she peered over Enrique's shoulder at us, eyeing us warily.

"These girls are here about Rafael," Enrique explained.

"You are friends of my son?" Rosa asked. The sadness

in her eyes nearly broke my heart, and I felt like an imposter. But we *were* honestly trying to help by getting more information.

"Well, sort of," I hedged. "We met him once, but Hailey and I are good friends of Josephine Coletti."

"Oh, you know Josephine!" Rosa clasped both hands to her breast. "Come in, come in. Enrique, move aside and let these young ladies through." She pushed past him and opened the screen door.

"Thank you," I said.

Hailey introduced herself, and we sat on a worn but comfortable maroon velvet sofa in the Martinezes' living room.

"Mrs. Martinez—" Hailey began.

"Aw." Rosa waved one hand. "Call me Rosa. Please."

"Rosa," Hailey went on, "Lexie and I are so very sorry for your loss. To tell you the truth, we're a bit upset that the police aren't doing more to look into Rafael's death. We're trying to find out whatever we can, to see if we might be able to figure out what happened to him."

"*Dios míos!*" Rosa exclaimed. "I too am so sick of the police and their stupidity!" She rattled off a few choice words in Spanish that I didn't understand but got the general meaning of. "They do nothing to find my son's killer! Nothing!"

"Rosa," Enrique soothed, laying a gentle hand on his wife's arm. "Don't get so worked up." He turned to us. "All they say is that the autopsy showed traces of mercury poisoning. They do not know how it got there, but they think Rafael was poisoned gradually, over a period of time."

"Poison!" Hailey looked appalled. "Who would do such a thing?"

"*No lo se.*" Rosa shrugged.

"The police are not even sure if this was an intentional poisoning," Enrique explained. "Or if he was exposed to mercury in his environment."

"He was killed!" Rosa exclaimed. "And I know this much." She wagged one forefinger. "The *policía*, they do not care to look too hard for my son's killer, and you know why? I'll tell you why. Because he was a stripper!" She went off into another stream of Spanish, and again Enrique calmed her.

"Our son had a bit of trouble finding work," he said sadly, "after he got out of prison. If you are friends of Josephine, you must know he served time for selling marijuana."

I nodded. "Yes."

"He made one mistake!" Rosa said heatedly. "He paid for his crime, and he turned his life over to God." She clasped the cross hanging on a simple gold chain around her neck as she spoke. "He was only working as a dancer because he could not find another job. No one wanted to give him a chance. I hated that he took off his clothes for women!" She began to cry. "My Rafael, he was a good boy—so young! Only twenty-five!" She held the crucifix to her lips and kissed it. "*Madre de Dios.*"

Enrique rubbed Rosa's shoulder and murmured to her in Spanish. She sniffled, then reached for a tissue from a box on the end table.

I felt awful for upsetting her.

"Are you sure you can't think of anyone who would want to harm Rafael?" Hailey asked gently.

Suddenly Rosa narrowed her eyes. "Yes, and I told the *policía* this also. It might be that *puta*, Bianca! *La hija de Diablo*—with her big, spooky eyes!"

"Who's Bianca?" I asked.

"She *is* the devil's daughter," Enrique said, his dark eyes furious. "She took advantage of my son when he was vulnerable, and he ended up having an affair with her."

An affair. Whoa. I shot Hailey a quick glance, and she raised her eyebrows at me as if to say, *Things are getting interesting!*

"Rafael met Bianca a few months ago," Rosa said. "He was depressed because he and Josephine had had a small argument over something stupid. He was staying with us for a few days while they worked things out. Bianca saw him at the club where he worked, got him drunk, and took him home with her. She sleeps with a man on the first night, that *puta*! That woman is no good!" Rosa waved one finger again. "She does drugs, and I know she was trying to drag my son back down again!"

Enrique nodded. "I think she was getting him mixed up with the wrong crowd. Maybe that is how he got killed."

"Do you know Bianca's last name?" I asked.

"No." Enrique shook his head. "We tell the police, but without the last name or address . . ." He waved his hands in a dismissive gesture. "They are no help."

"Rafael should never have gotten involved with that tramp!" Rosa reiterated. "He had Josephine—such a kind, sweet young woman." She began to sob all over again. "I think the world of her. She was good for my son, and she would've given me such beautiful grandbabies!"

I could barely contain my shock. *Grandbabies?* Hailey and I exchanged glances, Hailey's eyes widening briefly. Obviously, poor Rosa had no idea that Josephine was a transsexual . . . well, almost.

"I think we should go," I said, standing. I reached out and took Rosa's hand, then gave her a little hug. "Try not to be discouraged. I'm sure something will come to light. Hailey and I will do what we can to help."

"You bet we will," Hailey said firmly. "We'll go back to Fantasies and find out if anyone there knows this Bianca woman. Don't you worry, Rosa—Enrique." She put her hands on her hips. "I'm good at snooping."

"*Muy bien,*" Enrique said. "*Muchas gracias.*"

"No *problema*. If there was foul play involved, we'll find out." Hailey gave them each a hug. "Can we have your phone number, so we can call if we find out anything useful?"

"*Sí*, of course." Rosa wrote down the number, and Hailey and I gave her ours as well.

"We'll see you later, then," Hailey said.

"*Adiós.*" I gave a little wave and stepped outside.

Neither Hailey nor I said anything to each other until we were down the sidewalk, out of earshot.

"Grandbabies!" Hailey bit her lip, trying not to laugh. "Ohmygod, it's not funny, but . . ."

"I nearly peed my pants when she said that."

"It took all my self-control not to laugh out loud."

"How can she not know?" I went on. "I mean, how was Rafael going to explain no babies? Or were they going to dress Josephine with a fake belly and hire out a surrogate on the side?"

Hailey grimaced as we climbed into her truck. "Beats the hell out of me. But I wasn't about to spill the beans."

"I know," I said, getting serious again. "I feel so bad for them. No matter how Rafael lived his life, he didn't deserve to die like that."

"Poisoned." Hailey shuddered. "You think it was accidental—something he ingested somewhere without knowing it? Or do you think it was murder?"

"Well, we're just gonna have to find out—aren't we, Sherlock?"

Nine

Hailey

As much as we wanted to learn more about Bianca, Lexie and I decided not to head back to Fantasies right then. We also decided not to tell Josephine what we'd learned about Rafael's affair with Bianca. Josephine had been through enough stress already. And if she didn't know—which seemed likely, since she hadn't said anything about Rafael's infidelity when she'd been so distraught—then why add to her heartache and give her more reason to take a dive off her roof? Rafael was dead and gone, and it was all muddy water under a shaky bridge.

The next day—Thursday—Lex and I made arrangements to meet with Gina once more. She met us at the store, which was a scattered mess of half-packed boxes and partially emptied shelves. She'd quit packing things up once we'd offered to buy her out. The coffee counter with its latte maker and cappuccino machine was still intact as well, and Gina fixed us a treat that was one of her specialties—iced coffee topped with whipped cream and a cherry. She'd dubbed the concoction Whipped Delight.

"You hungry?" she asked, setting the drinks in front of us. "I brought some fresh-baked cookies from home."

"Thanks, Gina. You know I can't resist your cookies," I told her as she brought forth a Saran-Wrapped platter. I peeled past the plastic and scooped up a cookie. It was still warm.

"Yeah, thanks." Lexie stared wistfully at the white-chocolate, macadamia-nut cookies. "I'm sure going to miss these."

"If you're going to take over my shop, I want my customers to still enjoy these," Gina said. "It's tradition, so I'll give you the recipe. But you have to promise to keep it a secret."

"We won't tell a soul," I promised. "Not even my turtles." I'd finally gotten Speedy a mate, and I'd named her Missy B—in spiteful honor of Travis's new wife.

Gina sat on a stool behind the counter. "Look, girls. I know you're almost there on making your decision, and I really do want this thing to happen. So here's what I'm going to do for you. I'm going to drop my asking price— by ten big ones." She sobered. "My brother is really sick, and he needs this experimental treatment for his cancer as soon as possible. But it's pretty costly. I need the money ASAP."

"Oh, Gina, I'm so sorry!" I laid my hand on her arm, thinking of my dad's recent death. "I know how hard it can be to watch a loved one struggle with such a horrible disease. Is there anything Lexie and I can do to help? Besides buying your store, I mean?"

"Thanks, but I just need to get things tied up here so I can go on out to California. Taking over the bookstore is the best favor you can do for me right now. And I'll feel so much better knowing it's in good hands."

"Well, you're certainly giving us a good deal," Lexie said. "I'm ready to commit. Hailey?" She looked at me for approval.

I nodded. "I say we have a deal!"

"Oh, that's wonderful, girls! You have made me one happy woman."

"When do we sign the papers?" I asked.

"Can you meet me at my lawyer's office on Monday?" Gina asked. "Say, ten-thirtyish?"

"Monday's fine with me," Lexie said.

I nodded. "Monday works."

Gina gave us the address of her attorney's office. "I'll call and set up the appointment, and in case that time isn't good for my lawyer, I'll let you know. Otherwise, I'll see you there." Gina paused, stared at us each in turn. "Now, as for the money . . . how long do you think it will take to get a mortgage?"

"My bank isn't far from there," Lexie said. "I'll get a cashier's check made up for my half, then meet you two at ten-thirty."

"Ditto," I said.

Gina placed a hand on her chest. "You're going to pay me cash outright?"

"You bet," I told her.

"God bless you both." She lifted her cup of espresso in a toast. "Here's to a bright new future for all of us."

"Cheers!" Lexie exclaimed, and we all clinked glasses.

"Hey," I began, "if we're making a fresh new start, I think we need to give the store a new name. Any suggestions?" Sipping my Whipped Delight, I glanced from Lexie to Gina. But the look on Gina's face dimmed my excitement.

"Gina?"

"It's nothing," she said, waving a hand. "Of course you'll change the name. I still can't believe this store won't be mine anymore."

"Maybe not officially," Lexie said, "but the whole place has your touch written all over it. And I'm sure I speak for Hailey when I say that we don't want to lose that special touch. Hey—how about we make a miniature version of Gina's store sign and put it right in this area—along with a picture of Gina? It'll be our way of always honoring this store's heritage."

"What a great idea," I said.

"Oh, you two. You're gonna make me cry. That's so thoughtful."

"This is still your legacy," Lexie said.

Gina dabbed at her eyes. "Thank you. But it's your store now. How about calling it Lexie and Hailey's Used Books?"

Lexie wrinkled her nose. "That doesn't have the same ring to it as your name, Gina."

Gina shrugged. "Well, I'm sure you both will come up with something suitable."

"I have an idea," I said as a thought hit me. "Since Gina doesn't have many nonfiction titles left in stock, how about if we put them in a sale bin and get rid of them, then carry only fiction from now on?" I gave Lexie a playful nudge. "We could call the store Nothing But Lies. You know—since it'll be all fiction?"

Lexie laughed out loud. "Now, that's a great idea. And it'll surely grab people's attention."

"Nothing But Lies it is, then," Gina said. She stood, giving the coffee counter a firm slap with the palms of both hands. At least she was smiling again, no longer wistful.

Lexie and I did a high five.

"Now," Gina said, "if you girls will excuse me, I've got a million things to do."

"No problem." I slurped down the rest of my drink. "Thanks for the Whipped Delight, Gina."

"You're welcome."

Outside, Lexie and I squealed with excitement, grabbing on to each other's hands. "I can't believe it!" I said. "We're bookstore owners!"

"And partners." Lexie grinned. "Like always."

"You'd better know it. Man, I can hardly believe the deal Gina gave us!"

Lexie opened the driver's door on her Lexus and slipped behind the wheel. "Yeah, it's almost too good to be true."

"I hope she feels the deal was fair," I said as I buckled up. "Clearly she wants to get out of town to be with her sick brother, which is why she sweetened the deal."

"I'm sure she wouldn't have offered us that price if she didn't think it was fair." Lexie backed out of the parking spot, then whizzed onto Collins. "Wait a minute," she suddenly said.

I looked at her, saw her puzzled expression. "What is it, Lexie?"

"Hailey, I don't remember Gina saying her brother had cancer. Do you?"

I wracked my brain for a minute. "You know, you're right. My brain was a little fuzzy the night we found her packing at two A.M., but I thought she said something about needing money to leave town because she was trying to escape her obsessive ex-husband."

"That was it. Exactly."

"And something about her mother needing a heart transplant because of a weak ticker. Her words."

"That's right! We were both drunk, but it's coming back to me now. She mentioned her mom having to wait on the donor's list, and she also called her brother an 'irresponsible idiot'! Why would she say that if he's dying of cancer?"

"That's definitely weird. Either she's lying or she's got a

whole lot of shit going on in her family right now. And I can't see Gina lying . . ."

"Want to go back and ask her about it?" Lexie hesitated, slowing the car as we neared an intersection.

"No." I waved my hand. "I really don't care what her reasons are for selling, as long as she's giving us such a good deal on the store."

"You're right." Lexie shrugged. "And who knows— maybe she's so caught up in her personal problems with her ex, she made all that other stuff up because she's embarrassed or something."

"Could be. In any case, I'm not going to let it spoil our day. Woo-hoo!" I raised one fist in a victorious shake. "We are business owners, girlfriend!"

"Want to go to Fantasies tomorrow night to celebrate?" Lexie asked. "Or are you still not up for that yet?"

"No, I think I'm ready to rodeo." I grinned. "And I can't think of any better way to party than with naked men. Providing none of them end up dead. Besides, then we can question Sidney some more. See if he knows anything about Rafael and Bianca."

"Exactly what I was thinking, Sherlock. Exactly."

The next day, Lexie and I made plans to meet early that evening so we could get a good table at the club for when the show began at nine. We also wanted to have time to pump Sid for information before the place got busy.

"Hey, Lex," I said when I called her just before seven-thirty. "You ready yet?"

"Just about."

"Great. I can swing down to your place and pick you up."

"Uh . . . no."

"What do you mean? We have to get going."

"Here's the thing. As much as I have nothing against Montana or pickups in general, this is South Beach. And we're going out for a night on the town. We're gonna look sexy. And no offense, but we need a sexy ride."

"At least it's red," I said weakly, though I couldn't disagree with Lexie's logic. I already felt a little self-conscious driving my banged-up Ranger around in a city full of sleek, sexy cars and glitzy SUVs. I really was going to have to splurge on something new. Something fun.

"I'll pick you up," Lexie said sweetly. "It's along the way, anyway."

Fifteen minutes later, Lexie showed up at my door. When she saw me walk down my building's front steps, she lifted her sunglasses and whistled. "Girlfriend, when did you get *that* dress? Because you didn't get it when I took you to the Bal Harbour Shops."

"I took a trip to the Aventura Mall," I explained. "Decided I needed a whole new wardrobe—not just the pieces you helped me pick out." I'd had a blast trying on and buying sexier clothes. I felt like a new woman.

"Wow." Lexie made a sizzling sound. "You are hot!"

Smiling, I twirled. I knew I looked good in this dress. The ocean blue was just the right shade to highlight my eyes. And it was short—daringly so—and fit my body like a second skin. The spaghetti straps were made of rhinestones.

"Don't you love the shoes?" Lexie asked. "I knew the moment I saw them they would look amazing on you."

I glanced down at my feet, which looked sexy for the first time in forever. The jewel-encrusted Manolo Blahniks had been my first big splurge when Lexie took me shopping last week—a price tag I'd justified given what I'd saved on the bookstore purchase. And I was wearing toe rings! Sparkly toe rings that were bound to make any man melt like butter on a biscuit. I'd even had bold red polish painted on my toenails at a salon.

I was ready to party my butt off. And maybe even get lucky.

Lexie looked hot as usual, this time in a silver sheath that passed for a dress. Matching sandals with straps that crisscrossed over her calves completed the outfit. Her dangling diamond earrings made her look like a million bucks.

Never mind the exotic dancers being our fantasy. I walked into the club with Lexie, feeling like we could be *their* fantasy.

Lexie strolled past me around the back seating area, her hips swaying in a sexy swagger. I watched her and tried to do the same.

"You look so good, hon," I told her when she paused at

the entrance of the back hallway. "I give Sidney thirty seconds before he's telling you everything we want to know."

Lexie laughed. "You're looking pretty damned good yourself, girlfriend." She lowered her voice. "Sid doesn't stand a chance."

This time he wasn't in his office—he was behind the bar, overseeing things. Waiters in bow ties but no shirts whipped up drinks for the row of women sitting on bar-stools. A few of the women looked me and Lexie up and down—leered, really. I guess they were sizing up the competition, and I'm not trying to boast, but they didn't stand a chance either. I felt like Cinderella—Miami-style.

"Ladies!" Sid spotted us right away and waved us over. "I see you came to collect on those free drinks."

"And to see you, of course." With a delicate flick of her wrist, Lexie pulled her neon-green card out of her hand-bag. I did the same, handing mine over to the bartender, a well-built black guy who was yummy enough to be a dancer himself.

"Get these girls whatever they want," Sid told him.

We both ordered cosmopolitans.

As the bartender mixed the drinks, Sid came around the bar to greet us. He looked us up and down like a man on a diet who wanted something sweet. "Wow," he said. "You look amazing."

"Why, thank you," Lexie purred. She gave Sid's bicep a little rub. "You're not so bad yourself."

"Now, if only this was a female strip club, I'd hire you both in a second." His hot gaze made me tingle. "You'd bring me in the big bucks, for sure."

"You sweet-talker," I said, giving him a coy look.

Sid inhaled a deep breath as his gaze roamed over first me, then Lexie. "I'm gonna have to force myself away from you two if I ever expect to get work done tonight, you know? I'll let you pretty ladies get settled at a table, but I'll come around to check on you later."

"Actually"—Lexie placed a hand on Sid's chest to stop him—"Hailey and I have been wanting to talk to you all week."

His eyebrows went up—twin caterpillars on a twig. "Is that a fact?"

"Got a minute?" She gave him her sweetest smile, showing off her perfect teeth.

"For you, I've got all the time you need." Sid indicated his office with a jerk of his head. "Come on back, girls. Bring your drinks."

We took the cosmos Mr. Yummy handed us, then followed Sid to his office. As he closed the door behind us, I sipped my drink somewhat nervously. I hoped we hadn't just shut ourselves in the lion's den.

As before, Sid motioned us into chairs. He then slid onto the corner of his desk, folding his arms over his chest. There was no mistaking the hot look he was giving us, like he was hoping he'd get lucky.

"Ladies, I'm all yours."

"We won't keep you long," I told him. "We went to see

Rafael's parents after the last time we saw you, and they mentioned something interesting. That Rafael had been involved with a woman named Bianca." I studied him, closely watching his reaction.

"Know anything about that?" Lexie added.

"Ah, Bianca. Yeah." Sid gave a solemn nod. "She's trouble, that's for sure. Got herself knocked up."

My mouth fell open in shock. "She's pregnant? With Rafael's baby?"

"That's just what I heard, you know? She showed up at the club one night a while back and stayed late until Rafael was finished. I heard them arguing in his dressing room. Sounded like she was angry, saying that of course the baby was his. The next day, Rafael came into work looking real glum, you know? I asked him what was up, and he told me about the baby. Said Bianca was in her first trimester."

Holy moly!

"You think the baby is really his?" Lexie asked. She gave me a look I could easily read.

Poor Josephine.

Sid shrugged. "Who knows? I wouldn't trust a woman like Bianca as far as I could throw her. But Rafael believed her. It got him pretty upset, him being in a relationship with Josephine and all. I think Bianca was supposed to be more of a one-night stand than a full-blown affair, you know?"

I nodded, already plotting how we could get Sid to tell us more. Maybe we could find Bianca and talk to her too.

"Do you know where to find her?" Lexie asked.

Sid's lips twisted in a playful grin. "What are you two—Agatha Christie and Poirot?"

"Concerned friends," I answered simply.

"Determined to figure out who murdered him," Sid went on. "You're good friends. I admire that."

"Murder?" Lexie asked.

I perked up. "Is it officially a homicide now?"

"Apparently. The cops were back here just a couple of days ago."

"And?" I prompted, excited.

"Here's what happened." Sid lowered his voice. "I got a guy working here for me—cleaning, you know? Name's Manuel, and he's not exactly legal, you know?"

Lexie and I both nodded. Sid was hardly the only business owner in South Florida to employee illegal aliens. None of *my* business. All I cared about was finding out what had happened to Rafael.

"Anyway, I suddenly remembered that Rafael wasn't feeling so hot the night he died. He'd come in to work about seven o'clock, looking kinda peaked and sweaty. Seemed kinda out of it, but I figured he was distracted, you know? He had a lot on his plate with Bianca's news. I told him he could go home if he wanted, but he said he'd go ahead and work, 'cause he needed the money. So he stayed, and put on a helluva show based on the audience reaction, and I figured everything was fine, you know? Then, boom—you ladies find him dead in the bushes."

"His parents told us he'd been poisoned with mercury," Lexie said. "The police think it happened gradually, over a period of time. They weren't sure how he'd been exposed to it, or if it was even murder."

"Yeah, and the police got on my case something good for that, let me tell ya. Thinking there was mercury here in the club, that it wasn't safe. A team of people came in to check the place from top to bottom. I had to close down shop for a good coupla days. I had dancers threatening to quit—all scared, you know? Lost a shitload of money too. And who's gonna pay me back?"

"So what happened next?" Lexie asked, subtly urging him to get to the important part of the story.

"So the police do all this testing, right, and the place comes up negative for mercury anywhere. But get this." He leaned forward, eager to share what he knew, now that things had gotten juicy. "Manuel, the illegal alien—he'd been in Rafael's dressing room earlier that night, cleaning up like he usually does. And he sees some chocolate candy on the vanity—those Turtle things, you know? Manny's got a sweet tooth, so he snags a few out of the box and eats them. Later on, he feels sick. But he doesn't say anything, because he doesn't want to draw attention to himself, him being illegal and all that, you know?"

Goosebumps broke out on my skin.

"Chocolate Turtles?" Lexie asked, then shot me a look.

"Yeah, that's right. But when Manny heard about Rafael dying from mercury poisoning, and that the coroner found some nut and caramel chocolate in the contents of

Rafael's stomach, he came to me and fessed up. Scared shitless, he was. Thought he was gonna die and figured the decent thing to do before he croaked was at least tell the cops what he knew. They looked the other way, of course, not much caring that he'd come in on a raft from Cuba. The cops were just grateful for another lead, seeing as though they hadn't thought to analyze the Turtles right off. But they took them to their CSI lab or wherever they take that kind of stuff . . ." Sid's voice trailed off and he said with concern, "Hailey, you don't look so good."

I gripped the edge of my chair as the room started to spin. "Oh, my God . . . Oh, my God!"

"Hailey, sweetie." Lexie clutched my arm. "Are you okay?"

"Of course I'm not okay!" I shouted. I met Lexie's eyes, wondering if she'd lost her mind. "Lex, I *ate* one of those Turtles the other night! Ohmygod!" Already I could feel myself slipping away. I was going to die. Right here at Fantasies. Just like Rafael. And I hadn't even had post-marital sex yet!

"I feel sick." I gripped my stomach. "Oh, shit!"

"Hailey. Damn, girl!" Lexie gripped my arm harder as I stood up. "Take it easy. I'm sure you're fine."

"I'm not fine!" I felt my throat begin to close, and I clawed at it. I could barely breathe. "I've been poisoned! Somebody call 911. Ohhh, I think I'm gonna faint."

"Get her over here," Sid said, rising quickly and taking me by the other arm. "Let her lie down." He cleared off a leather love seat I hadn't noticed before, for all the magazines and papers piled on top of it. Then he hurried over and jerked the office door open. "Casey!" he shouted, making my head echo.

Was my brain swelling? I moaned and closed my eyes, slumping over on the love seat. My tongue had grown thick and dry. I tried to lick my lips.

"Casey, bring us a wet towel!" Sid barked as Mr. Yummy poked his head in through the open door.

I peered at him through one half-closed eye. "I've been poisoned," I gasped. "Call an ambulance."

"She's not poisoned," Lexie said, having the gall to shake her head. "Just get me the towel." She sank down on the edge of the love seat, patting my wrist. "Hailey, get ahold of yourself."

"How can I get ahold of myself when I've been poisoned?" I shrieked.

"You're gonna be fine."

"The room is spinning, Lex. And I can hardly breathe," I croaked. "I'm hot and cold at the same time."

"Shit," Sid said. "I think Rafael suffered the same symptoms."

With that confirmation of my pending doom, I squeezed Lexie's arm and screamed, "Lex, help me!"

"I am helping you," she said in a calm, patient voice. Good ol' Lexie. I was sure she was going to miss me.

Suddenly loud music filled the club, and I heard frenzied screaming. Great. I could just imagine my sister's reaction to learning that I'd died in a strip club. She'd probably think it was divine intervention.

"How much of that chocolate did she eat?" Sid asked.

"One," Lexie told him.

"Only one?"

"Yeah. That's how I know she's not dying."

"I *am* dying," I told them. "Feel my face, Lexie. It's clammy. Why would it be clammy if I'm not dying? You heard Sid. He said Rafael suffered the same symptoms."

"That's before I knew you ate only one candy," Sid commented. "Hell, Manny had at least four or five."

I moaned long and loud, effectively shutting Sid up. How dare he minimize my suffering?

Casey came back with the towel, and Lexie laid it across my forehead. It was cool and damp, and man, it felt good. Casey hovered nearby, staring at me with genuine concern.

"Lex," I said softly, trying to save my strength, "see if Mr. Yummy over there will give me a good-bye kiss. Send me from this world a happy woman."

"Enough of that," Lexie told me. "You're making yourself sick, thinking about that candy."

"Gaaawd," I moaned. My hand shot to my stomach. "I think I'm getting cramps. It's gotta be the mercury poisoning mixing with the alcohol. I'm going to die with a mercury-cosmo in my stomach. And I'm wearing my first pair of Manolo Blahniks!"

This was *so* not fair.

"You are not dying," Lexie said. "It's all in your head."

"No, it's not—it's in my stomach." I groaned, trying to focus. "Kiss me good-bye, Casey. I'm fading fast."

Sid laughed. And that was all it took to piss me off. Here I was, dying right in the guy's office, and he thought it was funny?

"I'm glad you think it's so amusing," I said, half sitting up. "You'll be lucky if Lexie doesn't sue you once I'm gone. You're the one who let us into Rafael's dressing room."

"Hey!" Sid frowned, looking defensive. "I told you girls you shouldn't go back there. But you sweet-talked me, and what's a guy to do, you know?"

"Enough." Lexie glared at both of us. She pressed me back down on the love seat. "Just lie here for a few minutes, Hailey, and you'll be fine. Nobody's suing anybody, and you are *not* dying!"

"You need another drink," Sid said. He motioned to Casey. "Bring her a fresh cosmo."

"Right away," Casey said. But from the corner of my eye, I caught the wistful look he gave me. I think he was hoping for the kiss I'd requested.

"I don't know," I said. "Maybe I shouldn't drink any more, on top of the mercury and all."

"You ate *one* chocolate," Lexie said. "And even if it had mercury in it, it must not have been enough to do anything to you, or you would've noticed it long before now."

"Don't be so sure," I said, rising up on one elbow again. "It took Rafael days to die."

"Yeah, but he was really sick," Sid said. "I'm not kidding. Like I said, he was sweating and all that. Looked like hell." He shook his head. "What a waste. He was my best dancer."

Casey came back with my cosmo, and I eyed it suspiciously. God knows who might've poisoned Rafael. But one look from Lexie was enough to make me take a risk. If I died, so be it. I took a sip, then another. My head was starting to feel a little less foggy, but my stomach still hurt.

"Are you sure we shouldn't call an ambulance?" I asked, giving Casey my best pitiful look.

He grinned. "Whatever you want, babe. An ambulance . . . a kiss. I'd be happy to give you a proper send-off, whether you're going to heaven, hell, or home to my place later." He wriggled his eyebrows, and Sid graced him with a look that had him backing out the door. "Sorry." Hurriedly, Casey left.

I pouted.

"You okay now, Hailey?" Sid asked.

"I . . . I'm not sure. Well, maybe." My stomach had calmed, and my sweaty palms weren't quite so damp. The cosmo had started to give me a pleasant buzz, and I felt a little silly.

"Tell you what," Sid said. "Never mind the free drink cards. You ladies can be my guests here tonight." He waved a hand. "Anything you want. On the house."

"Thanks, Sid," Lexie said. "That's sweet."

Sweet, hell. He probably just didn't want to get sued.

"No problem." Sid placed his hands on his hips. "Guess I'd better get back out front. Hailey, you stay here as long as you want. Then come on out and have a good time. I'm sure the naked guys will cheer you up."

I shot Sid a fierce look before sitting the rest of the way up. I swung my feet to the floor and wriggled my toes. My shoes still looked good, and my toe rings sparkled. I felt better just appreciating how pretty my feet looked.

"I think I'm okay now."

"One more thing, Sid." Lexie left my side and slipped her arm around Sid's waist. "Do you know where we can find Bianca?"

His lips twisted, and his gaze wandered. He definitely looked uncomfortable. "Lex . . ."

"We need this info, Sid," Lexie told him. "Please."

"Some ritzy high-rise in Aventura."

I saw the slightest flash of discomfort in Lexie's eyes— so brief, I'm sure Sid missed it. In fact, she went right back to being sexily coy, cocking her head and looking up at him from beneath her thick dark lashes. "Do you have the address?"

He shrugged. "I know the name of the apartment, because I gave Bianca a ride home one night when she got too drunk to drive. But I'm not so sure I should be getting you girls involved any more than you already are. I probably shouldn't have even told you where to find Rosa and Enrique, you know? The cops might not like it."

"It's not against the law to tell us the name of Bianca's apartment," Lexie said. "Come on, Sid. We won't tell a soul."

"Oh, hell," I said, looking right at Sid as I clutched my stomach once more. "Maybe I'm not feeling so hot after all."

"She did eat that chocolate," Lexie added with a little sigh, catching on right away.

Sid wagged his finger at her. "You girls are bad."

"So bad, we're good." Lexie gave his waist a squeeze. "Come on, baby, you can tell us. We want to ask Bianca a couple of questions—that's all. For Josephine's sake."

"Oh, all right. She lives at the Peninsula. About ten minutes north of here, somewhere off Biscayne Boulevard."

"Northeast 183rd Street." Again, I saw something that resembled unease in Lexie's eyes. "I know it. Do you know which unit?"

"Apartment seven-eleven. That stuck in my head, you know? But remember, you didn't hear it from me."

I went to Sid, smiling sweetly as I handed him the damp towel. "I feel better already."

"You're a doll, Sid." Lexie stood on tiptoe, and instead of a peck on the cheek, she kissed him on the mouth. Sid's eyes widened in shock, but the kiss was over before he could enjoy it.

I shot Lexie a curious gaze, but she was already walking toward the door. I followed her.

"Lex?" Sid said.

Lexie stopped at the door, throwing her gaze over her shoulder at him. "Yeah?"

"You ladies be careful, you hear? I want you alive so you can take me up on my offer for dinner. I'm serious."

Sid's words were somewhat ominous, making me wonder if we were about to get ourselves into some trouble.

"We'll be fine," Lexie assured him. "And we'll be back here for those free drinks you promised before you know it." She gave him a sexy smile that would've melted ice in an igloo. "And we'll do dinner. Definitely."

Sid grinned from ear to ear. "I can't wait, babe."

Ten

Lexie

Hailey and I didn't bother to stay for the show. Instead, I told Hailey that I wanted to get going on this new lead, so we headed for the exit, catching only a glimpse of a hot guy dressed as a policeman onstage as we walked back through the club.

Outside, we climbed into my car. "Are you feeling okay?" I asked her. The crisis had passed, but I wanted to know how she was emotionally.

"I'm fine," Hailey said, waving my concerns aside. She looked somewhat embarrassed. "You were right. It was all in my head."

"Are you sure?" I felt a little guilty. After all, she *had* eaten one of Rafael's chocolates. And I would absolutely die if anything happened to her. "We can stop by the ER if you want to play it safe."

She shook her head as I drove toward the parking lot's exit. "I think you're right. We should head to Bianca's apartment right away, and see if we can catch her at home. And hey—what was with you in Sid's office?"

"Because I kissed him on the lips? It wasn't an open-mouth kiss, Hailey. And I just wanted—"

"That's not what I'm talking about. And I think you know that."

I didn't meet her gaze as I turned left onto Northeast 163rd Street.

"Come on, Lex," she said. "What's up?"

"It's just . . . I've been to that condo, okay?"

"And?"

"And it doesn't exactly hold fond memories for me."

"Alexandra Muller, you look at me right now."

Grudgingly, I glanced to my right. "Yeah?"

"I've been your friend forever. Sure, we weren't in touch for years, but you have to know you can still trust me. I love you, girlfriend. So tell me what's bothering you."

I sighed, long and loud. But Hailey was right. We did go way back. If I could confide in anyone, it was her. And I hadn't really talked to anyone when all this drama in my life had gone down. I'd just held my pain inside and tried to move on. Clearly, I hadn't done a one hundred percent great job at that, considering how tense I was at the thought of heading to the Peninsula.

"Remember that guy I told you about? The one I said bought me my place?"

"The married guy?"

"He lives at the Peninsula. At least, he did. I've been to his place several times. I even had a key."

"Where was his wife?"

"I guess at the house they had in Miami Lakes. A house I didn't know about until I learned I was the other woman. He had this whole charade going, with the bachelor pad on the beach, so I had no idea he had another family. I guess his wife knew he was a cheating dog and hired an investigator to follow him. That's how she found out about me."

"Holy shit."

I turned left onto Biscayne Boulevard. "Yeah, that's what I said when she approached me in the parking lot of my building. And Hailey, it was priceless. She was holding a baby, maybe five or six months old. Tears streaming down her face. Begging me not to ruin her happy home. The whole nine yards."

"Happy home, my ass. Who was the bastard, and how could he afford to keep two homes?"

"Richard Ford. He was a star on the Miami Dolphins. I guess I was flattered by his attention. I didn't question the gifts he bought me, since he could afford them."

"Oh, Lexie." Hailey patted my arm. "You were in love with him, weren't you?"

Had I been? Oh, who was I kidding? Hailey's question alone had my stomach twisting painfully. "Yeah," I answered honestly. "And he broke my heart."

"How long ago was this?" Hailey asked.

"A year ago. We dated for six months. Six months, and I never had a clue!"

"Right after his wife would have given birth."

"I guess so." I shook my head, remembering the awful day I'd learned the truth. "Shithead."

"Now I get it. Why you don't trust men."

"Yeah, well, that was an easy one, Sherlock."

We fell silent, and a short while later, I turned right onto Northeast 183rd Street. The gorgeous white building with blue-tinted windows stood proudly in the distance.

"Stunning," Hailey whispered.

"Yeah," I agreed. "It's quite something. You should see the view of the Intracoastal Waterway and the Atlantic Ocean. And like practically all the high-priced neighborhoods in Miami, it has a gated access. Aren't you glad we brought my car?"

I smiled sweetly at Hailey's questioning look. Then I stretched an arm past her to open the glove compartment.

"You still have the gate key?" Hailey asked me.

I pulled up to an electronic sensor outside of an iron gate and held the white card key up to it. "Not for the reason you think. I'm a pack rat. It's been at the bottom of my glove compartment for a year. It wasn't taking up any space, so I left it."

That was the truth—mostly. I also kept it as a reminder of Richard's lie and a warning never to give my heart to another man.

I drove to the back of the condo's parking lot and whipped into one of the spaces for visitors.

Hailey glanced around the vast parking lot, her eyes wide with wonder. "I guess taking your car was the best plan after all. My truck definitely would not fit in here."

On the water behind the building, yachts floated. I remembered the times Richard and I had traveled on his yacht along the water, taking in the sunset.

I yanked my gaze away. I had to forget about Richard and focus on the reason why we were here.

"Does that card access key work to get us in the building too?" Hailey asked.

"You bet. Now we have to hope Bianca's home. It's Friday night. She could be out on the town. Although she should be home grieving, if she had any feelings for Rafael."

"We'll see about that."

We entered the building and strolled across the lavish lobby to the bank of elevators. An elevator opened right away, almost noiselessly. I swallowed a spate of nervousness as the elevator ascended to the seventh floor. Thank God it wasn't the penthouse level—I wasn't sure I would have been able to face that floor. I had no clue if Richard still lived in this building, but I had no desire to run into him.

We found apartment 711 and knocked. I glanced nervously around as we waited for someone to answer. Someone was there, though, because I could hear the sounds of Gloria Estefan playing on a stereo from inside the unit.

"Try again," I said.

Again, Hailey knocked. Louder this time.

"Fuck, Gordy, I'm not dealing with more of this shit," a woman said as the door swung open.

A woman wearing a black, leather miniskirt, and a purple crop top appeared startled when she saw us. She had short, spiky, cherry-red hair, and body piercings wherever she'd been able to find a place to add another hole. Her heavily made-up eyes looked a little glassy, and I caught a whiff of weed drifting from the cluttered living room.

Not exactly the type of person I'd expect to be living in a high-end condo unit.

"I already got a church." She started to close the door.

Now I knew she was high, because since when did the Jehovah's Witnesses wear sexy dresses, high heels, and toe rings?

"Wait a minute." I put my hand out to prevent the door from closing. "Are you Bianca?"

She eyed me warily. "Who wants to know?"

"We're friends of Sid's," Hailey said. "You know—the guy who owns Fantasies?"

"This about Rafael?"

I shot Hailey a glance, unsure what to say.

"It's an . . . urgent matter," Hailey explained. "And private. Sid sent us with a message."

"Yeah? Well, Bianca ain't home. She's workin'."

"Oh, no." I bit down on my bottom lip. "We really need to talk to her. She'll be pissed if we don't."

"Yeah?" She frowned as if half believing us.

"Oh, yeah," Hailey elaborated. "Sid told us to be sure and find her right away. You know, because of the sensitivity of the issue. So, if you could just tell us where she works . . ."

For a minute, I thought Ms. Pincushion was going to question us some more. Instead, she shrugged. "No skin off my nose. She's a waitress at the Clevelander."

"On South Beach?" I asked.

"Is there another one?" the woman asked tartly.

"Thanks," Hailey said. But she was already closing the door.

We both looked at each other and rolled our eyes.

Hailey and I hurried for the elevator. "Who do you suppose that woman is?" she asked as we descended.

"I don't know. Bianca's roommate, I guess."

"Some roommate."

We stopped talking as we hit the lobby and the elevator doors opened. A young woman who looked like a porn star got on with a well-dressed man old enough to be her grandfather.

I snorted my derision as we crossed the lobby. "Girlfriend—or a prostitute?" I asked Hailey.

"A prostitute?" she exclaimed, then quieted when she saw that there was a woman with two small children standing near the window. In a whisper, she asked, "You think so?"

"I told you, this—"

"—isn't Montana anymore," she finished for me. "Sheesh, I guess not."

148

Outside, we went to my car. As I started to drive, Hailey said, "Back to the roommate."

"Not exactly the type I'd expect to find living in the lap of luxury. Maybe she's a family member. The kind that comes to visit and never leaves. You know—the kind that doesn't pay rent, doesn't know how to cook or clean . . ."

"You might be right about that. One of Travis's cousins showed up at our place once for a one-week visit—and stayed for eight months. We finally had to kick him out. He sat around drinking beer all day, then hit the bars as soon as the sun went down. It was a nightmare."

"I'll bet."

I got to Biscayne Boulevard and turned left, heading toward the South Beach strip. Forty minutes later—great time, given the busy Friday night traffic—I was pulling the Lexus into a parking garage on Tenth. I didn't want to try my luck getting a meter on Ocean Drive, given the certain gridlock I'd find on that street. Every out-of-town guest within a twenty-mile radius was sure to be cruising the strip in high-end rental cars, all there to get wasted and have weekend affairs with strangers. I hoped we wouldn't have a hard time finding Bianca among the hordes of drunken partygoers.

Catcalls erupted around us as Hailey and I exited the parking garage, reminding me that we'd dressed for a night on the town. A quick glance over my shoulder, and I saw a convertible stuffed with inebriated guys who didn't even look old enough to drink.

"My feet look great," Hailey said, "but they're killing

me. I don't know if I should take my shoes off or what."

"You take them off, you know you're not getting them back on tonight. The club's the one on the corner, anyway. Not too far."

"The sacrifices women have to make for beauty!"

A guy strolling past us looked Hailey up and down and said, "Ooh la la, mamasita."

Hailey beamed, bright as a beacon. "I guess I won't lose the shoes. Not yet."

We strutted onto Ocean Drive, where the music from various clubs filled the air with a pulsing beat. The Cleve-lander Hotel/Restaurant/Bar was absolutely packed with people dining at tables that lined the street and in the outdoor part of the club that surrounded the pool.

"This is an absolute zoo," Hailey said, stopping at the corner. "I don't think there's this many people in the whole town of Sage Bend."

"I completely forgot—Friday night is Fiesta Night at the Clevelander. Always draws a huge crowd. Maybe it's not the best time to be here. You want to come back to-morrow?"

Hailey shook her head. "We're already here. May as well try to find Bianca. Especially before her roommate tells her people were looking for her."

"Good point." I pasted a big grin on my face and said, "Follow me."

We went through the obligatory pat-down with the bouncer, though I was certain that the brawny Italian could tell we weren't hiding any weapons on our person. It was a nice excuse to grope us.

I weaved through the massive crowd, Hailey on my tail. I looked left and right, through the dancing bodies, trying to spot the wait staff.

"I don't think she's out here," I said after a while, speaking loudly so Hailey could hear me over the Britney Spears tune. "Maybe she's working inside the restaurant," I added, pointing in the direction of the doors that led inside.

"Let's go."

We continued walking, and I had to fight wandering hands all the way there. Finally, I was at the entrance to the restaurant. That's when I turned—and saw Hailey nowhere in sight.

"Hailey?" I called. "Oh, shit."

I headed back the way I came, and spotted her within seconds. Some bear of a guy had her wrapped in a tight embrace, the kind that might squish the very life out of her. I charged—pushing people out of the way in my single-minded goal to save Hailey's butt.

"Lex . . . ie . . ." Her face was flattened against this guy's chest. What the hell was wrong with him?

"Hey, you big lug. Do you mind letting go of my friend?" I was ready to whip a heel off and stab him in the eye.

"Holyshityou'regorgeoustoo," he said, one big slur.

Okay, so he wasn't dangerous—just a drunken pig.

"Yeah, whatever. Can you let her go now?"

"I'mgonnamarryher."

I rolled my eyes, then reached for Hailey's hand and yanked on it. No luck. Hailey wasn't moving.

"H-yelp, Lex!" Hell, Hailey's voice even sounded squished.

"Look," I began, trying a different tactic. "My friend really likes you. I can tell. It's just that we have to . . . to go potty."

The drunk's eyebrows shot up. "Potty?"

"You know," I went on. "The ladies' room. Then she'll come back out, and you can get married on the beach."

"Yeah?"

"Yeah. I've got a friend. He's a priest. I'll call him."

The poor lug smiled, even as his eyes glazed over. "Allrightsweetheart. I'llbehere, okay?"

He loosened his grip on Hailey and she audibly gulped in air. I grabbed her arm and hurried with her through the crowd to the restaurant door.

"Okay," she said, her breathing labored, "that time I was *sure* I was going to die."

"I say we ask the manager if Bianca's in tomorrow, then come back early to chat with her." I stopped talking as Hailey's eyes bulged. "Oh, shit, Hailey." I turned to follow her line of sight. "Not the big lug!"

"No," she answered, her voice an excited whisper. "I think it's Bianca."

My eyes scanned the room. "Where?"

"That cocktail waitress passing out drinks to the table with the four potbellied guys. Before she turned, I saw her face. And she had just the kind of eyes Rosa described!"

The middle-aged men, all wearing Hawaiian-print shirts and Bermuda shorts, were loud and rowdy with Bianca. They loved her eyes, they said, her hair, and her huge, knockout tits.

Potbellied guys? Potbellied pigs was more like it.

One of the pigs ran his hand up the back of Bianca's honey-brown legs, then gave her ass a squeeze. She jumped backward and whipped around—and then I saw exactly what Hailey was talking about.

The woman's eyes were hazel—almost gold—and furious, now that the men could no longer see her face. She was beautiful, nearly as tall as Hailey if you counted her three-inch spiked heels. And she sure didn't look pregnant, except, possibly, for those huge breasts—though I was sure one of the many cosmetic surgeons in South Florida had been responsible for those. Her black hair hung midway down her back, tumbling over her shoulders in soft curls. Though she looked African-American, I thought she might also have Cuban blood in her family tree. She glanced at Hailey and me as she headed our way, and rolled her eyes in regards to the guy with the roaming hands.

"Hi," I said, stepping forward. "You're Bianca, right?"

"That's right." Her Cuban accent proved my hunch

correct. She paused, holding the empty serving tray tucked beneath one arm. "Can I help you with something?"

"Sid sent us," Hailey quickly said, and I nearly laughed at the way her Sid alibi kept growing. "Have you got a minute?"

"Sid?" Bianca looked puzzled.

"I'd rather tell you what he had to say in private," Hailey went on.

"Yeah," I echoed.

"Sure," Bianca agreed, but she sounded wary. "I could use a quick break." She crooked her head toward a corner table. "We can talk over here."

Thankfully, the interior of the restaurant was less than half full. People clearly preferred to be outside jamming it up to the DJ's funky music, or eating at one of the outdoor tables that gave them a view of the beach.

I slid onto one of three chairs grouped around the small round table, trying to think of a good way to open the conversation.

Before I could say a word, Bianca began. "So, what's the deal? One of you is Sid's girlfriend? I'll tell you, like I told him, that he doesn't have to worry. First of all, we only hit it once. Second, we used protection. Third, I wasn't lying when I told him what happened, so tell him to stop freaking out."

I was stunned into silence. My mind scrambled for a sensible comeback.

"Well, yes," I said. "I—I did want to make sure." Beneath the table, I kicked Hailey's foot.

"But that's not the only reason we're here," Hailey said. "We're the ones who found Rafael," she blurted out. "Dead in those bushes!"

Bianca's eyes bulged.

"And we're so sorry for what happened to him," I interjected, trying to smooth over Hailey's bull-in-a-china-shop approach.

Hailey leaned in close to Bianca. "It was awful. Seeing him lying there like that. His eyes open. Really freaked me out."

What the hell was Hailey doing?

I cleared my throat. "We were hoping you could answer a few questions for us."

Bianca graced us with a distasteful look. "What are you guys—cops?"

"No, no, not cops," I said, laughing lightly. "It's like she said," I went on, deliberately not saying Hailey's name. "We're friends of Sid's. And Josephine's." I studied her reaction.

Her mouth pinched into a thin line. "Ah, so this is really about Josephine, isn't it? Look, things were over for me and Rafael long ago. I don't know what Josephine is trying to pull, but I don't have time for this crap. God, I need a smoke."

"No, no," Hailey said quickly. "Josephine doesn't even know we're here. I told you—Sid sent us." Hailey darted me a clever, girl-detective look. "He was worried about you."

"Yeah?" Bianca looked skeptical.

"You know," Hailey said. "Because of your delicate

155

condition." This last she stage-whispered. Then she eyed Bianca's flat stomach. "Boy, you sure aren't showing yet. How far along are you? And did you say you're smoking? Do you think that's wise, being pregnant?"

Bianca stood, and her hazel eyes aptly fit Rosa's description as they sparked with fury. She turned on me. "Look, bitch—I don't know who you and your friend are, but I don't have any 'answers' for you. And it's none of your business whether I'm pregnant or not!"

Hailey smacked her palms against the tabletop and rose to her feet, making Bianca and I both jump. In her own three-inch heels, she towered over Bianca. "Nobody talks to Lexie that way," she said, narrowing her eyes. "For your information, we're not trying to butt into your business. We just want to know what happened to Rafael."

Bianca drew back, her "devil eyes" looking a little less scary in the face of Hailey's anger. "I don't know anything about it."

"That's not what we hear," Hailey said. "Come on, sister, cough it up!"

"Hailey." I put one hand on her arm. "Settle down." To Bianca, I said, "We're just trying to help Josephine find out what happened to Rafael."

Bianca put one hand on her hip, wagging her head, her gumption back. "I could care less about helping that wannabe ho! Tell her to get over herself. She knows I lost the baby!"

Hailey's jaw dropped—literally. "What?"

"You heard me. No more questions. You two get out

of here." She gestured dismissively. "Go on, or I'll call a bouncer and have you thrown out!"

"That won't be necessary," I said. "Come on, Hailey." I took her by the arm and marched her toward the exit.

"No, not this way, Lexie. My fiancé—remember?"

"Right." I turned and led Hailey to the street exit.

Outside, we stared at each other in disbelief. "Shit, Hailey. You heard what Bianca said?"

"So, Josephine *did* know about Rafael and Bianca's affair!"

"Then why was she so distraught over his death if she knew he'd gotten another woman pregnant?"

Hailey thought for a minute. "Well, just because you're angry with your lover doesn't mean you don't still love him. Know what I mean?"

"Yeah, I guess." But I knew exactly what Hailey was talking about. It was hard to just turn off your feelings, no matter how devastating the betrayal.

I started with her toward Tenth. "I couldn't tell if Bianca was upset over Rafael's death or not."

"Yeah, it was hard to gauge her reaction," Hailey agreed. "That's why I kept going on about how awful it was when we found Rafael. To see how she'd react."

"I think we need to talk to Josephine again."

"I don't know." Hailey's nose wrinkled. "I keep seeing her on her roof. I don't want to do anything to upset her."

I pondered Hailey's concern as we went into the parking garage and retrieved my car. I didn't like that Josephine hadn't told us about the affair. But I knew from firsthand experience that didn't mean Josephine's grief was any less intense. And the truth was, Bianca could have been lying. She hadn't exactly been forthcoming with information.

"I feel so frustrated," Hailey said when I pulled out of the parking garage onto Tenth. "We're running out of leads."

I studied her in profile, then burst out laughing.

"What?" She glanced at me.

"You." I shook my head. "Going all *Terminator* on poor Bianca. I thought you were going to punch her or something."

Hailey laughed. "I almost did. Nobody calls my best friend a bitch."

"She called Josephine a ho," I said. "Guess I should've decked her too."

"I didn't want to hit a pregnant woman," Hailey said. She sobered. "Only I guess she's not so pregnant after all."

"And oh, my God—what a revelation that was. About Sid. She basically said that he was worried he could be the father, though she'd assured him he wasn't. I wonder when he slept with her. But more important, did Sid not believe her about losing the baby?"

"Can you believe the guy?" Hailey asked. "He had nothing but great things to say about Rafael, yet he screwed Bianca. Some friend."

"Maybe he slept with Bianca before she got involved with Rafael," I said. But I knew I was making excuses. I couldn't find Sid guilty without proof, but he was a guy, and guys were so lame about keeping their dicks in their pants.

Hailey arched one brow. "What if Rafael didn't know Bianca was no longer pregnant? Maybe she was trying to trap him into marriage."

"It's possible." I headed north on Collins. "Or what if it was a love triangle—Sid, Rafael, and Bianca? Now Rafael's dead. Let's face it—Sid had access to Rafael's dressing room."

"Lexie! Do you really think—"

"I don't know. I'm not sure we should trust him." Thank God I hadn't yet taken him up on his offer for dinner. "And here's something to think about. Bianca lives in this lavish condo, and I don't care how busy it is at the Clevelander—how can she afford that place? Sid—now, he just might be able to foot the bill. He's a successful business owner."

Hailey's eyes lit up. "Want to go back there now? See if Sid sweats a little?"

I grinned at Hailey. "I like the way you think."

Fantasies was significantly more crowded by the time we got back, and the parking lot was packed full. I squeezed my Lexus into a space meant for motorcycles, and we headed for the bar.

Casey's eyes lit up when he saw Hailey. "Hey, gorgeous. I see you're feeling better."

"Yep."

"There's an empty table up front for VIPs. I say you

both are VIPs. Let me take you there. The next show's about to start."

"Cool!" Hailey said. She leaned toward me. "We can talk to Sid later. I'm in the mood for eye candy."

"Me too."

"Cosmopolitans?" Casey asked.

"Please." I gave him a smile as I slid into the booth.

"Make mine a beer," Hailey said. "Coors Light. Oh— and if you run into Sid, tell him we found Bianca."

"Gotcha." Casey hurried away, and I eyed his cute butt with appreciation.

"You were serious about making Sid sweat," I said to Hailey.

"You bet."

I tried not to think about Rafael and just enjoy the show. Hailey and I were soon caught up in the fun, and this time she waved a twenty over *my* head, and got a gorgeous "fireman" to give me a private dance. *Lord, he could use his hose on me any day!*

Since I was driving, I switched to orange juice after my cosmo, but lack of alcohol didn't hinder my good time. We had so much fun watching the dancers, we nearly forgot to talk to Sid. I spotted him over in the corner, and his eyes were scanning the crowd. Was he looking for us?

"There's Sid." I raised my hand and waved at him.

Just as I thought, Sid saw me and started for our table. *This could get interesting.*

"Ladies." Sid grinned at us as he sat at our table. "You made it back."

I smiled at him. "Of course we did. You didn't think we'd miss out on the show, did you?" I sidled closer and gave him a gentle nudge. "You ought to be up there dancing, big guy." Somehow, I flirted with him as though everything was normal, even though I wondered if he'd deliberately lied to us.

"I hear you found Bianca. Maybe we can go to my office and talk?"

Maybe I was projecting, but Sid seemed awfully anxious.

Inside his office, Sid didn't offer us chairs before he asked, "So, what did Bianca have to say?"

"Did you know Bianca lost the baby?" Hailey blurted.

Sid raised his eyebrows. "No shit? Rafael didn't tell me that." He frowned. "You sure?"

"That's what she said," Hailey replied. She sounded a little too chipper. No doubt because she was drunk.

I watched Sid closely. After a moment, he shook his head and sighed. "That's too bad, but it's probably for the best. Considering what happened to Rafael."

I couldn't help asking, "Is that how you really feel?"

" 'Scuse me?"

"Sid, Bianca told us you two had been involved. She also made it sound like you knew she'd lost the baby—but you didn't believe her. Why wouldn't you tell us that?"

Sid looked down, but he didn't say a word.

"I think you owe us some answers," I told him.

"All right." He blew out a ragged breath. "I did lie—by omission. I'm sorry, babe."

161

"Go on."

"Yeah, I slept with Bianca. But it was before she got involved with Rafael. She was always coming to the club, and one night she hung around flirting with me." Sid paused. "Next thing I know, she was seducing me in my office."

"How long was this before she got involved with Rafael?" I asked.

"Only about a couple weeks."

"A couple weeks!" Hailey exclaimed. She plopped down onto the love seat. "Woo, that girl gets around!"

I shot Hailey a look I hoped she'd understand, given her state. *Leave this to me.*

"I told you—Bianca is trouble," Sid went on. "When I gave her that ride to her place, she told me about the baby but assured me it wasn't mine. Then one day she calls and says she lost it. But I never quite believed her, you know? I kinda got the feeling that she'd hold the pregnancy over my head if it suited her."

That didn't surprise me in the least. "So that's why you didn't mind sending us to find her—because you were hoping we'd get some answers about the baby."

Again, Sid didn't speak. But I saw confirmation of my assumption in his eyes.

"Well, now we know," I said.

Sid moved toward me, put a hand on my arm. "No, you don't know," he told me, his voice full of contrition. "Bianca—she's a little slut, you know? I was never into her. I'm not proud of what happened between us, but it was a one-night stand, that's it. I was terrified when I learned she was pregnant, you know? I don't know what that girl's capable of."

Sid explained this all to me like I was his lover or something. I nodded and simply said, "Fine." But in my heart I didn't believe he had any feelings for Bianca, which made him an unlikely suspect in Rafael's murder.

"I don't know what happened to Rafael. But maybe it's not smart for you to keep digging around asking questions."

"Meaning?"

"Just let the police handle this, you know?"

"But that's the problem," I said. "They don't really seem to be doing anything."

"Lexie, seriously." Sid's gaze was full of concern. "I don't want you getting hurt."

He stopped short of putting his dinner offer on the table again, and for that I was glad. Right now my feelings were all mixed up, and I needed time to think.

I had to put an arm around Hailey's waist and lead her out of the club, since for most of my chat with Sid she'd sat on his love seat, her head tipped back as she lightly snored.

But she was wide awake by the time I helped her into my car—or at least she was trying to pretend she was.

She looked at me with glassy eyes. "So, Lex," she said a little too loudly. "What are you thinking?"

"About Sid?" I shrugged. "Well, my gut says he didn't kill Rafael. But I wouldn't be surprised if there's more he knows. It's the way he keeps warning us to leave this to the police."

"Hmm."

We drove for a while longer in silence. I wondered how much of this evening Hailey would remember.

The warm evening air blew our hair around, and Hailey laid her head against the headrest and closed her eyes. She should sleep well tonight—thanks to all those Coors Lights.

When we got to her apartment, I had to wake her up. Her eyes flew open, and she looked shocked to be there.

"Time to go, sleeping beauty."

"Oh, Lexie." She gave me a hug. "That was a fun night. We'll have to do it again soon."

I grinned, remembering the way she'd tucked bills into the G-string of more than one dancer. "I think I've created a monster." I laughed.

Hailey chuckled. "You'd better keep an eye on me, or I'm liable to spend all my money on eye candy. We're business owners now, girl. We've got to think about investing in the store."

"Exactly." But right now I wasn't as excited about the store as I should have been. And not because I was having second thoughts.

I guess I was a little disappointed in Sid—and surprised that I cared so much.

But I was also wondering if there was anything behind his worries that Hailey and I might be in danger if we kept asking questions.

It was all I could think of as I drove home.

Eleven

Hailey

When my phone rang the next day, I thought a nuclear bomb was going off in my head. I popped an eye open, and a piercing pain shot through my skull. Somehow, I eased myself up onto an elbow to glance at my digital clock. Nearly three in the afternoon! Holy crap, I'd slept that long?

The phone kept ringing. I reached for it and grumbled a hello.

"Hey," I heard. It took me a moment to realize it was Lexie's voice.

"Oh. Hi."

"God, you sound awful."

"My head feels like a herd of mustangs stampeded through it."

166

"Ouch."

"I'm feeling every bit my age, Lexie. Maybe I have to cut down on all this partying."

"Or maybe you just need a roommate to take care of you."

"Huh?" I asked, not sure if I heard correctly. "Oh, like a guy. Hey, Casey certainly is fantasy material, but my divorce is barely final. Did I make a fool of myself with him last night?"

"I was talking about me, dimwit."

"Oh. Ohhhh."

"I thought about it all last night after I dropped you home. Part of it was wondering how you'd fare after all that beer. And another part . . . well, don't think I'm crazy, but I'm a tad bit concerned about what Sid said. Warning us to leave the questioning to the police."

I had to wrack my brain to remember what Lexie was talking about. I couldn't. "What did Sid say—exactly?"

"Just gave a general warning to be careful, leave the questioning to the police. It's the second time he's said that, and I'm starting to wonder."

I couldn't do any serious wondering without some coffee. "Maybe Sid didn't mean it in a specific way."

"Could be, but why take chances? I think living together just makes sense. And not just for safety, but on a friendship level. Don't you get a little lonely?"

"Yeah," I admitted. "It would be great to have you around to talk to all the time."

"Exactly. My apartment is plenty big enough for the

both of us. I've got three spacious bedrooms and a view to die for. And it's paid for," she added in a sugary voice. "Other than the yearly taxes and monthly expenses. Can you get out of your lease?"

"I signed up for a month-to-month lease, so that won't be a problem."

"Excellent!"

"Hey—can I bring my turtles?"

"Of course, silly. Maybe I'll even get one."

"Cool." That made me smile. "Then it's all settled—roomy. Now I definitely need coffee."

"Then let's celebrate over a latte at Starbucks. Same one as before. Half an hour?"

"Make it fifteen minutes."

Fifteen minutes later, I was standing outside of Starbucks when Lexie showed up. Today she was wearing black shorts and a V-neck red cotton shirt with her signature blue-tinted sunglasses. It didn't matter what she put on, she always looked amazing.

"My treat, roomy," she announced. "Get the works."

"I'll try the one you had last time—the caramel one? The largest size they've got. Hey, do they come in a horse-trough size?"

Lexie grinned knowingly, then made her way to the counter. I sat at a small table near the door.

"One Grande Caramel Macchiato for you," Lexie sang, putting the coffee cup onto the table before me. "One tall one for me. And two slices of carrot cake. I hope that's okay."

"Are you kidding?" I took a huge, ungraceful bite of the carrot cake. "This is the *best*."

Before Lexie could sit down, her cell phone rang. She rolled her eyes before answering it with a pleasant hello.

"Josephine, hi. How are you doing?"

I swallowed my mouthful of coffee, my eyes lighting up.

"Right." Lexie pulled the phone from her ear, pressed a button, and suddenly Josephine's voice sounded loud enough for me to hear.

". . . has finally released my dear Rafael's body. His funeral is set for next Wednesday. Can you and Hailey come?"

She sounded so forlorn, it broke my heart.

"Oh, sweetie. Of course we will," Lexie said. "Do you need help with the arrangements or anything?"

"No, sugar, but thanks for offering. Rafael's family is taking care of things for me, God bless them. They're just the sweetest people."

"They are." As soon as Lexie said the words, she screwed up her face in a grimace.

"You've met them?" Josephine asked.

"Um, yeah. Hailey and I went to see them the other day."

"Really? Why on earth would you do that?"

I couldn't tell if Josephine was curious or appalled. I decided it was best not to jump into the conversation.

"We've been worried about you, Josephine," Lexie continued. "And the police aren't doing enough to find out what happened to Rafael, so we decided to do a little investigating on our own. We weren't going to mention it unless we found out something significant."

Josephine's sniffle came across loud and clear. "That is the sweetest thing. You girls are really good friends."

Lexie's face relaxed with relief. I gave her two thumbs up. "Hey, no problem," she told Josephine.

"Rosa and Enrique are just devastated. I hate seeing them so sad. They're like a second mom and dad to me." She sniffed again, then blew her nose. "Were they able to tell you anything helpful?"

"Um . . ." Lexie shot me a look, and I had a feeling she was debating mentioning our meeting with Bianca. I mouthed the word *No* at her.

"Not really," she finished. "But we're not giving up."

"You be careful," Josephine said in her husky mother-hen voice. "I don't want anything to happen to you or Hailey. My God, that's all I need."

"Don't worry about us. You just take care of yourself. Where is the funeral going to be?" Lexie reached for a napkin, then gestured to me with her hands. I dug in my purse and retrieved a pen for her.

She scribbled the information on the napkin.

"The viewing is Tuesday," Josephine said sadly. "If you want to come."

Lexie shook her head, but said, "I'll see what Hailey says, but I'm sure we'll be there. Call us if you need anything."

"Will do, sugar. 'Bye."

Lexie groaned as she ended the call. "How could I

have been so stupid? Letting it slip that we met Rosa and Enrique?"

"Josephine didn't sound upset, so it doesn't really matter. She knows we're asking questions because we're trying to help her."

"I guess you're right." Lexie broke off a morsel of her carrot cake and delicately put it in her mouth.

"We're going to the funeral—right?"

"You know we have to be there. As for seeing Rafael's body at the viewing—I already saw him dead. Hell, I hope they have a closed-casket service."

"Oh, my God," I said, a brilliant idea hitting me. "I've got a *great* idea!"

"What?" Lexie asked warily.

"We can look for suspects at the funeral. You know how the police always do that? They say the killer usually shows up to relish the aftermath of his crime." I felt like a verified detective. "The killer is bound to be there."

Instead of high-fiving me for my genius, Lexie twisted her mouth and shook her head. "Hold on one second, Sherlock. How would we know who to look for? We don't even know Rafael's friends or family, other than his mom and dad and Josephine, so it's not like we could pick out a stranger in the crowd."

"Hmm. I didn't think of that. Maybe we can get Josephine to help us?"

"That might be too much. She's grieving, Hailey. Not trying to be Nancy Drew."

"You're right." My mood dampened, but only for a

second. "No, this can still work. All we have to do is keep an eye out for somebody suspicious-looking. With the two of us working together, we're bound to see something."

Lexie smirked at me. "You're too much."

"I think it can work," I said defensively. And I'd certainly read enough detective novels to get an idea of how to pull this off.

"I guess it won't hurt to try," Lexie said after a moment.

"There you go!" I exclaimed. "Oh, Lex. Real live undercover work. I think we have a knack for this, girlfriend."

"Hey—did you notice that Josephine expressed concern about us not getting hurt? Just like Sid did?"

"You're right. What—you think there's something she knows that caused her to say that?"

"Other than that we might be pissing off a murderer?" Lexie raised her eyebrows in a look of concern. "Let's hope we don't find out."

"We'll be fine, Lexie," I told her. But I couldn't deny that in my soul, I was starting to feel a tiny bit of fear.

What if we *did* piss someone off? Were we getting in over our heads?

Lexie and I decided that we'd wait until after Rafael's funeral to start moving my stuff into her apartment. Sunday night, weather warnings began about a tropical storm brewing. I hoped it wouldn't turn into a hurricane. That's all Rosa and Enrique needed. I pictured Rafael's coffin sailing away on a wind-fueled wave and shuddered.

On Monday, Lexie picked me up and we drove to our respective banks, got a check drawn up for Gina, then met her at the attorney's office. It felt good to make everything official, and we walked out of the building arm in arm, grinning like we'd won the lottery.

"Yahoo!" I pumped my fist in the air. "Nothing But Lies, here we come."

"We need to celebrate," Lexie said. She sobered. "But I guess we should wait until after the funeral."

I nodded. "It's only right. Speaking of which, what should I wear? I don't really have anything appropriate."

"Then let's go shopping. We'll make that our bookstore celebration for now."

"You're on." We headed for downtown Miami, where we strolled the Bayside shops selling women's wear. And I was looking forward to her offer of having a couple margaritas at one of the restaurants overlooking the bay. In Miami, I was living the life. Let Travis put that in his snuff can and chew on it.

We strolled through the quaint shops, checking out several stores before we found what we wanted. Lexie helped me pick out a simple black peasant dress and granny boots.

"You look so cute!" she said.

"I'm supposed to look sad and serious."

"It's perfect," she assured me. "Now let's find something for me."

Lexie chose a black sheath dress for herself, black lace shrug, and lace-covered black flats. She looked divine. Leave it to Lex to look good even for a dead guy.

Lexie's cell phone rang, and she fished it from her purse, going back into the changing room to talk. She came out a few minutes later in her own clothes, the outfit she wanted to buy draped over her arm. I held her shoes. "That was my agent," she said. "I've got a commercial to do on Thursday. Wanna come with me?"

"You bet! I'd love to see how all this movie-star stuff works."

Lexie laughed. "Well, I'm hardly a movie star—yet."

"It's comin'," I said, doing a little Sarah Jessica Parker strut.

Wednesday morning started out rainy and dreary, but we'd gotten lucky, and the predicted storm blew around us, leaving behind a little sun. I thought it appropriate that the sun should shine on Rafael. I hadn't known him, but he'd been such a hottie, and Rosa and Enrique were really sweet.

"Poor Rosa," I said as we pulled into the church parking lot in my truck. "This has to be the hardest thing to face . . . losing your son."

"Mmm-hmm." Lexie nodded. "They say there's nothing worse than burying your child, no matter how old he is."

I found a parking space, then reached beneath the seat for the handheld video recorder I'd tucked there. I pulled it from its case and checked it over.

"What are you doing?" Lexie stared at me.

"Making sure the battery is fully charged. I forgot to check it last night. I don't want to miss a single thing."

"Hailey!" Lexie's jaw dropped. "Surely you're not going to record the funeral service!"

"Well, yeah. I told you, cops always case out funerals to see if the killer shows up."

"I know, but you didn't tell me you were planning to *film* it!"

I shoved the small camera into my shoulder bag. "Don't you think that's the best way to get hard evidence?"

"Not at the funeral." Lexie emphasized each word as though I were dense.

"Don't worry," I told her. "I'll be discreet." I got out of my truck and locked the door, and Lexie and I hurried toward the red-brick building that housed St. Peter's Catholic Church in Hialeah.

"Wow," Lexie whispered as we stepped into the church's vestibule. "Guess Rafael was pretty popular."

The church pews were packed with people, with more still wandering in, including us. "How in the world am I supposed to film the killer in all this crowd?"

Lexie rolled her eyes. "Exactly. This is a time for respect."

"Hey, look," I said. "There's Josephine."

"Holy . . . moly!" Lexie finished, I assumed because we were in a church and with her comment about respect, she didn't want to be disrespectful to God Himself.

Lexie and I stared. We couldn't help it. Josephine was walking down the aisle, leaning on the arm of a man I assumed was one of the funeral directors. She wore a black sequined dress that hit her midthigh and a veiled hat.

Her shoes, purse, and belt were also sequined—in a fiery red. From our rear view of her, I noticed her black nylon hose had seams that ended in black sequined bows just above the heels of her stilettos.

"Holy moly is right." Lexie and I exchanged a look.

"Guess her pizzazz is back," Lex said. "Even if her fashion sense is sorely lacking. Red at a funeral?"

"She must be trying to draw attention to herself," I said. "Not to be catty, but why else would she wear such a loud outfit to her lover's funeral?"

I watched as the funeral director seated Josephine in the front pew next to Rosa and Enrique. Josephine dabbed at her eyes with a black-lace hankie, and Rosa slipped her arm around Josephine's broad shoulders.

"I think she's trying to cope with her loss the only way she knows how," Lexie said. "By being the center of attention, as usual."

"Poor thing." I started down the aisle, speaking softly. "Let's go pay our respects."

We slipped around the crowd and worked our way to the front pew. I looked at the coffin, wishing it weren't closed. Unlike Lexie, I felt the need to say good-bye to Rafael in a way that didn't involve seeing him lying flat on his back in some shrubbery. I shivered at the image, forever burned into my mind. I supposed I'd have to settle for looking at the eight-by-ten photograph of him that stood amid a spray of white lilies atop the linen-draped coffin. His smiling image looked sweet and innocent, nothing like the man who'd danced naked for us a couple of weeks ago.

"Josephine," Lexie said, bending to give her a hug. "We're so sorry for your loss."

"Thank you." Josephine sniffled, making an obvious effort not to break down and sob. "Thanks for coming. You too, Hailey." She grasped both my hands and gave them a squeeze, leaving the lace hanky in her lap.

I tried not to think about germs. "Of course," I said. "We wouldn't think of not being here." My half-truth made me feel a little guilty. I wanted to support her, but she obviously had enough friends and family to lean on. What I really wanted was to catch the killer on the mini DVD camcorder I'd purchased specifically for this occasion. The new-generation video recorders were much smaller and easier to conceal—making my job today much more simple. I hoped.

Lexie and I greeted Rosa and Enrique as well, then moved past their pew to a row designated for nonfamily members. We had a side-angle view of the coffin. Perfect for filming everyone who filed past to pay their respects. I dug the camcorder out of my bag and discreetly slipped it into my lap, ignoring the elbow jab Lexie gave me.

Carefully, I watched the crowd, using the camera's window viewfinder to focus so people wouldn't be as apt to notice what I was doing. The service was a long one, but beautiful, with the priest waving over the coffin a silver thing on a chain with puffs of smoke coming from it.

I reached for a Kleenex, jostling the video camera as I dabbed at my eyes. "I'm really going to miss Rafael," I whispered to Lexie.

She raised her eyebrows. "You barely knew him," she reminded me.

"I know." I sniffed, caught up in the whole funeral thing. "But this service is just *so* sad."

It finally ended, and we all filed outside once more. I still kept watch over the crowd. I'd discreetly studied everyone over and over again inside the church, making sure to memorize as many faces as possible. I wanted to see if anyone new showed up at the cemetery.

Back in my truck, Lex and I followed the funeral procession to Peaceful Acres. I'd never seen so many cars in a single row—except last Friday night on the South Beach strip—headlights on, solemn-looking police officers on motorcycles, wearing helmets and sunglasses, escorting us along. The hearse led the way, white and shiny with lots of chrome. Rafael's family had done things up right.

We drove beneath the ornate arch at the entrance of Peaceful Acres, and wound our way through the lanes that crisscrossed between row upon row of headstones and markers, to where Rafael's coffin had been taken. The priest gave a brief sermon over the coffin, where Rosa, Enrique, and their family were seated in folding chairs around the graveside, weeping and wailing. I knew how hard it was to lose a loved one, but to lose one to murder? That had to be a whole other kind of pain.

I felt so bad as I watched and listened to the family

grieving, it made me more determined than ever to find the creep who'd killed Rafael.

That thought in mind, I scanned the crowd again, noting many faces I remembered from the church. Then my back straightened as my gaze fell on a blond woman I didn't remember seeing. She stood near the rear of the crowd, hanging back a little from the other mourners. She wore dark glasses, a floppy-brimmed hat, and a plain black dress. Her medium-length hair was clipped back in a neat ponytail—one that looked classy rather than casual.

I elbowed Lexie and whispered, "Look."

"What?" Frowning, she scanned the crowd as well. She met my eyes again and gave a puzzled shake of her head.

"That woman," I said, leaning close to her ear. "Back there, standing by herself." I jerked my own head in a subtle motion, then reached inside my purse for the camcorder. Discreetly, I stepped to the edge of the crowd, swung it around, and got the woman on film. If anyone saw me, I could explain that I was making a video for the family. Morbid, perhaps, but it was a logical explanation.

I made a quick sweep of everyone there, then tucked the camera back in my purse as the service ended.

"Come on," I said to Lexie. "Let's follow her."

"Hailey. Don't you think you're getting a little carried away here?"

"No. I have a feeling." I took her by the elbow. "Hurry—she's leaving!"

But before we could go more than a few steps, a police officer stepped in front of us, blocking our path. "Can I have a word with you, ma'am?" He crooked a finger at me.

I gulped and exchanged a look with Lexie. "Sure."

Ever loyal, she stuck beside me as the officer and I stepped over to the curb near some parked cars. He was a tall, muscular black man—good-looking enough to make me feel a little less intimidated by his size. His badge read R. ROBERTSON. At least it wasn't Montoya or Schaefer, our buddies from the night at the strip club.

Robertson stood with legs slightly spread, hands clasped in front of him. His biceps were quite impressive, even underneath the uniform, and I tried not to lick my lips.

He frowned at me. "May I ask what you're doing filming the funeral service?"

"Oh. That." I gave him a friendly smile. "I thought it might help."

"In what way?"

"Well . . ." How did I tell him that I didn't think his fellow officers were doing a bang-up job on the investigation? "You know how on those crime shows the killer always shows up at the funeral?"

"Uh-huh." Wary, he eyeballed me.

"I thought maybe if I filmed the crowd, it might help the police locate the person who killed Rafael Martinez."

"Is that right?"

"She meant well," Lexie said, coming to my defense. She batted her lashes, but this time it didn't work. R. Robertson looked at us both with an uncompromising, stone-faced gaze.

"Hand it over." He held out one big hand, staring me down with his sexy dark brown eyes.

I narrowed mine. "Do you have a search warrant?"

"Hailey!" Lexie's jaw dropped.

"He can't just take my camcorder for no reason," I said, feeling a surge of satisfaction as Robertson hesitated, then dropped his hand to his side.

"I thought you wanted to help the investigation," he said.

"I do."

"Then why won't you give the tape to me?"

I couldn't really think of a good reason, other than I wanted to view the DVD with Lexie and see if we noticed anything we'd missed at the actual service. Maybe we could show the video to Josephine when she wasn't feeling so distraught. Surely *she* would know who did or did not belong in the crowd.

Maybe she'd even know the blonde.

I set my jaw and stared Robertson down. "Because. It's also a gift for Rafael's life partner."

"A gift?"

"Yes," I said. "You know—a memento." I held my breath, not really one hundred percent sure he couldn't demand I hand over the DVD. "Is there something illegal about videotaping a funeral?" I gave him a wide-eyed innocent look.

He narrowed his eyes. "I suppose not."

"Then you can't take her camera," Lexie said. "Come on, Hailey." She took me by the arm and marched me toward my pickup.

"Crud—now I've lost sight of the blonde." My eyes frantically raked the crowd. "Oh, there she is." I pointed. "Damn, she's getting away!" I fumbled for my camera.

The woman climbed into a silver Beemer and took off.

"Hailey."

"The license plate! Did you see the license plate?"

Lexie gave my arm a firm shake. "Hailey—"

"We have to go after her! She could be the key to this whole thing!"

Lexie threw a gaze behind her, I guess checking out the cop. "Get a grip, girl," she told me when she looked me in the eye. "You're way out of control."

As I stared at her, I realized she was right. I blew out a long breath and put the camera away. Robertson was still watching us.

"We have to be careful, Hailey."

"Sorry," I mumbled.

"I want to find out who killed Rafael too," Lexie said, "but we can't go around making a scene. And we certainly don't want to make the cops think we're getting in their way."

I wrinkled my nose. "I didn't think of that. Oh, darn."

"I think we're fine," Lexie assured me. She threw another glance over her shoulder at Robertson. "Nonetheless, I say we go now. We've already paid our respects to the family."

I nodded, and Lexie and I went to my truck. But I couldn't help wondering who the blonde was, and why she'd been standing back from the crowd.

Twelve

Lexie

The next day, Hailey went with me to my commercial shoot. It was nice and easy—no cleaning toilets and smiling, and no mopping staged spills off of otherwise spotless floors. This time the gig was for a promotional spot advertising the city of Miami. The production team cordoned off a section of Lummus Park Beach, and I got to frolic around in the sand in a bathing suit, smiling like this was the best place in the world to visit.

It wasn't a hard sell for me. I loved Miami.

The shoot was mercifully short, only five hours of actual hair/makeup/wardrobe, sitting around and waiting, then the shot itself, which the director got in less than an hour. I'd done many a shoot that was fourteen hours or longer, so the bonus of finishing quickly yet still getting the minimum pay for eight hours made me leave the set a happy woman.

With the extra time I hadn't counted on, Hailey and I used the afternoon to begin moving her stuff over to my apartment. "Good thing you've got a truck," I commented as we loaded boxes into the back of her Ford Ranger.

"Hey, you made fun of my truck before!" Hailey said.

"I didn't make fun of it. I just said it isn't cool for cruising."

We both had a little chuckle, then went back to work.

"At least we don't have to move any furniture," Hailey said, plopping a box down in the truck bed with an "*Oomph.*"

Her rental unit had come completely furnished, so all we had to worry about was Hailey's personal belongings—most of which consisted of mega-heavy boxes of books.

"Lord, girl, you've got enough books here to stock our store."

She laughed. "Hey, at least now we have a great way to recycle them."

By Friday, Hailey was all settled in at my place. I'd given her one of my two guest bedrooms for her own. It faced Biscayne Bay and Virginia Key while mine faced the wide expanse of the Atlantic.

"I can't get over this view!" Hailey said for the umpteenth time. She gave me a hug. "I'm so happy you let me move in with you."

"Are you kidding? We're going to have a blast, girl-friend. Running our own business, setting our own hours . . . and partying whenever we want."

Hailey chuckled. "I don't know how much partying time we'll get in, when you think about it. It's not as if we'll have the money to hire a bunch of employees right off the bat."

"True," I said. "But we can at least get a couple of part-timers. Business is great, but we don't want to be slaves to it. Let's make sure we always have one week-end night off."

"Speaking of which," Hailey said, "want to go to Mango's tonight?"

"Why not? I'll even treat you to dinner beforehand. Steak and lobster?"

"You're on! But only if you let me buy drinks."

"Deal." I moved over to the small round marble table that was Hailey's one and only piece of furniture, now in the far corner of the living room. "You know, your turtles are really cute," I commented. "Maybe I will get one."

"You should! Too bad I already got Missy B. or you could've gotten a girlfriend for Speedy."

"Who says he can't be a player?"

We laughed. I picked up the phone and made reservations at Monty's, a popular seafood place at the Miami Beach Marina, and by seven o'clock Hailey and I were seated at a booth in a quiet corner. We both gorged on steak and lobster, then groaned when the waitress later asked if we wanted dessert.

I settled the bill, leaving a generous tip, and then we were off to Mango's.

"Oh, Lexie, no!" Hailey exclaimed after we'd parked on the street and were making our way to the club. "Please tell me you didn't."

"Didn't what?"

Hailey grabbed hold of my arm, making me halt. "Look. That's Cedric standing out front." She narrowed her gaze at me. "You know I said I didn't want to see him again."

"Hailey, I had nothing to do with this."

"Really?"

"I swear. Want to go someplace else?"

"No," she said after a moment. "I'm not going to have some man dictate where I can and cannot party. I already let Travis dictate where I could and couldn't go, who I could and couldn't hang with. No more of that crap."

"That's the spirit," I told her. She'd filled me in on how controlling Travis had become over the years, especially since he'd had her isolated from friends and family.

As we strolled the sidewalk to Mango's front door, Cedric's eyes fixed on Hailey. We'd dressed up for the occasion, me in a lemon-colored skirt and tank top, Hailey wearing a cute powder-blue sundress. Based on the heated look in Cedric's gaze, Hailey's dress was a huge hit.

"Hailey!" He stepped toward her immediately, holding his arms out wide. Then he gave a little pout. "Where's your cowgirl outfit?"

"I left it at home with my horse," she quipped. "What are you doing lurking out here?"

"Lurking?" He laughed hoarsely, spraying spittle. "I'm not lurking, silly. I was waiting for you."

I frowned. "How'd you know we'd be here?" I hoped he wasn't stalking my friend.

Cedric shrugged as he regarded me. "It was a good bet. Tyrone told me you like to come here most Fridays, Lexie. I thought I'd take a chance and hang out for a while, see if I saw you, and here you are!" He tucked Hailey's arm through the crook of his elbow. "Allow me."

She cringed and cast me a desperate look over her shoulder. I shrugged and mouthed *Sorry* at her. We'd find a way to ditch him once we got inside. As soon as Hailey and I had ordered our drinks—which Cedric insisted on paying for—I thought of a way. Thanks to the band, which was playing a salsa dance number that had my feet wanting to move all on their own.

"Come on," I said to Hailey, tugging her arm where she stood at the center bar. "Let's dance, girlfriend."

"Gladly." Hands raised above her head, Hailey snapped her fingers and wriggled out onto the dance floor.

We shook our hips and put on the moves, really getting into the Latin music. Then Kanye West's voice filled the club, and we kicked up the moves even more. I extended my arm straight out to point at Hailey, and she pointed back, lip-syncing the words to the song with me. We laughed and wiggled, and spun in circles. I was having so much fun with a shoulder-and-hip-shaking move that I actually danced clear across the floor before turning to realize that Hailey was no longer with me.

My eyes volleyed over the area, searching for her. And then I saw her. To my horror, she was dancing about ten feet away—albeit reluctantly—trapped by Cedric.

Good Lord! Not only could white men not jump, they couldn't dance either. Something I'd always known, but Cedric proved the stereotype true. He moved like he had a load of fire ants burning his crotch.

"Oh, no, Hailey," I muttered—and I couldn't help suppressing a laugh. Cedric was just too funny to watch.

Hailey, on the other hand, looked tortured, and I was determined to rescue her. I started to shake my hips again, moving her way, but a hot-looking Latino guy appeared in my path. He was sweet, all right, even if he was a good inch shorter than me. He did a salsa-meringue move toward me, and in that moment, I thought of Rafael.

But I pushed the thought aside as the Latin hottie took me by the hand.

"*Que bonita!*" he purred, taking me in with his sexy dark eyes from head to toe. "Would you do me the honor of dancing with me, *por favor*?" He rolled his *r*'s, making my heart leap. Was there anything sexier than a Spanish accent?

Then he kissed my hand, and I knew I couldn't deny him. "*Sí, señor.*"

I let him tug me closer. We shook and swayed and spun to another snappy salsa number, and before I knew it, I'd completely forgotten about Hailey and Cedric. Not on purpose—it just happened that way. It wasn't until a couple of songs later when Juan offered to buy me a drink that I remembered them. I looked for Hailey, but didn't see her anywhere.

I excused myself from Juan and went to the bathroom, but didn't see Hailey there either. On the way back, a hot brother who looked a lot like Jamie Foxx blocked my path, as though ready to tackle me. Hey, what's a girl to do? I let him lead me to the dance floor, but after one song, I finally spotted Hailey. She was practically pinned against the bar, Cedric hovering over her.

"Sugar, I have to get my friend," I told my current dance partner.

"Come back and dance with me?"

"All right," I told him, though it remained to be seen if that would happen. Hailey was going to need me by her side, given Cedric's leechlike quality.

"Hey, you!" I exclaimed as I made my way to her. "There you are!"

She narrowed her eyes at me, none too pleased. "*I* wasn't the one who disappeared."

"Hey, one minute I was dancing with you, the next you weren't there," I said sweetly. But Hailey's stone-faced gaze made it clear she wasn't impressed. "Sorry," I added.

"Let me buy you another round," Cedric said, flagging down a waitress from behind the bar.

I sidled up to Hailey and wrapped an arm around her waist. "Well, at least he's good for free booze."

She snorted. "Yeah, if you don't mind having it served with a side of saliva." She shot a glance at Cedric, then gritted her teeth as she spoke under her breath. "Help me ditch him!"

"Yeah, okay. Just chill, babe." I gave Cedric a warm smile and thanked him as he passed me a cosmopolitan.

"No problem," he said, winking at me. "Anything for Hailey. I'm crazy about this girl."

Behind his back, she gave me the look.

I cleared my throat. "So, Cedric, where's Tyrone?"

"Working. Man, that guy's a workaholic at times. But then, I guess that's why he gets paid the big bucks." He turned his attention back to Hailey. "So, Hailey, what's your work schedule like? I wouldn't mind dropping by your apartment sometime."

"Oh, she doesn't liv—"

"I don't have much free time anymore," Hailey interrupted me. "Lexie and I are business owners now. We're practically working around the clock. Except tonight. We took a break."

"Business owners, huh?" Cedric leaned against the bar, trying his best to look cool, which was hard to do when you were wearing polyester pants, a white disco jacket, and white patent-leather shoes. John Travolta he was not. "What sort of business are you in?"

"We just bought a bookstore," I explained, wracking my brain for a way to ditch Cedric. Poor Hailey. He obviously had it bad for her.

"No kidding!" Cedric grinned. "I love to read."

Hailey rolled her eyes behind his back.

"Do you?" I asked. "Well, please stop by our store

sometime. We won't be open for a little while yet, but we're in a strip mall on Collins. Corner of Twenty-third Street."

Hailey was glaring at me, but I couldn't help myself. After all, we needed every customer we could get. And what could he do to her in a bookstore?

"I'll do that," Cedric said. He raised his glass in toast. "Here's to your bookstore, ladies. What's the name of it?"

I told him, and he chuckled. "Clever. I like it." He took a gulp of his scotch and water. "So, Hailey, want to celebrate your new store? I'll take you out to dinner."

"Thanks," she said, "but Lexie and I already ate."

He laughed again. "Yeah, but you got to eat tomorrow, don't ya?"

"I don't know," she stalled.

"You don't know? You're not on one of them starvation diets, are ya? Cuz honey, you look *fine* to me! C'mon, babe. Have dinner with me."

"Um," Hailey hedged. "I'll have to check my calendar. We're pretty busy right now, getting the store set up and all."

"You need any help with that?" Cedric draped an arm around Hailey's shoulders. "I'm good for the heavy work."

She tried to shrug out of his grasp, and I could tell her patience was coming to an end. Hailey's sweet—until you piss her off. "Cedric, how about a dance?" I grabbed him by the wrist.

"Sure thing, brown sugar." He laughed as though he

thought himself clever. I bit my tongue as Hailey mouthed *Thank you* to me.

There was no way I was actually going to dance with this fool. But I'd just spotted someone who might be able to help us out.

Josephine.

She stood near the bar, sipping a glass of something blue. She wore an aqua tank dress that fit her like a glove, jet earrings, and a matching bracelet. Her stiletto heels were black and had cute little crisscross straps at the ankles.

Her eyes lit up as she saw me. "Honey, how *are* you?"

Up close, she looked sad and tired. I imagined she was trying to drink her sorrows away.

I air-kissed her cheeks. "I'm fine. How are you holding up, babe?"

"One day at a time," she said. "I just had to get out of the house for a while. I promised Aunt Gina I would stop moping around and go somewhere this weekend. But so many of the guys here remind me of my Rafael."

"Oh, sweetie." I rubbed Josephine's arm. I felt bad that I hadn't thought to ask her to come with us. "I'm sorry. But I agree with your aunt . . . it's a good thing for you to get out."

Josephine merely shrugged. "Aunt Gina told me you and Hailey bought the bookstore."

I nodded, a smile on my face. "We did."

"Congratulations." She gave my arm a little squeeze. "I

hate to see the store leave the family, but I'm just tickled to pieces you and Hailey are the ones who bought it. In a way, you are family. I've known you forever."

Cedric slipped his hands onto my waist, probably his way of trying to remind me that I was supposed to dance with him.

"Oh, I'm sorry," I said. "Where are my manners?" I turned toward Cedric. "Josephine, I'd like you to meet a friend of mine and Hailey's. Cedric . . ." I hesitated, realizing I didn't know his last name.

"Jones," he said, holding out his hand. "It's a pleasure."

"Oh, the pleasure's all mine, sugar," Josephine said, eyeballing Cedric's broad shoulders.

Overall, the guy wasn't bad-looking. And he was built fairly nice. Maybe Josephine could use a little something to distract her from her grief. "Why don't you two dance?" I suggested. "Josephine's going through a hard time," I added to Cedric. "She needs some cheering up."

Before Cedric could respond, Josephine stood and took his hand. She towered over him by at least four inches in her heels.

I tried not to laugh as Josephine led Cedric toward the dance floor. If Cedric had any reservations, he quickly got past them. He wriggled onto the dance floor, britches on fire. Josephine didn't seem to mind. I sighed happily and found my way back to Hailey.

"Thanks," she said, giggling as she watched Josephine and Cedric.

"No problem, sweetie." I giggled with her.

A short time later, we made a trip to the ladies' room. When we neared the restroom entrance, Hailey suddenly tensed up.

"Not Cedric?" I asked.

"No. That guy. The one with the long beard."

I saw a guy fitting that description hugging the wall near the walkway to the restroom. When we passed him, I said, "What about him?"

"I've got such bad luck with the leeches, I wanted to make sure he didn't see me."

"He hit on you?" That was a total shocker. "When did he have time, with Cedric all over you?"

"No, not tonight. But the last time we were here," Hailey told me, her tone hushed. "Actually, he didn't so much hit on me as he offered me X."

"Ecstasy?"

"Yeah. And he was standing in the same spot. I wonder if he's here all the time, selling it or something."

"Sherlock, can you take a break from the detective stuff for one night?"

"I'm just saying—"

Hailey stopped short when my cell phone rang. I groped for it, hoping it was my agent, who'd said he might have another gig for me. It was Gina.

"Lexie, I was wondering if you and Hailey can stop by the store tomorrow," she said. "There's something I need to talk to you about." She sounded serious.

I stood back in the restroom while Hailey went into a stall. "Sure, Gina. Is something wrong?"

"I can't get into it over the phone," she said. "Besides, I forgot to give you the extra key for the deadbolt on the back door, and the one to the storage room."

"Okay. Hailey and I are out celebrating. What time do you want us there?"

"It doesn't have to be early," she said. "Around noon is fine. I'm keeping the door locked so that people don't wander in, so use your key."

"We'll be there."

"Hey, one more thing. Since you and Hailey are out partying tonight, can I ask you a favor?"

"Sure."

"If you're close to South Beach, do you mind stopping by Mango's? I'm trying to get Josephine to get out of the house, and she promised me she'd go there. It's her favorite club. I'd stop by myself to check on her, but the crowd's a little young for my liking."

"Not to worry," I told her. "We're already here, and Josephine is out on the dance floor as we speak."

"She is? Well, good." Gina sighed. "I've been really worried about her, and I feel like hell, having to leave her like this."

"Don't beat yourself up, sweetie. You can't be in two places at once. Hailey and I will look out for Josephine."

"I appreciate that. Well, tell Hailey I said hi, and I'll see you two tomorrow."

" 'Bye, Gina." I tucked my phone into my purse and checked my makeup as Hailey came out of one of the stalls.

"Did I hear you talking to Gina?"

I nodded. "She wants us to come by the store tomorrow to get some keys. She also said she needs to talk to us about something."

"Really? What?"

"I don't know, but she sounded strange." I frowned. "Maybe it's just because she was worried about Josephine. She wanted us to look after her tonight."

"I feel sort of guilty pushing Cedric off on her," Hailey said.

"You can always go dance with him yourself," I teased as we headed back out to the bar.

"Bite your tongue."

"Speak of the devil . . ." I nudged her in the ribs as Cedric zeroed in on us and hurried our way.

"Lord," Hailey said. "I think I need a shot of Jack Daniel's."

"Better make it a double," I said as the band kicked things up a notch with a reggae tune and Cedric's eyes lit up.

"There you are!" he called out. "Come on, Hailey, let's strut! Ouwwww!" He let out a wolf howl, and I burst out laughing. I couldn't help it.

"Not funny, sister," Hailey hissed at me over her shoulder as Cedric took her by the hand. "Get me that Jack!"

"Yes, ma'am." Still chuckling, I whirled around to head for the bar.

And slammed right into Bianca.

Thirteen

Hailey

Partway through the reggae song, as I wracked my brain for a way to ditch Cedric for good, I looked behind me and saw Lexie standing toe to toe with Bianca.

And it looked like they were having a heated discussion.

"Excuse me, Cedric."

"Hey—"

I hurried away, leaving him on the dance floor. I reached Lexie and Bianca just in time to catch the last of what Bianca was saying.

". . . a public bar, and I'll go any damned place I please, sister!"

"She's not your sister," I said, stepping up in front of Bianca. I shot a glance at Lexie. "What's going on here?"

"I was trying to get Bianca to show some respect," Lexie said, casting her a dark look, "for Josephine. Josephine's here tonight to forget her troubles, *sis-tah*." Hands on hips, she imitated Bianca's head wag. "And she damned sure doesn't need a reminder of Rafael's past with you by seeing you here."

"She's right," I said, glaring at Bianca. "So mosey on along. There are plenty of other bars on South Beach." And maybe a few in Timbuktu . . .

"Like I told your friend," she said, staring me down, "this is a public bar, and I'll damned well party here if I want to."

"And will you cry at your party if you want to, too?" I leaned toward her until we were nose to nose. "Wanna take your party outside, girlfriend?" Now it was my turn to head-wag. Lexie often tells me there's a black woman in my soul. Either way, Lexie *is* like a sister to me, and I was sick of Bianca's attitude.

"Who you callin' 'girlfriend,' cracker bitch?"

"And who are you calling 'cracker bitch,' girlfriend?" I shot back. I narrowed my eyes.

"Ladies, ladies. Is there a problem?"

I turned to see Cedric, who'd clearly followed me from the dance floor, a few feet away.

"No problem," I said. "*She* was just leaving—weren't you, Bianca?"

She gave me those devil eyes. "*Puta!*" she snapped, tossing her thick black hair over one shoulder.

"Ho!" I returned.

"Now, now." Cedric stepped between us. "Maybe you'd better leave, Miss."

"I'm going." Bianca gave me one last evil-eye glare before starting for the bar's exit, hips swaying, long legs strutting her stuff atop her four-inch strappy stilettos.

Worried Josephine might have seen her, I hurriedly looked around. I didn't see her anywhere.

"Well, then," Cedric said cheerfully. "Can I buy you ladies a drink?"

Suddenly I felt tired. "I don't think so. Come on, Lexie. Let's blow this pop stand."

She chuckled, and my anger seeped away—somewhat.

"Whatever you say, Annie Oakley."

I quirked my mouth. "I thought I was Sherlock."

"You're both. And Nancy Drew. And the Terminator." She tucked her arm through my elbow. "Bianca's lucky you didn't have your six-shooter with you." I kept the Ruger Blackhawk .44 Magnum—that Travis had taught me to shoot—underneath my bed . . . just in case. "Let's say good night to Josephine," Lexie said. She looked over her shoulder at Cedric. "See you around, Cedric. Tell Tyrone hi for me, will you?"

"You know I will. Hey, maybe the four of us can get together tomorrow night for drinks or something."

We pretended not to hear him.

It took a while to find Josephine in the crowd. I approached her as casually as possible, hoping my hands weren't still shaking. I shake when I get pissed, and sometimes I even cry. When that happens, look out.

"Hey, Josephine," I said. We found her in the back section of the club, sitting alone on a lounger. "You doing okay, hon?"

She shrugged, then raised her blue drink in the air. "This helps."

"Are you here alone?" Lexie asked. "Do you need a ride home or anything?"

"Thanks, sugar, but no. I'm with some of the girls from my club. We're putting on a show tomorrow night at the Blue Onion. You and Hailey are welcome to come if you'd like." Her features clouded over. "I figured the best way to keep from thinking about Rafael is to get back to work."

I nodded. "Good idea. And we'd love to come see your show, right, Lex?"

"Absolutely." Lexie gave her arm a pat.

"Fabulous. The show starts at seven." Josephine gestured with one long-fingered hand. Tonight her nails were painted blue to match her drink of choice—and her outfit. "Come early and I'll buy you ladies an apple martini. They are to die for."

"Thanks," I said.

"Just remember," Lexie added, "call us if you need anything."

"I will, sugar, I will." Josephine gave us a little wave. "Drive safe, ya hear?"

We left and drove to the Waffle House for a late-night breakfast. There's nothing like strawberry waffles and whipped cream to ease your troubles—or calm your nerves when you'd like to kick the crap out of someone. I was still fuming at Bianca.

"What do you suppose is up with Bianca anyway?" I asked, slicing into my waffle with the side of my fork. "Something doesn't seem right, if you ask me."

"Ah—Sherlock is back," Lexie teased. "Or is it Nancy Drew?"

"You don't think something's up?" I asked her.

"Hailey, give it a rest, babe. We'll sort it all out later. FYI, I'm not through snooping either."

I grinned at her. "Good." Then I frowned. "I wonder what Gina wants to talk to us about."

"I dunno. Guess we'll find out tomorrow."

We finished our breakfast, headed home, and crashed. I woke up the next morning a little after ten-thirty, and took a quick shower in my private bathroom while Lexie slept. When I padded into the kitchen, she was up, also freshly showered, sitting at the table sipping coffee. She was wearing a cute little peach camisole and matching silk pajama shorts. I had a cup of Belgian Hazelnut with her, and a short time later, we headed for the bookstore.

"We need to start planning for our grand opening," Lexie said as she pulled into the strip mall's parking lot.

"When do you think we should have it?"

"As soon as we can put the store in order, I guess."

"Oh, this is so exciting! Maybe we can enlist some help to get the shelves stocked faster."

"Yeah, maybe," Lexie said, "but for the first day or two, I'd like for it to be just us, you know?"

I giggled. "Now you're starting to sound like Sid, 'you know'?" We both laughed. "But yes, I do know what you mean, Lex. Just us partners."

"That's right." She smiled.

Lexie tried the front door and found it locked. "Oh, yeah. Gina said she'd keep the door locked because she doesn't want people wandering in."

Lexie presented the key with a little flourish. "Here we go. The start to a new and wonderful phase in our life."

"A key to the bookstore!" I clamped both hands to my chest. "Be still, my heart."

Lexie laughed as she pushed the door open. "Gina!" she called. "Are you here?"

No answer.

"Maybe she's at the coffee counter," I said.

"Probably."

But a quick perusal of the store showed no sign of her. "She must not be here yet," I said.

Lexie frowned at her watch. "We're fifteen minutes late, and Gina's always been a stickler for being on time, if not early."

"True." Suddenly the hair stood up on the back of my neck. "You don't suppose something's happened to her, do you?"

"Like what?" Lexie waved a hand. "Hailey, we're going to have to cut you off from reading detective novels for a while. Maybe you need a stack of erotica."

I flashed Lexie a syrupy grin. "How about I make you a cappuccino while we wait?"

But even as we sipped our frothy drinks, I continued to have a bad feeling. When Gina still hadn't shown up thirty minutes later, I got up from my stool at the coffee counter and paced.

"I don't like this, Lex. Maybe we ought to call the police."

"And tell them what? That Gina's late for an appointment to turn over extra keys to us?"

"Okay. I guess it's possible that she came early, we weren't here yet, and she had to leave."

"Maybe she's waiting outside or something." Lexie set her oversized mug on the counter and stood. "If not, we'll try calling her at home."

We glanced outside the front window, and not seeing Gina anywhere, we went to the back room to look out the back door. Again, we didn't see Gina.

I rested my elbow on a stack of boxes that housed books that needed to be unpacked and shelved. Some of them were stacked in the far corner, near the storage room door.

And then I had an odd feeling. "Lex . . . we didn't check the storage room."

Lexie rolled her eyes. "If she were in there, don't you think we'd have heard her moving around?"

"Not if she had a heart attack or something."

"Oh, Hailey. Stop thinking the worst. Let's just call Gina—"

But I was already rushing for the storage room door.

"The storeroom is probably locked," Lexie told me. "That's one of the keys Gina said she forgot to give us."

Ignoring Lexie, I tried the knob. At first I thought the door *was* locked, since it didn't want to open when I pushed inward. Then I realized the knob had turned, but something was blocking the door, keeping it from swinging open. I gave it a hard shove, then stuck my head through the crack. And let out a scream.

The "something" was a body.

"Jesus, Hailey!" Lexie hurried over. "What the hell is it? A rat?"

I jerked back from the partially opened door, déjà vu shooting through me. Only this time I felt ten times sicker than before.

"It's Gina," I squeaked, my throat closing. "She's dead."

Fourteen

Lexie

I pushed past Hailey and forced the storage door open as far as I could. Then I shouldered my way into the room and dropped to my knees beside Gina. She was lying on her back, strands of ash-blond hair covering her face. Blood pooled beneath her head and also covered her face and neck.

My pulse quickened. She had to be dead. All that blood . . . But I didn't want to accept that, and I reached for her neck to feel for a pulse while simultaneously lowering my cheek to her face to see if I could feel her breath on my skin.

Nothing.

"Oh, God, Gina!" I screamed.

"Is she . . . is she . . . really dead?"

I brushed a tear from my cheek as I got to my feet. "I think so. Yeah."

Hailey came into the room beside me and reached for Gina's hand. "She's cold, Lex." Hailey sobbed. "Who would do this?"

"Come on." I took Hailey by the arm and lifted her to her feet. "We can't do her any good now. We have to call the police."

Hailey bawled as we exited the room. I threw one last look at Gina, lifeless and covered with blood on the storage room floor. My heart ached and my stomach twisted painfully.

I ran for the store phone on the back room's wall. As I lifted it, I saw the blood on my hand. It was like a brutal slap in the face telling me that I wasn't in the middle of a nightmare.

I dialed 911. Behind me, Hailey couldn't stop crying. I told the emergency operator what was going on, gave him our address, and then fumbled to replace the phone's receiver.

"Oh, God," Hailey said. "I've got blood on me!"

"Me too." I sniffled. I was trying my best to hold it together, but I didn't know if I could keep it up much longer.

"So much blood," Hailey said. "How could there be so much?"

"Someone stabbed her?" I asked softly. "Or bludgeoned her? Oh, God!"

More tears fell down my face. I wiped the back of my

hand across my face, then realized I had to be smearing blood on my skin.

I left the back room and hurried behind the coffee counter to the sink. I poured water, washing my hands, then swishing it over my face. Finished, I grabbed a wad of paper towels and went back to Hailey, where she still sat crying on a chair. I wiped Gina's blood off her wrist and forearm as best I could.

"Your sleeve," Hailey croaked.

I groaned when I glanced at my shirt and saw the crimson stain. I went back to the coffee bar sink, realizing only once I was there that I'd forgotten about the small bathroom in the back room. My brain was only barely functioning.

I tossed the bloodied paper towels into the trash, then ran a little cold water on the cuff of my blouse. It didn't come out, so I used a little liquid soap, rubbing vigorously. Suddenly I realized what I was doing. The police were going to see my wet sleeve and think I had something to hide!

Too late now. I dried my hands, then ran some water into a paper cup for Hailey.

"Here," I said. "Take a little sip, then put your head down between your knees before you pass out." She responded as if she were on autopilot. I pulled a chair beside hers and sat. Then I massaged her shoulder blades, trying to comfort her and calm my own nerves. But my gaze was riveted on the partially opened storage room door.

Fuck!

I jerked my gaze away. "Hailey, you okay?"

She took a shuddering breath and sat up straight, pushing back her hair. "I think so." Tears swam in her eyes. "Gina can't be dead. My God, what the hell is going on?"

"I don't know, but I hear sirens."

I rushed to the front of the store, where I held the door open. I was surprised to see a cruiser instead of an ambulance. The cruiser door opened, and I got my second shock for the day.

"Oh, shit! *Hell* no."

"What?" Hailey appeared at my elbow, poking her head through the doorway. "Montoya?" Her jaw dropped.

"And Schaefer." I could not believe our luck.

"Ladies," Montoya said, coming through the door as we stepped back out of the way. "We meet again."

"H-hi," Hailey stammered.

I tried to hide my wet sleeve.

"Where's the body?" Schafer demanded.

"Where's the ambulance?" I retorted. To me, Gina appeared dead, but maybe paramedics could revive her.

"The ambulance is on its way," Montoya calmly said. "But you need to tell us where the body is."

I swallowed painfully. It was hard to hear Gina referred to as "the body." I pointed toward the back room with my arm that wasn't stained. "In the storage room in the back. You'll see it."

Schafer and Montoya headed for the storeroom, and

Hailey and I lagged behind them. We held on to each other for emotional support.

"You know this woman?" Montoya asked.

"Yes." Hailey and I spoke in unison.

"She's our friend," I added. "We just bought this store from her."

"Is that a fact?" Schaefer cocked a suspicious brow.

Montoya spoke into his police radio, and a moment later another set of cops came into the store. They were immediately followed by a team of paramedics. Schaefer and Montoya led us to the coffee bar, where we were allowed to sit while they questioned us and took notes. We explained what had happened, starting with Gina's phone call last night.

"You two seem to have a knack for digging up bodies," Montoya commented when we were finished, smirking as though he thought his dark humor was actually funny.

I wanted to slap his face. "For your information, Gina happens to be the aunt of the woman whose lover was Rafael Martinez—the guy murdered at the strip club."

"The aunt of who of what?" Montoya shook his head in confusion. Pen poised, he took notes as I repeated myself, more slowly this time.

Schaefer's brows arched with interest. "What's the woman's name?"

"Gina Coletti," Hailey said, as though he were dense.

He glared at her. "Not the victim. The stripper's lover."

"Oh. Josephine Coletti. Only she used to be Joey Coletti. When she was a man."

Mentally, I groaned. *Too much information, Hailey.*

"You know, this just keeps getting better and better," Schaefer said. He scowled at me. "What happened to your sleeve?"

Damn! "I got blood on it," I said, deciding honesty was the best policy. "When I checked Gina for a pulse."

Montoya lifted a wad of bloodied paper towels from the garbage can. "Did you dust her too?"

"I also had blood on me," Hailey said. "I checked Gina's pulse as well."

"You both checked her for a pulse?" Schafer narrowed his eyes at her.

"Well, yeah. She's our friend." Hailey threw her hands up in a gesture of frustration. "We were upset. What would you do?"

"Not disturb a crime scene and call the police."

"Well, sue us," I snapped. "We saw our friend in a pool of blood and we wanted to help her." My stomach lurched, and I thought I might finally break down.

"I think you ladies better come down to the station and answer a few questions," Montoya said.

"The station?" Hailey looked horrified. "The police station?"

"No, the gas station," Schafer quipped. "Yeah, the police station. You got a problem with that?"

"No." I pulled myself together and laid my hand on Hailey's arm, giving her a warning look. "We don't."

"Good." He gestured with his notepad. "After you, ladies."

I cast a final look over my shoulder, wondering what the paramedics were doing and if they were having any luck. I shivered, knowing they wouldn't. Gina was dead. She had to be.

Still, I hated leaving her alone with the police officers, like she was nothing more than a piece of evidence. Again, anger churned inside of me. Schaefer was a real wiseass, and I wished I could do something to get him in deep shit with his supervisor. If he were a doctor, his bedside manner would've made his patients keel over. Inwardly, I winced at my own poor choice of words.

At least Hailey no longer looked pale. She looked as pissed as I was, and she darted me a glance as we were unceremoniously deposited in the back seat of Schaefer and Montoya's patrol car.

"I feel like a dog in the pound," she said, just loud enough for me to hear. She glared at the wire mesh divider between the squad car's front and back seats.

A third cop car had pulled into the lot, and Schaefer rolled down his window to speak briefly with his fellow officer before speeding away.

I glared at his reflection in the rearview mirror. "Late for the donut shop?"

He shot me a dark look. "I'd watch my mouth if I were you, little lady. You and your friend here aren't exactly in a position to be wisecrackers."

I bit my tongue. I was surprised he hadn't handcuffed us.

Hailey and I were taken to separate rooms for intense questioning, making me feel even more like a criminal. This time Montoya questioned me, while Schaefer had his fun with Hailey. Two hours later, they let us go.

"How are we supposed to get back to the bookstore?" Hailey asked me.

"We'll give you ladies a ride to your car," Montoya said, "but you can't go into the store. It's a crime scene now, and it's off limits."

"But it's our store!" Hailey protested.

"Off limits," he repeated. "Until we tell you different."

"Fine," she grumbled.

We got back in the squad car, and a short time later we were in my Lexus, driving homeward with the top down. *Talk about Thelma and Louise.*

"Well, that was fun," Hailey said. "Not."

"I suppose they're just doing their jobs. But that Schaefer really pisses me off."

"Tell me about it." She snorted, then said somberly, "First Rafael, now Gina. What the hell's going on here?"

"This is Miami," I answered. "Anything can happen. Although the crime rate has dropped severely over the years and it's not nearly as bad as some people think." I shuddered. "Who would break into the store and murder Gina?"

"Do you think this was a coincidence—Gina's murder? Or is it connected to Rafael's death?"

"Well, first of all, the modus operandi is different. Rafael was poisoned. Gina . . ." I had to stop and take a deep breath. "Gina was clearly not poisoned. Oh, Gina . . ."

"It was probably a robbery," Hailey said sadly. "Someone who thought Gina had cash stashed away, with the store closing down and all."

"But the store's been closed down for a while now. There's no reason anyone would think Gina still had money there. And who would break in to steal used books?"

"Hey, wait a minute. You tried the door, but it was locked. So how did it get locked unless someone had a key?"

"Oh, my God. Good point." But a moment later, I frowned. "No—we never tried the back door. That very well could have been open. It had to be. Would someone stab Gina and then take time to lock up?" I shook my head. "No, they'd just run out of the closest door—the back door."

"But the back door locks automatically, doesn't it? So Gina had to have opened the door for her killer."

"And she wouldn't let a stranger in—unless he overpowered her." I was thinking out loud. "Unless she thought it was a would-be customer, which I think is unlikely." Sickness filled my stomach, making me want to puke. "Oh, Hailey. What if her ex-husband was still harassing her? She said he'd been bugging her for money, and maybe that's why she said all that stuff about her brother being sick—you know, as a cover because she was too embarrassed to tell us the truth. Women often are when it comes to abuse by a lover." I gasped as another idea struck me. "Maybe she and the ex fought over the money we gave her for the store! He could've killed her if she refused to give him some of it!"

"You might be on to something," Hailey said. "We need to find out the guy's name. I'm sure Josephine will know." Her eyes widened. "Lexie, if it *was* Gina's ex, then Josephine could be in danger. The guy might figure she'll be suspicious of him, just like we are."

"Good point." I swung the car into the far right-hand lane, making the split decision to head to Coconut Grove instead of back home. "Let's go to her house. She needs to hear about this from us anyway, not from the cops."

But we were too late. A squad car was pulling away from Josephine's place as we neared. I waited until the car disappeared down the block, then parked in Josephine's driveway.

When she answered our knock, I nearly gasped at her appearance. Sans wig and makeup, save for some smeared mascara, she looked more like the Joey we'd known when we were teenagers. Well, other than the fact that her breasts still loomed large beneath the T-shirt she wore. Her dark hair was cropped short, and looked tousled as if she'd just gotten out of bed, and her eyes were blood-shot. She stood in the partially open doorway, and I could tell she'd been crying.

"Oh, God," Josephine sobbed. "Lexie and Hailey, some-thing awful has happened . . . the worst possible thing!"

"We know," I said. And I couldn't stop my own tears. "That's why we're here, sweetie. To make sure you're okay."

"Can we come in?" Hailey asked. "We'll take care of you. Fix you some tea."

"No." Josephine dabbed at her eyes. "I'm really not feeling very well, as you can imagine."

"Of course you're not," Hailey said. "Which is why you shouldn't be alone right now. Hon, this is a devastating blow. Let us in. Let us help you."

"And," I began slowly, "there's something else. Something important we need to talk to you about."

"I don't know . . ."

Not taking no for an answer, Hailey gave the door a little push, and Bling-Bling let loose with a volley of spastic barking. Hailey gasped and took a step back, stumbling in her haste.

Surely she wasn't afraid of the chihuahua?

"Oh, you—you've already got company." She shot me an odd look, and I raised my eyebrows.

"Ohhh . . ." Josephine groaned. "I'm so embarrassed." She began to sob. "I'm not a slut . . . really I'm not."

"What?" I stepped up closer to the doorway. "What are you talking about?" I peered inside and saw why Hailey had gasped. A good-looking black man, wearing nothing more than a skimpy pair of leopard-print briefs, hovered in the living room just behind Josephine.

Oh, my!

"You might as well come in." Josephine sighed. She

scooped Bling-Bling into her arms and held the door wide.

"Oh," I said. "Well, maybe we can come back."

"No, no. It's okay. You're already here."

I exchanged an uncomfortable glance with Hailey. Then she took a tentative step forward, and I did as well. We did have important business to discuss with Josephine.

The good-looking guy gave us a shy smile. "Hi," he said, in a soft voice that contrasted with his buff, macho physique.

"This is Rueben," Josephine told us. "Rueben, Hailey and Lexie. They're good friends of mine."

We exchanged awkward greetings, then Rueben excused himself and disappeared up the spiral staircase.

"Josephine, what the hell is going on?" I demanded, a bit too harshly. But I was confused.

"Sit down," Josephine said, sinking onto a couch. Bling-Bling perched on her lap and growled menacingly at me and Hailey. "I guess I've got some explaining to do."

"We're listening," I said. I didn't want to be mean to her, but I'd had a brutally long day.

Josephine let out a long-suffering sigh. "I met Rueben a few weeks ago at one of my shows. He took me out for drinks afterward."

"But Rafael—" Hailey began.

"Let me explain," Josephine interjected. She grabbed a pink tissue from the end table beside the couch, then dabbed the smeared mascara from beneath her eyes.

"Rafael was cheating on me. With some bitch named Bianca Sanchez."

Hailey and I exchanged surprised glances. "Go on," I said, deciding it was best not to mention that we already knew about Bianca and had met her.

"He—he got her pregnant!" Josephine's voice quavered as she lowered it so Rueben wouldn't hear. "We'd been together for two years, then he gets some bitch pregnant! It killed me, sure as anything. I couldn't even get out of bed, I was so depressed. We even broke up—briefly. But Rafael apologized, said he wanted my forgiveness. That I was the only woman for him. We worked things out, but a small part of me felt . . . I don't know . . . unsatisfied about the whole thing. Then about a week before Rafael died, I met Rueben. I know this might not make much sense, but even though I forgave him, I wanted to get back at Rafael for what he did by going out with Rueben."

"I can understand that," I said.

Hailey nodded. "My ex-husband cheated on me," she said, moving to lay a comforting hand on Josephine's knee. Bling-Bling took a snap at her.

"Bling-Bling, baby, that's not nice," Josephine cooed to the little dog, plucking her gently back onto her lap by the dog's sparkling collar.

"I know what it's like to have a rebound relationship," I said. Lord knows, I'd had my share of them.

"See—we girls know how it hurts to have a man rip your heart out. Rafael promised me he wouldn't see Bi-

218

anca anymore, and that he'd make sure she got an abortion. But he lied." Pain filled Josephine's eyes. "I saw Bianca's number on his cell phone after that—a few times—so I know they were still talking. I felt guilty for even going on a date with Rueben, but when I saw Rafael's cell phone log . . . I couldn't stop myself from sleeping with Rueben. Then Rafael died and I was wracked with guilt. It's part of the reason you found me on my roof that day. But Rueben's been so sweet through everything that's been happening. He's more than a fling, know what I mean? I thought I was finally getting over my grief. And now Aunt Gina's dead!" She burst into tears.

Leery of the chihuahua, I scooted as close to her as I dared. "I'm so sorry, babe. What can Hailey and I do to help?" I was dying to ask her about Gina's ex, but I didn't want to seem callous.

"What can you do? What can anyone do? No one can breathe life back into my dear, sweet Aunt Gina!"

Josephine sobbed, and we didn't interrupt her as she got it out of her system. Then Hailey gently said, "You don't look like you've had much sleep." She ignored Bling-Bling long enough to hand Josephine some more tissues. "Your eyes are red."

"I haven't. Rueben's been spending a lot of time here." Josephine looked sheepish. "And . . . I smoked up a little last night. Rueben and I like to do that. It makes our lovemaking so much richer."

I fought to hide my reaction, once more exchanging

glances with Hailey. I didn't need that visual, thank you very much.

"And smoking weed is the only way I can get past the guilt of being with Rueben now that Rafael's gone," Josephine continued. "I mean, at first it was all good, getting revenge on him for Bianca and everything, but now that he's dead . . . well, I feel so guilty. I still love Rafael with all my heart, but a woman has needs."

Too much information!

Hailey cleared her throat. "Yes, well, this is true." She hesitated. "Josephine, is weed all you're doing?"

"What do you mean?" Josephine blinked at her, looking insulted.

"I found a syringe in your bathroom the last time Lex and I were here. I'm not trying to judge you," she added hastily, "I'm just worried about you, that's all. So . . . are you doing stronger drugs? Cocaine, maybe?"

"I'll have you know that I have no tolerance for drugs. Well, other than weed. But that's harmless. Not like cocaine." Suddenly Josephine gasped and her face crumpled. "Oh, Lord. I hope Rafael didn't put it there."

"Rafael?" I frowned.

"Oh, I shouldn't have said anything. I don't want to tarnish Rafael's name, God rest his soul." Josephine crossed herself. "But he was into cocaine, and sometimes he did heroin."

Now I gasped. "But Sidney said he only did a little weed."

"Weed?" Josephine snorted. "That's what he wanted

220

everyone to think. He was always down in that private entertainment room, claiming he wanted space to relax." Josephine made air quotes as she said "relax." "I hardly used that bathroom. The syringe you found in there must have been his. I'd be cooking dinner in the kitchen, and he'd be in that room getting high. Even his parents don't know why he really went to prison."

"Oh, my God," Hailey said. "Remember, Lex? Rosa told us that she was afraid he was getting into drugs again— under Bianca's influence."

"I wouldn't be surprised." Josephine's eyes flashed fire. "I hate that woman! Did you know she was married to a drug lord?"

"What?" Hailey and I exclaimed in unison.

"Oh, yeah. Louie, otherwise known as Big Lou. He hangs out all over Miami, but mostly in Little Havana. I'm not so sure he and Bianca are even divorced. They might just be separated." She huffed disdainfully. "You can bet that's where Rafael was getting his drugs from. Louie kept Bianca well supplied. As a matter of fact, I'm pretty sure she had something to do with trafficking the Ecstasy that killed those teenagers—the ones on the news right around the time Rafael was killed?"

My mind was spinning from information overload. I tried to process it all.

"Are you bullshitting me?" Hailey's mouth gaped, but there was something in her eyes—the hint of excitement like a lion on the hunt.

"No, I'm not." Josephine shook her head vehemently.

"Bianca loved doing X. She gave it to Rafael all the time. He became addicted. Even tried to get me to do it, but I said no. Like I said, all I do is a little weed now and then." She sniffed, reaching to brush back long hair that wasn't there.

"Did you tell the police about this?" I asked, stunned.

"Not hardly." Josephine drew back, giving me a horrified look. "Louie is dangerous, girlfriend. I ain't even messing with anything that has to do with him and his boys. I'd be liable to end up in the deep end of the ocean."

"But Josephine," I began, "what if Louie killed Rafael?"

"Why didn't you tell us this before?" Hailey asked. "If I were a betting woman, I'd say Louie killed Rafael for sure. He was messing with his wife, and like you said, he's dangerous."

Josephine began to sob. "Why do you think I've been so upset? It's not just that I miss Rafael so damned much I could die! I feel so guilty that I can't tell the police what I know. I'm way too scared, ladies. I don't want Louie coming to my door and blowing me away. Besides, anything I say won't bring Rafael back."

"I understand what you're saying," I told Josephine. And I finally understood Sid's warnings, and Josephine's. I was beginning to wish Hailey and I had never started digging into this whole mess.

"You can't let creeps get away with murder," Hailey said, a little animated. "Do you think you'll ever be living free of fear where Louie's concerned? If he knows you can point a finger at him—"

Josephine started to cry again, and Hailey stopped talking. I went to the kitchen and made her some tea.

Josephine drank most of it and had regained her composure.

"I don't mean to scare you," Hailey said gently. "Nor be too hard on you. But I do think you should reconsider. Especially given what happened to Gina."

"How did you find out about Gina so quickly?" Josephine asked. "The cops barely left before you got here."

"We found her," I said. "That's why we came over here. We were hoping to tell you before the police got to you."

"And we wanted to ask you something," Hailey said. "Do you know where Gina's ex husband is?"

"Walt? You think he had something to do with this?"

"It's a possibility," I said.

"So, where is he?" Hailey pushed.

"LA, last I knew." Josephine ran a hand over her hair. "The bastard. He said he wanted to put as many miles between him and Aunt Gina as possible. After she did everything for that man! I don't care if he's my dad's brother or not. He treated Aunt Gina like shit."

I arched an eyebrow and glanced at Hailey. Then I said, "Gina told us he was here in Miami—harassing her. And she said she was going back to California—partly to get away from him."

"She did?" Josephine looked genuinely shocked. "I had no idea. When did she tell you that?"

"When she sold us the store, she said Walt was one of the reasons she wanted to get rid of the bookstore quick.

She gave us a deal so she could get the money and leave."

"She also said her brother was sick," Hailey added with a frown. "But I could've sworn she said her *mom* was sick the first time she mentioned it."

"And," I added, "she told us her ex was dogging her for money."

"I'm not surprised." Josephine's face reddened. "The bastard! He's a real piece of work. He used to hit Gina. Did she tell you that?"

Hailey's eyes grew round with rage. "What a scumbag! I'd love five minutes alone with him and my Ruger."

"I have no patience for wife abusers," I said.

"But I don't understand," Hailey went on. "Why would Gina want to live in California if he's there? Did she tell you about any of this—what she told us?"

"No." Despair streaked across Josephine's face. "I thought she was selling the store so she could retire early. She told me she wanted to travel."

"Damn." I sank back against the couch, my mind whirling. Now I was in full amateur detective mode, just like Hailey. "I'd love to know what the hell is going on."

"Me too," Hailey said, looking determined. "And we're damned sure going to find out."

Fifteen

Hailey

After giving Josephine our cell phone numbers again in case she needed to reach us, Lexie and I left. My head was spinning nonstop with all the new information we had.

"What do you make of all this?" I asked Lexie. "Do you think Gina sold the store because she'd gotten mixed up in something illegal?"

"I sure wouldn't have thought so, but with the lies she was telling . . . I guess it's possible." Lexie chewed her bottom lip.

"I think we should go talk to Bianca again," I said.

"I don't know, Hailey." Lexie's brown eyes were serious. "Do you really think we should, given what Josephine told us about Louie?"

"We won't mention anything about him," I said. "We'll

just talk to Bianca and see if we can get her to tell us anything that might have to do with Rafael. I have a hunch this is all connected somehow."

"Okay, but I doubt she'll be very happy to see us, after last night at the club."

"Probably, but it's worth a shot. Let's just drive by the bar and see if she's at work."

We drove to the Clevelander, and at first I thought Bianca wasn't there. But as my eyes adjusted to the dimly lit interior, I spotted her at the bar, loading a tray full of drinks. I hurried over, Lexie right behind me.

Bianca turned, skillfully balancing the tray on one hand. Her eyes narrowed immediately. "You!" she said. "What the hell are you doing back here?"

I swallowed my pride. "I came to apologize, Bianca. Will you just listen to what I have to say?"

"I'm not interested in anything you have to say."

"Five minutes?" I held up my hand, fingers spread. "Please? That's all I ask."

She heaved a sigh. "All right," she huffed. "If it will get you to leave me alone. But you'll have to wait a minute."

"That's fine," Lexie said.

We slid onto barstools and ordered club soda and cranberry juice. I sipped mine, waiting impatiently for Bianca to come back. From the corner of my eye, I watched her serve her customers. I'd swear she was purposely taking her sweet time, just to tick us off. Finally, she came back our way.

"Okay, five minutes," she said, tossing her hair over her shoulder. She waited expectantly.

"Can we sit over there?" Lexie pointed to a corner booth.

The barroom wasn't all that crowded, but I knew she didn't want anyone to overhear us.

"Fine." Bianca cast a glance over her shoulder at another waitress. "I'm taking five, Denise." She strode toward the booth, walking as if she owned the place and we were a burr in her shoe.

I slid into the booth beside Lexie. "I'm sorry I lost my temper last night," I said, "but it's only because Lex and I are so worried about Josephine." I leaned forward and lowered my voice. "And this morning her Aunt Gina was murdered."

"You're kidding." Bianca looked mildly curious. "And you're telling me this why?"

In spite of my resolve, I lost my patience. "Bianca, Josephine told us about your husband—Louie."

Her pale brown face turned to scarlet. "Louie's my *ex*-husband, and what the hell does he have to do with anything?"

"That's what we're trying to find out," Lexie said. "It just seems strange that someone would break into a bookstore. That's where Josephine's aunt was found."

Bianca shrugged. "People are killed every day. Any lunatic could've done it, so why are you asking me about Louie?"

"Josephine told us about your drug use," I said, deciding it was time to fish or cut bait. "We know you got it from Louie, and that you also got Rafael involved in drug use during the time you were having the affair with him."

Bianca's face scrunched with fury. "How dare you?"

"We're not judging you. We just want—"

"Josephine is a fucking bitch! She's filling your minds full of shit!" She gestured emphatically. "Josephine and her stories about my drug use. She called the fucking cops on me—weeks ago. They came and questioned me and everything. But you don't see me in jail, do you? Josephine's a liar, the *puta!*"

"Okay," Lexie said. "Calm down. We're just trying to figure things out, here."

"Then figure this." Bianca leaned forward, staring from Lexie to me. "I didn't lose Rafael's baby—I had an abortion! I didn't want anything more to do with him when I found out he'd been involved with some transsexual freak, only he couldn't take a hint. So if Josephine thinks I'd help him get drugs, she's even crazier than I thought!" She slid from the booth.

"But what if Louie was jealous of the fact that you were sleeping with Rafael?" I asked, scrambling to keep her from storming off. "Angry that you'd gotten pregnant with his baby? Don't you see—he could have killed Raf—"

"Your five minutes are up." Bianca shot us a last venomous look before storming off.

"That went well," Lexie quipped as we walked outside to her car.

"I'm more confused than ever." I slid into the passenger seat and Lexie drove out of the metered spot and slipped into traffic. "Why would Josephine lie to us about having called the cops on Bianca?"

"Could be Bianca who's lying."

"Could be, but we need to talk to Josephine again."

"Then let's do it," Lexie said. "Are you up for going to the Blue Onion? We can watch Josephine's show, then buy her drinks and talk to her about Bianca."

I raised my eyebrows. "What, now *you're* going into Nancy Drew mode?"

"Hey, we got started on this. We might as well finish it."

By six-thirty that night, Lexie and I were sitting at one of the dozens of tables surrounding the stage at the Blue Onion, sipping apple martinis.

"Ooh, these are good," Lexie said.

"Mmm-hmm," I agreed. "I bet this show's gonna be something." I couldn't wait to see it, even if I was more interested in talking to Josephine afterward. I wondered what the folks of Sage Bend, Montana, would think if they could see me now.

Lord have mercy!

"Good evening, ladies and gentleman!" the emcee, dressed in a silk pin-striped suit, spoke into the microphone. "Thanks for coming out. If this is your first time to the Blue Onion, then you're in for a special treat tonight. Three hours of adult entertainment starring the finest women in Miami. If you've been here before, you know what the rave is all about. And you know that one of our most popular performers is the lovely Tequila Sheila."

There were hoots and howls of agreement.

"Don't you worry. I won't make you wait another minute. Put your hands together for Tequila Sheila!" The emcee began to clap. "Oh, yeah!"

A tall and slender brunette walked out onstage, all sultry in a sequined gown. "Thank you, thank you," she purred into the mike. Her voice was noticeably deep.

I leaned over and whispered to Lexie, "Is that a five-o-clock shadow on her face?"

"Shh." Lexie smothered a giggle. Then, "And a hint of a mustache, too, I think."

I bit my lip and listened as Tequila Shelia sang a sexy song about being sad south of the border. Whew! Maybe they ought to have a tongue-twister competition during happy hour.

Five performers later, Josephine took the stage, and the crowd went wild. You could tell a lot of them were regulars, and fans to boot.

"Thank you, my sweets," Josephine crooned, blowing kisses with one hand while holding the microphone with the other. "You know I love you all."

More cheers. Josephine strutted her stuff across the stage. She wore a flesh-colored dress that left little to the imagination, its sequins barely covering her nipples and her pelvic area. She had on glittery silver spiked heels and lots of jewelry. A sparkling tiara topped her flame-colored hair, which she'd piled high on her head in the way of an old-fashioned movie star.

"Now let me entertain you," Josephine purred. She broke into song, doing a Marilyn Monroe number. Her hips pumped and jiggled as she worked the stage, making the crowd go wild. Not that I was biased, but she was clearly the best of the bunch so far.

I leaned toward Lexie. "I've been to a rodeo, a greased-pig-catching contest, and a goat auction—and I thought I'd seen it all!"

"Miami, baby. Land where anything and everything is possible." Lexie giggled. "Josephine really knows how to work the crowd, doesn't she?"

And how. She topped off her performance by whipping off a silk scarf from around her neck and throwing it out into the audience. Three men and four women made a dive for the scarf, knocking over a couple of drinks in the process and nearly upsetting one of the tables.

"Lord!" Lexie drew back in her chair, one hand to her chest. "Maybe we're in the wrong business."

I laughed, then signaled the waiter for two more apple martinis. By the time Josephine joined us at our table, I had a nice little buzz going. *Better slow down.*

"Ladies, I'm so glad you could make it!" Josephine had spotted us at our table a few minutes earlier while still up onstage. "What do you think of the show so far?"

"Amazing!" I exclaimed.

"Fabulous!" Lexie assured her.

"Wonderful." Josephine beamed. "I'm so glad you like it."

The waiter set two more apple martinis in front of us.

"Those are on me," Josephine said. "For the rest of the night. So how goes everything? You ladies keeping out of trouble?"

"We're trying," Lexie said. She looked pointedly at me before continuing. "If you have time, though, we were hoping to talk to you about Bianca."

Josephine's smile slipped. "What about her?" Her Adam's apple rose and fell as she looked from Lexie to me.

"We went to the bar where she works," Lexie said. "We wanted answers," she quickly said when Josephine's eyes bulged. "Now that we know about Louie, we think it's quite likely he had something to do with Rafael's murder. She flat out denied being involved with Louie anymore. And she also said . . ." Lexie hesitated. "She said you called the police and told them about your suspicions about her weeks ago."

For several seconds, Josephine didn't speak. All we could hear was the current drag queen onstage belting out a Liza Minnelli tune.

"Josephine?" I prompted.

"May I?" she asked, indicating my apple martini. I nodded, and Josephine downed the rest of my drink in one swallow. "Don't worry. I'll buy you another one."

"Josephine, what is it?" I asked her.

She glanced down, blushing. "I feel so silly. Yes, I did call the cops, but I didn't want to say anything to you girls."

"Why?"

She placed her hand on my knee. "Honey, this is dangerous shit you're digging into. I'd hate to see anything happen to either of you. I called the cops on Louie—anonymously—but I figured Bianca would know I was behind it. And now I'm watching my back like a hawk. I don't want you to have to do the same."

"Ahh," Lexie said, understanding.

"You're good friends," Josephine continued. "But the truth is, I think you're probably right. I think Louie is knee-deep in this. I'm sure he killed Rafael, and my God, what if he killed Aunt Gina as a way to hurt me? And if you two keep asking questions . . ." Tears filled Josephine's eyes.

"Shit," Lexie mumbled.

I felt a stab of fear in my gut.

"You know, maybe it wasn't Louie. Maybe someone else was responsible for Rafael's death. Maybe Walt finally murdered Gina. Domestic violence always escalates." Josephine paused, her eyes looking sad. "Hopefully the cops will track down those vicious murderers sooner rather than later."

"We hope that too," I said.

Josephine frowned, and her smooth skin wrinkled. "What an awful coincidence—you found poor Rafael *and* Aunt Gina. It's hardly believable."

"That's what the police think," Lexie said wryly.

"Oh, no." Josephine waved a hand, flashing her red-colored nails. How did she have time to get so many manicures? "I'd never believe you two could ever hurt a fly, much less anyone close to me." But as she said the words, I wasn't sure if I saw doubt in her eyes.

"Maybe God had a hand in us being there both times," Lexie said.

"Yeah," I concurred. "Like we were meant to be there. You know—as your guardian angels. Maybe that's why we feel so compelled to solve this, since the police can't."

"How was it?" Josephine asked in a shaky voice. "Seeing Aunt Gina. Did you see—do you know—how she was killed? The police aren't releasing any details until the killer is caught. You know how they hold back certain information from the public—things only the killer would know about?" She chewed her bottom lip. "I can't even get full closure."

A vision of Gina lying in a pool of blood zapped into my head. I shivered. "You really want to know?"

"Yes—no. God, I don't know." Josephine put her head in her hands. "I keep having nightmares. In one, Aunt Gina has been shot. In another, she's strangled . . ." She gave us a forlorn look. "Just tell me."

"I think she was either stabbed or bludgeoned to death."

Josephine cringed, making me feel guilty for being so brusque. But she'd asked.

"The cops said they didn't find a murder weapon." Tears welled in her eyes. "Poor Aunt Gina! She must've been terrified. Lord, I can't take going to one more funeral!"

"We'll help you with the arrangements," Lexie quickly offered. "You've been through enough. And like you said before, we've known you and Gina for ages . . . you're practically family to us."

"That would be nice." Josephine smiled softly at us. "Thank you."

"No problem," I said. Then I spoke without thinking to run this by Lexie. "If you're really concerned about Louie, and I think you're right to be, why don't you stay with me and Lexie for a while? We're living together now. And we've got an extra bedroom." I looked to Lexie to see her reaction.

She nodded vigorously. "Great idea, Hailey. Josephine, you're more than welcome."

Josephine suddenly frowned, and I did the same, wondering why she didn't like the idea. "You could have your own bathroom," I offered.

"I just thought of something," she said, still frowning. "Maybe Louie isn't the bad guy here. Don't get me wrong. He's a son of a bitch, but I just remembered that Bianca is on parole."

"What?" Lexie and I echoed.

"That's right." Josephine nodded vehemently. "According to Rafael, she did some time for stabbing her boyfriend."

"Wait a second," Lexie said. "I thought she was married."

"The skank-ass ho gets around. But I think this was before Louie."

"Hmm." Lexie's lips twisted, and I'd bet dollars to donuts she was thinking about Sid.

But I wasn't concerned about how much of a slut Bianca was. "She stabbed someone? As in murdered?"

"No, she didn't kill him, which is probably why she saw the light of day again instead of the dark four-by-six cell she deserves. But she messed him up pretty good, from what I hear. Caught him messing around on her, honey." She pursed her lips, waving her hand. "No man's worth all that, if you ask me. There are more fish out there in the ocean."

I wondered if she was thinking about Rafael.

"If she killed once in a jealous fit . . ." Lexie said.

"Who's to say she wouldn't do it twice?" I took another sip of my drink. Maybe we were finally on to something concrete. "Josephine, do you think Bianca could've killed Rafael?"

"Hell, yeah. That jealous slut is obviously capable of anything—sleeping with my man, then aborting his baby! I think she couldn't handle the fact that he'd dropped her like a hot potato and came back to me."

"So if Bianca killed Rafael," Lexie began, "then I think someone else killed Gina—since Bianca would have no reason to go after Gina."

"Not that I know of," Josephine said. "Unless—"

The roar of applause deafened us as one of the performers finished her act, and I assumed that that's why Josephine didn't finish her statement. Now I gazed intently at her, eager for more clues. "Unless what?"

"No. It's too much."

"Tell us what you're thinking," Lexie said.

"I saw lights on at Aunt Gina's store, on more than one occasion, late at night. She told me she was taking inventory, but I couldn't help but wonder if she was up to something else."

"Like what?" I asked.

"I don't know." Josephine shrugged. "I just found it odd. Maybe I'm overreacting."

"Maybe not," Lexie said. "Gina was at the bookstore in the wee hours of the morning on the night Hailey and I found Rafael."

I nodded. "That's right. We thought it was weird too, but then she told us she was just trying to get things packed and ready so she could sell the store and leave town."

"Come to think of it," Lexie said, "why would Gina close the store down and pack everything before she even had a buyer?" She looked at me.

"I never thought about it that way," I murmured. "But you've got a point. We didn't even talk to her about buying the store until that very night, when we found her already packing."

"Wow," Lexie said. "This is getting weirder by the minute."

"Ladies, I've got to get backstage." Josephine stood. "But if you want more drinks or something to eat, tell your waiter I said to put it on my tab. Evan will be cool about it."

She took one of mine and Lexie's hands in each of hers. "I can't thank you two enough for all you're doing."

"We'll call you Monday about Gina's funeral," Lexie promised. "Like I said, we'll help with the arrangements."

"Thank you, dolls. Bye-bye, now." Josephine gave a little finger wave, then sauntered away.

My head was whirling, and not just from the apple martinis.

"I'm feeling tired," Lexie said suddenly. "You want to go?"

"Fine by me." I'd seen enough drag-queen stuff to last for a good long while. Maybe even a lifetime.

"I wonder where this Louie character is," Lexie said as we drove home. We were in her car, but I was the one behind the wheel, cruising toward our building. I loved this car. Maybe I'd get one of my own.

"You want to try to find him?"

She cast a sidelong glance at me. "You think that's smart?"

"I don't know," I admitted.

"Maybe we ought to tell the cops about him, see if there's a way to link him to Gina. Or Rafael."

"You really want to talk to Montoya and Schaefer again? They think we're guilty as hell. Probably think we're pleasure killers, like in that movie *Natural Born Killers*."

"This is true," Lexie muttered. "I don't know, Hailey. Maybe we need to back off for a while."

I nodded my agreement, but I wasn't interested in doing any such thing. As far as I was concerned, there was a killer out there—and if someone had so easily bludgeoned Gina in the store, what was to stop the person from doing the same to us? At this point, only God knows what this person's motive was.

But if I had anything to say about it, Lexie and I would know too. Before we opened the bookstore, so we could put all this behind us and get on with our lives.

Sixteen

Lexie

The cops kept our store under their control for the investigation of Gina's murder for nearly a week. When they finally cleared away their yellow crime-scene tape, they left a helluva lot behind—a huge mess to clean up.

I stood with Hailey in the back room, my hands planted on my hips as I stared at the entrance to the storeroom. "I can't believe they left all that blood for us to clean up!"

"Me neither."

"I sure as hell am not crazy about cleaning up Gina's blood." She'd been a friend, and the thought was more heartbreaking than horrifying. In fact, a big part of me wondered how we would ever run this store, with the dark cloud of Gina's murder hanging over us every time we came in here.

"Maybe we should call someone to do it for us," Hailey suggested.

"Like who?"

"You think Merry Maids handles this type of thing?"

I shrugged. "It's worth checking out."

Hailey walked to the small table in the back room. "At least they were kind enough to leave us the yellow pages." She snorted with derision.

She opened up the phone book and made half a dozen calls while I tried to busy myself with sweeping the floor and reorganizing boxes—anything to avoid heading into the storeroom.

Finally, Hailey hung up the phone and looked at me, frustrated. "Nobody wants the job."

"Surely *someone will*," I said. "Please tell me we don't have to do this ourselves."

"I'll keep looking."

After about five minutes, Hailey said brightly, "Hey, here's one. 'Crime Scene Clean-Up,'" she read aloud. "'Your loss is our gain. We'll clean up after your dead loved one, so you won't feel the pain.'"

"You're making that up!" I smacked Hailey's arm while peering over her shoulder at the phone book.

"I'm not! I swear. Listen. 'Will clean up bloodstains and body fluids. We specialize in murder crime scenes— multiple homicides not a problem.'"

I looked at Hailey skeptically. "Does that say 'Miami-Dade CSI' at the bottom of the ad?"

"Nope."

"Could be a trick. You know—for the murderers dumb enough to call. And bang, Horatio hauls them off to jail."

Hailey's mouth twisted with doubt.

"I guess not," I said. "But seriously, I've never heard of such a thing. That would be funny if it weren't so morbid."

"You're right." Hailey scowled. "Bad idea. It really is morbid. And completely insensitive."

"Talk about capitalizing on people's pain!"

"Who would even *think* of such a business?"

"Someone with some serious screws loose, that's who."

For a moment, neither Hailey nor I said anything, just looked at each other as though contemplating what to do next.

"Well," I finally said, slapping a hand against my thigh. "Shall you call them, or shall I?"

Hailey was already reaching for the phone.

By the time the weekend came, Hailey and I had sorted through the jumble of half-packed boxes Gina had left, and we'd given the store a good overall cleaning. The crime scene cleanup people had done an amazing job—you couldn't even tell a pool of blood had soaked into the storeroom concrete. Still, I shivered every time I got anywhere near the storage room. No amount of cleaning would erase the mental picture in my mind.

"We're going to have to do something different to that room as soon as our budget allows," I said to Hailey as we unloaded and shelved a box of office supplies. "Maybe put carpet down there."

"With the humidity we get here?" She wrinkled her nose. "And that room isn't accessed by the central air system."

"Then we can tile it over," I went on, liking that idea. "Yeah, new tile is good. Looking at that room the way it is gives me the willies. I can still see that bloodstain so vividly in my mind."

"I know what you mean," Hailey said. "I can't shake the image of it either. My God, to think how Gina must have suffered!"

"I wonder if she saw her attacker or was surprised. If the first blow knocked her out or she knew she was going to die."

"Thinking like that will drive you crazy . . . but I do it too."

"Guess we have to concentrate on the fact that she's beyond pain now, in a better place."

"Yeah." Hailey sighed wistfully.

"I didn't say this earlier, but the thought crossed my mind that we should sell the store. I just didn't know if I could deal with coming here every day, knowing Gina had been murdered here." Hailey stared at me in mild surprise, and I shrugged my shoulders. "I don't feel that way anymore. Now I feel that by going ahead and opening our store, we'll be honoring Gina's memory."

"And instead of just putting up a version of her old sign in the coffee area," Hailey said, gesturing excitedly, "we can include a nice picture of her too. We can ask Josephine for one."

"Exactly what I was thinking."

We both grinned at the idea, the only ray of sunshine in a sky of dark clouds. In my heart I knew that Gina would still want us to run the store, and I wasn't about to let some asshole murderer shut us down before we opened shop.

"When we finish up here, let's go to the grocery store." I wanted to change the subject to something happier. "I need to pick up a few things so I can cook a nice dinner for us tonight." Cooking always relaxed me. "Do you still love lasagna?"

"Are you kidding?" Hailey grinned. "Be still my heart!"

I laughed. "You can make the garlic bread."

"Now you're talkin'," Hailey said. "We can cook and figure out when to have our grand opening."

By five o'clock, we were home and unloading bags of groceries. With that done, I shooed Hailey out of the kitchen while I got to work on the main dish. This was my treat for her.

I heard the television come on in the living room, and seconds later the sound of Bill Kurtis's voice as he spoke on one of A&E's ever-popular crime shows. I smiled to myself. Hailey was addicted to them. Little Miss Sherlock.

In the kitchen, I had one of those fancy metal fridges with a built-in TV, and I switched it on before I went about seasoning the ground beef. "I've perfected my lasagna recipe since I first made it for you back in high school," I announced, not sure if Hailey was hearing me over Bill Kurtis. My mother had taught me the recipe, and making this dish was one of the ways that I felt close to her. For the past ten years, she'd been living hundreds of miles away in Orlando. She was constantly involved in charitable work for severely abused children, which kept her busy—and happy. "I've added some ingredients my mother never used, and I actually think it's better than hers—"

I stopped talking abruptly and lowered the bowl of ground beef onto the counter. Had I just heard Bianca's name?

I walked closer to the thirteen-inch set and stared at my favorite newscaster from Channel 2 news, who was talking about a "breaking news" story.

On the screen was an image of a spectacular car wreck along a stretch of interstate. Something made the hairs on my nape stand on end.

"Oh, my God, Hailey," I called out. "Come quick! I think I just heard the newscaster say something about Bianca Sanchez!"

Hailey hopped off the sofa and hurried to my side. "The hell you say!"

Using a knuckle, I turned up the volume on the television, my gaze riveted to the screen. A reporter stood in front of a flipped and mangled SUV along a twisted guardrail. ". . . hit and run here on I-95, a little over an hour ago. Again, we now know that the driver of the vehicle was Tommy Castellano of Aventura, thirty-three years old. Earlier this year, he was charged by police for his role in a money-laundering scam, and was on bail until his trial, slated for next January. Castellano was killed on impact, but the passenger, a Bianca Sanchez, twenty-six years old, also of Aventura, has been rushed to Jackson Memorial Hospital and is reported to be in serious condition. The police are asking for anyone with information on the vehicle that fled the scene, reportedly a gold-colored SUV, to call Miami-Dade police . . ."

"Bianca Sanchez?" Hailey's eyes grew wide as she stared at me. "That's obviously our Bianca, don't you think? I mean, what are the chances?"

"Exactly—what *are* the chances? I have no doubt it's her. And how convenient is that—her being run off the road? I don't believe for one second that it was an accident."

"Holy shit," Hailey said.

"It makes sense now. She *had* to have lied to us. I'll bet anything she was still involved with Louie. How else was she able to live in a ritzy condo while working as a waitress? Drug money, baby. Drug money supplied by her not-so-loving husband."

"She must have talked to Louie about our conversation with her. Oh, shit." Hailey looked worried.

"This is really heating up. Maybe we should call the police."

"And tell them what? That we just happen to know the victim of this crime too? They'll have us in jailhouse orange before you can say Manolo Blahnik!"

Damn, she has a point. I could just picture the look on Montoya's and Schaefer's faces if they got ahold of that info. "Well, we've got to do something."

"Maybe we should go to the hospital and see Bianca."

I shook my head. "That reporter said she was in serious condition. I doubt she'll be up to receiving visitors, much less talking. And if you think she talked to Louie . . . if *he* did this to her because he thought she talked to us . . . Hailey, it's not smart. We shouldn't go anywhere near the hospital."

Hailey groaned. "You might be right about that." She slumped against the counter, resigned to our fate. But the next moment, she snapped her fingers, her eyes lighting up. "The DVD! From the camcorder at Rafael's funeral! We only skimmed through it once and didn't see anything significant, but what if there's something we missed?"

"Like a shot of Louie?" I was hopeful, even if that was unlikely.

"Who knows?"

Hailey disappeared into her room and came back with the DVD she'd recorded of the mourners at the funeral. I hadn't been particularly keen on watching the DVD the first time we'd put it on, hours after the funeral, thinking that Hailey had gone overboard with her detective antics. But now I had to admit she was right for doing what she did. Maybe some vital information *had* been recorded. And it would certainly help to have an idea of what Louie looked like—*if* he was on film.

"Let me get the lasagna started, then we'll watch it."

"I'll get the garlic bread ready and make a salad."

We soon had the lasagna in the oven and the DVD playing. I had to admit, Hailey had done a good job of covering the crowd of mourners at both the church and the cemetery, something I appreciated now that we were viewing the video for a second time. Still, I didn't see anything or anyone that would lend us a clue.

"There's that blond woman," Hailey said, pointing. "I wonder who she is."

"Probably just someone who knows Rafael or his family," I reasoned.

"Then why's she standing back away from the crowd, like a red-haired stepchild?"

"Maybe she secretly had a crush on Rafael." I shrugged. "I don't know. But babe, I hate to say this—I think you're looking for clues that aren't there."

Hailey sighed. "Maybe." Then she gasped. "That's Bianca!"

"What?" I squinted at the screen. "Where?"

Hailey grabbed the remote. "I *know* that was her! Let me rewind this thing."

In her haste she fast-forwarded instead, then rewound too far. I pried the DVD remote from her fingers. "Let me do a slow rewind."

I did, and Hailey dashed to the TV in excitement. "*There!* Go back a little bit." I did, and she ordered me to stop. "Bianca—that sneaky little devil." She plopped down on the rug and jabbed a finger against the screen. "I didn't see her there!"

"Neither did I." I stared at the woman Hailey indicated. "Are you sure that's her?" The woman on the recording *could* have been Bianca, but it was hard to tell. She was wearing sunglasses, a wide-brimmed black hat, and a plain black dress—like many other women in the crowd.

"It's her," Hailey insisted. She pointed again. "She's tall—I can tell by that guy she's standing next to. He's Rafael's cousin—I heard Rosa say so—and I know he's about six foot, because he was standing with the family when we passed by to give our condolences, and he's just a little taller than me."

"Okay, but Bianca's not the only tall woman in the world besides you."

"Yeah, but watch how she carries herself, like a strutting peacock." Hailey gestured with one hand. "Rewind a little."

I rewound to where the woman in question walked up to the graveside. Her head was hanging low, so I couldn't see her face, but still, I realized Hailey was right. Bianca had a certain way of strutting that she couldn't hide—not even at her former lover's funeral. And those strappy black stilettos were the same ones she'd been wearing at Mango's!

"It *is* her! And look!" I rose partway off the couch. "Watch that guy who walks up behind her."

Again, I rewound the DVD a bit, then hit play. A stocky guy in a charcoal-gray suit stepped up behind Bianca and put his hand on her shoulder. She startled visibly, then the guy leaned close to her ear and said something. Unfortunately, Hailey had picked that moment to focus the camera elsewhere in the crowd.

"Oh, damn!" Hailey clenched her fist, giving the area rug on the floor a smack. "I should've paid better attention to who I was filming."

"You couldn't have known," I said. "Bianca blended into the crowd. Besides, you didn't want to be too obvious."

"Do you think that guy was Louie? He looked like someone who'd be nicknamed Big Lou."

"Oh, yeah? And you know that why?"

"Big and burly, has a sort of mafia, drug-dealer look to him." She nodded toward the freeze-framed video.

I couldn't deny she was right. "I bet you saw lots of those in Montana."

"No, but I saw Mob Week on A&E."

"Ha!" I chuckled. "I should have known."

"A&E's great. Very informative."

"Well, at least you caught Bianca on film. Of course, it doesn't prove anything except she was there."

"But if she and Rafael parted on bad terms—and she certainly made that clear—then why was she at his funeral?"

"Paying her respects?" I offered.

"I wouldn't go to Travis's funeral. Well, unless it was to line-dance on his grave."

I laughed at that image. "You know, Hailey, you could be on to something."

"Then let's talk to her—once she's feeling better. We can ask about the guy in the gray suit."

"Couldn't hurt to try, but we're not exactly her best friends."

"But we'll have the element of surprise. And if she's stuck in a hospital like a sitting duck, it's not like she can run from us. We'll catch her off guard. If she's up to something sneaky, she won't want to piss us off when I tell her we caught her on a video recording. Besides, if Louie *is* responsible for what happened to her, she might be ready to tell us the whole truth."

We watched the rest of the video, but saw nothing of interest. I checked the lasagna, and Hailey put the garlic bread in the oven. When dinner was ready, we sat at the table with two heaping plates, plus bowls of the salad Hailey had put together.

"God, this is good!" Hailey closed her eyes in ecstasy as she placed a cheese-drenched forkful of pasta in her mouth.

"Thanks. And girlfriend, the garlic bread is divine." I broke off another slice. "So, shall we make a to-do list for getting the bookstore ready? We need to pick a date for our grand opening, so we can run an ad in the paper . . . maybe put up some flyers."

"I think we can have things ready to go in a couple of weeks, don't you?" Hailey asked.

She grabbed the calendar off the kitchen wall, and we began to plan in earnest, picking a date in mid-September. Where had the summer gone? August had flown by.

And the next few days did too, as Hailey and I got down to business. We still had a lot of work ahead of us, but things were gradually falling into place, the bookstore starting to really feel like ours. We'd kept an eye on the news, but nothing significant had happened in regards to the hit-and-run driver who'd put Bianca in the hospital. Follow-up news reports said only that the unidentified driver had not been found.

On Tuesday, Hailey and I decided to make a trip to Jackson Memorial. Since there'd been no news of Bianca's death, I assumed she had to be recovering—but I hoped she was confined to bed with an IV tube in her arm. That would make it harder for her to take off when she saw us.

"So, Sherlock," I said to Hailey as we headed across the street from the pay parking lot to the hospital. "How're you feeling?"

"Nervous. But excited."

"I hope we don't send Bianca into cardiac arrest when she sees us," I said half jokingly. I was trying to lighten the mood, but I was nervous too. I didn't imagine Big Lou to be the type to back down if a job wasn't finished. What if he happened to show up at the hospital at the same time we did?

"She'd better not," Hailey said, sounding serious. "I'm more than ready to get the truth from her—even if I have to shake it out of her when she can't fight back."

"Forget Sherlock—sounds like you're going into Terminator mode again. It's a good thing you never worked at the post office."

Hailey roared with laughter at that.

"Seriously, though," I went on, "let's try not to scare her. Even if that means being sickly sweet to her. Anything to get her to talk. And there's the chance that her accident was just that—an accident. A lot of people are involved in hit-and-runs. It doesn't mean the driver purposely ran her off the road."

"But it doesn't mean he didn't either," Hailey insisted.

Inside the hospital, we approached the receptionist at the front desk and asked for Bianca's room number.

"I'm sorry," the woman said. "Miss Sanchez has been transferred."

"Transferred?" Hailey frowned. "Transferred where?"

"I'm sorry. I'm not allowed to give out that information."

"Can you tell us when she was moved?" I asked.

"Two days ago."

The receptionist looked bored, as though she couldn't care less if Bianca had been sent to another hospital or to Mars.

"But we have to know where she is," Hailey pressed. "It's a matter of life and death."

The woman raised her eyebrows, causing the silver hoop in the left one to twitch. "I'm sorry," she said again. "I can't help you." She swiveled her chair around to face her computer, and tapped away at the keyboard.

"Great!" Hailey turned reluctantly away from the desk. "Now what?"

"I don't know." I walked beside her, back to her truck. "Maybe we should go to Bianca's apartment."

"Couldn't hurt," Hailey said. "It's possible she might've just gone home. Maybe that's the hospital's story so the news crews don't bother her."

Unfortunately, the card access key was in my car, so we had to make a stop at our place before heading to the Peninsula.

"Let's go upstairs for a second," I told Hailey.

"Huh?" She looked at me blankly. "Don't we want to get to Bianca as soon as possible?"

"I have a hunch about something."

"What kind of hunch?"

"You'll see," I told her, then got out of the truck.

When we hit the ninth floor, Hailey looked at me and asked, "Why won't you tell me what you're doing?"

"Because." I entered our unit, and she followed me. "I have a few tricks up my sleeve too, Sherlock."

Inside, I headed to my bedroom and my computer, where I logged on to the Internet. "Okay. What was the name of the guy who died in the accident with Bianca? Tommy Castellano?"

"Yeah, that sounds right."

"Then let's see what we can find out about him." I typed in his name, feeling pretty smart.

The first articles that popped up were about the fatal hit-and-run. The next were about his arrest in the money-laundering scam. As I skimmed one of those articles, my hunch was proved correct.

"Aha!"

"What?" Hailey asked.

"It says here that Tommy Castellano was also under investigation for possible drug dealing—Ecstasy in particular—and that he was a known associate of Louie Delvecchio."

I glanced over my shoulder, looked up at Hailey, and grinned. "Bingo, baby."

A short while later, we were at Bianca's condominium door. I rapped on it urgently, excited to talk to her.

No answer.

"I wonder if she's here," Hailey said, sounding worried. "I can't hear anything in there."

"That doesn't mean she's not home." I knocked on the door again, willing it to open. After a couple of seconds, I raised my eyebrows at Hailey when I thought I heard a sound inside. Then I heard the lock turn, and I held my breath.

The door swung open. But instead of Bianca, a thin man of about six-foot-four, with dark-rimmed glasses and a dress shirt open at the collar, stared down at us with an annoyed expression. "Yeah?"

"We're looking for Bianca Sanchez," Hailey said, narrowing her eyes in confusion. "We thought this was her apartment."

"Let me guess—you're here for another drug-induced low-life party?" The man scowled. "Well, you're shit out of luck."

His tone shocked me, and I glanced beyond the man into his condo. It was in complete disarray. "We're not here to party," I explained. "We're here to . . . to ask Bianca some questions."

"You two cops?" the guy asked. He looked like a computer nerd sort, and I wondered what his affiliation with Bianca was.

"No, we're not cops," Hailey told him.

"Bounty hunters, right? I wouldn't be surprised."

"No," Hailey said. "We're . . . friends."

He looked us up and down, his eyes saying he didn't believe us. "Really?"

"Business associates, really," Hailey amended.

"Is Bianca here?" I asked. I didn't know what was going on, but it was possible that the guy was hiding her.

"Here?" His eyes widened. "You're kidding me, right? Look at this place, and you tell me if you think she's here."

Both Hailey and I glanced behind him at the floor littered with cups and dishes and all sorts of garbage. Even the blinds were broken at one end and sloping toward the floor. It was clear now why he was pissed.

"I don't understand," I said. "The last time we were here, Bianca was living here."

"She was *house-sitting*," the man said venomously. "Or so I thought. I came back from my extended business trip to find my condo turned to shit. And all my exotic fish are dead."

"Oh," I said, turning the word into a moan.

Hailey and I glanced at each other. Then she asked, "Do you know where she is?"

"If I knew where she was, I'd already be there. The little bitch owes me big time."

"Do you know she was in the hospital?" I asked. "Did you hear about her accident?"

"I got off a plane from Thailand eight hours ago. I didn't hear a damn thing. Obviously she's still alive. Too bad."

"So you have no idea—"

"None whatsoever. But if you find her, you tell her that she owes me ten grand for those fish alone. Not to mention what the cleaning bill's gonna be. There are syringes all over the place, pills, strange vials . . ." The man shook his head. "Someone warned me about her, said she was involved with some big drug dealer, but Bianca swore it was a case of mistaken identity. That white people always think all black people look alike."

"Louie?" Hailey asked. "Was that the name of the drug dealer?"

"Yeah, that sounds like his name. You know him?" The man's voice rose on a hopeful note.

"No," Hailey told him. "But quite frankly, we've heard he's not someone you'd want to piss off."

"That right? Well, I don't give a damn who the sonofabitch is. I tried to help out a woman in need. And this is how she repaid me." He gestured behind him. "I'll bet she was still fucking this drug-dealer guy, right here in *my* home, if the state of my condo is any indication. I work my ass off to afford a decent life. Drug-dealing scum—they could care less about people's property, people's rights. For them, it's easy come, easy go. They think they can run this city, fuck up people's lives. Well, that Louie guy can kiss my ass."

I could only imagine the battle between Twiggy here and Louie. I'd bet my money on Louie—and my car, my condo, my closet full of designer shoes . . .

"I'm a bit confused," Hailey said. "How much did you know about Bianca?"

"Not enough, clearly. But my ex-girlfriend warned me about her. Too bad I didn't listen."

An elderly couple strolled behind us, staring at us all with concerned gazes. "Do you mind?" Hailey was already stepping forward. "Maybe we could step inside for a couple minutes to talk a bit more?"

The man shrugged, his face still twisted in a scowl. "Sure, whatever."

We stepped inside the condo, and it was even clearer why the guy was as pissed as he was. I saw the giant aquarium on the left wall, the water dark and murky. No fish could be alive in there. He hadn't mentioned having a cat or a dog, but near the large window in the corner there were pieces of feces on a newspaper, so someone had to have had a small animal in there. Further testament to that were the gashes in the man's leather sofas—probably from a cat's claws. The white sofas were also stained with colorful spills.

Yikes. What a disaster.

"She cleaned me out too," the guy said. "My silverware. China."

"You mentioned your ex-girlfriend had some knowledge of Bianca?"

"She said that as far as she knew Bianca looked a lot like a woman who was married to some big-shot drug lord. Said some of her friends, who always hang out on South Beach, knew who she was."

"But you didn't believe her," I stated.

"My ex and I, we'd had our problems. When it came to Bianca, I didn't want to hear what she had to say. I figured she was just jealous because I'd moved on."

With someone as hot as Bianca, he may as well have added.

Well, that solved the mystery of why a hot girl like Bianca would be with a geeky-looking guy like this one. Why else would this guy have let her stay in his place to house-sit? I could just imagine it now, Bianca on the prowl for a man who looked like he had money, perhaps while she'd been waitressing. A guy like this one would be flattered by the attentions of a sexy young woman—and probably did everything to please her. His ex had been smart to warn him to stay away from Bianca, but love—or lust—was blind.

"I started to have my doubts when Bianca never answered the phone, and one of my neighbors called my cell and left a message to say he saw a woman who looked like she had a million body piercings coming out of my place on several occasions. And other scary-looking sorts. Lots of noise and late-night parties. I cut my trip short to return home. And found this freakin' disaster zone."

The man looked so frustrated, I didn't know what to say.

"I'm so sorry," I told him. "My name's Lexie, by the way, and this is Hailey. Maybe we can give you our numbers in case you learn anything else and you can contact us?"

"Sure. And I'll give you my card so you can do the same."

The man's card read Adam Page, and he was some executive with GRON Technology—whatever that meant. Clearly, it meant he was well paid.

Adam suddenly laughed, albeit mirthlessly. "The property manager left me a note in my box. Before I left, I told her I was getting a house-sitter. In the note she asked if I knew that I'd turned my place over to a drug lord's wife and some stripper."

Stripper? Hailey and I exchanged glances. Bianca's roommate had looked more like a punk rock groupie than an exotic dancer.

"Stripper? Was she sure?"

"Yeah, said she talked to the freak herself, and that she'd bragged about how much she got paid taking off her clothes."

"Well, thank you for your time," Hailey said, moving toward the open door.

"Yes," I agreed. Clearly, we couldn't learn anything more helpful from Adam.

"If you find Bianca, you'll call me?"

"Sure," I told him, though I didn't think that was wise. "I wish there was more we could do to help."

He huffed. "Know anyone who will clean up a mess like this?"

I looked to Hailey, then to him. My lips curved in a smile and I said, "As a matter of fact, Adam, yes, I do."

Seventeen

Hailey

"So, Bianca's taken off," Lexie said to me when we were back in her car. We'd left my truck at our condo after our short visit there to check the computer. Like the first time we'd gone to the Peninsula, we took Lexie's Lexus—where she had the card key to the Peninsula conveniently stashed.

"Looks like," I said.

"Do you think Bianca's disappearance has anything to do with Rafael's murder, or do you think it's because of something between her and Louie?"

"Why wait till now to take off if she had something to do with Rafael's murder? But Louie—I can see that."

"She could have waited because she thought she got away with it. An obscure poison—she probably thought his death would be ruled a heart attack or some other natural cause. Then we started asking questions, and she starts to get scared . . . or Louie tried to kill her and she knew she had to skip town. It could be anything, really."

"What if—and hear me out on this one—this all ties in with the Ecstasy that killed those teens?" I stared at Lexie, my brain churning. "Josephine said she thought Rafael had gotten involved with drugs again, and she sure seems suspicious of Bianca."

"True. And so did Rafael's mom. In fact, Rosa said something about Bianca and the wrong crowd—would she say that if she simply thought Rafael was doing drugs? Or was she suspicious of something more?"

"What if Rafael got in deep with something he shouldn't have?" I chewed on my bottom lip as that thought played in my mind. "You know, I'll bet Louie had him whacked."

"*Whacked?*" Lexie asked as she passed a slow-moving car in front of us.

"Yeah. That's what drug lords do. They want you out of the picture, they whack you."

Lexie chuckled softly. "I guess all those A&E crime shows have helped you get the mobster lingo down." Suddenly she frowned. "Hailey, maybe we're messing with something we shouldn't be. I don't want to end up with poison in my chocolate."

"Don't worry. We're going to look out for each other. That's part of why we're living together, right?"

"Right."

"Anybody tries messing with us, I'll show 'em a Clint Eastwood 'make my day.'"

Again, Lexie laughed. "Okay, Montana. But seriously, maybe we ought to take a step back for now and just focus on the bookstore."

"I suppose." I sighed. We *did* have to concentrate on our business, but I didn't want to let this go. "I don't want to give this up, Lexie. I'm too into finding answers to quit now."

"We won't quit. We'll just take a break. Give our brains a rest."

"Yeah," I agreed. "And maybe when we take a break, something we're missing will come to mind."

"All right, then. Let's go home and finish our to-do list."

Back at the apartment, we'd just sat down at the kitchen table with pen and paper when the phone rang. I hopped off the chair and answered it.

A man's voice boomed into my ear. "Hailey, darling. That you?"

Travis? No, it couldn't be. "Who is this?"

He chuckled hoarsely. "It's Cedric."

"Cedric." I said his name so Lexie could hear. "How'd you get this number?"

"Tyrone gave it to me. I figured I'd call Lexie and find out what happened to you. I went by your apartment, but no one seemed to know you there, Pink Sugar."

I rolled my eyes. "That's because they're dimwits."

"So, you're living with Lexie now?"

"For now, yeah. But I might be moving out of state."

Lexie whacked my arm. I looked at her and she mouthed, *Cedric's nice.*

"Well, I won't be moving for a while yet. If I do."

"You owe me a dinner, babe. How about tonight?"

"Gee, I'd love to Cedric, but I'm afraid I'm too busy right now. Lex and I are trying to get the store ready for our grand opening."

"Yeah, that's right. I can help you. Remember—I told you I'm good for heavy lifting—among my many talents."

I grimaced. I could just imagine what he thought he was talented at.

Lexie poured us some lemonade and I gulped it down, wishing it were whiskey.

"When's the grand opening?"

"A week from Saturday."

"I'll be there. But I sure hope you call me before then—for that dinner I promised ya."

"Well, we'll have to see, thanks." I hung up and slumped into my chair beside Lexie.

"How'd he get this number?"

"Tyrone. He figured he'd call you to track me down."

"You gotta admit, the guy's resourceful."

"He said he's coming to our grand opening. He wants to help."

Lex laughed airily. "Looks like you've got your own personal stalker, babe."

"It's not funny, Lexie. You try putting up with skunk breath and spittle."

Lexie's lips pulled into a thin line. It was clear she was trying not to chuckle.

"Okay," I said. "That's fine. Go ahead and laugh. I guess free help is free help, right? And a customer is a customer. I'll get back at Cedric by making him buy a whole ton of books."

"There you go. The perfect revenge."

I cooked dinner that night, and we settled in to watch movies, taking our plates of barbecued chicken and potato salad to the living room. After dinner, we telephoned Josephine, and helped her plan for Gina's funeral. Gina had requested cremation, and a simple memorial service with only her close friends and family in attendance.

Since she didn't seem to have much of the latter, Lexie and I sat with Josephine a few days later, in the front row of the church where the service was held. Afterward, we went out on Josephine's yacht to scatter Gina's ashes at sea. She'd loved the water, and I couldn't help but feel a little sad that I hadn't had a chance to go on a boat ride with her until now. Imagine—my first time on a yacht, and the circumstances were these. Tough cowgirl that I am, I buried my face against Lexie's shoulder when Josephine opened the urn.

I was still sniffling when Josephine presented us with a small cylindrical object attached to a silver chain. "Here," she said. "I know Aunt Gina would have wanted you to have this."

"What is it?" Lexie asked.

"It's a memorial necklace," Josephine said, wiping her

own eyes. "A little bit of Gina's ashes are in there." She gestured toward the sterling cylinder. "I've got one too."

Lex and I exchanged somewhat horrified glances.

Who the hell would want to wear a dead person—well, part of one—on a chain around her neck?

"Thanks." Lexie managed a graceful smile.

Me, I was grateful Josephine hadn't given us each one.

Lex and I spent the rest of the week going through inventory, and by the weekend, we were ready to begin stocking the store shelves. It was hard, hot work, and Lex and I took a break to make iced coffees, which reminded us of Gina all over again. We'd been keeping a close eye on the news broadcasts and the papers, but nothing more was said about her murder, or Rafael's. Just another couple of Miami homicides, as far as the police were concerned, I thought dryly.

I looked around the store. "We really need to do something to pep this place up. So it doesn't say Gina so much, you know?"

"I hear you, Sid," Lex said and chuckled.

"Hey, how about we come up with some sort of a theme? We can get some decorations to make the store look more inviting."

"Sounds good. What kind of theme did you have in mind?"

"How about 'Get lost reading' or 'Lose yourself in a book' or something like that? We could do a cardboard cutout of Hansel and Gretel and maybe some trees. And the gingerbread house, only instead of the witch waiting for them with a preheated oven, she's got a storybook to read to them."

"That's kind of cute, Hailey. But what about for the rest of the store?" Before I could say anything, Lexie's eyes lit up. "Oh, I know. We could make footprints on the floor that lead to different sections in the store, and paint things on them. Like 'This way to romance' and 'Follow the clues.' What do you think?"

"I like," I said. "Oh, and cardboard trees here and there, to make it look like the footprints are leading the reader through a forest."

"And a sign that reads NEVER MIND THE FOREST. JUST LOOK FOR THE TREES. Each section can have a tree labeled with mystery, or romance, or whatever."

I nodded. "Yeah. We're such a good team."

"But can we do all that in a week? Too bad we didn't think of this sooner. We've still got a lot of shelves to stock."

"Nothing's impossible, right? How about I go to the party favors store and see what I can find? Surely they've got something we can use, and we'll make the rest. Heck, we can get Josephine to help if she's up for it, or even good old Cedric."

"Now I know you're desperate."

I shrugged, then held up my glass of iced coffee. "When life gives you cold coffee, you make a Whipped Delight."

I left Lexie to finish her iced coffee and went out to my truck. En route to the bookstore from my old apartment, I'd noticed a store called Party On at the corner of Euclid and Sixteenth that looked like a good place to buy decorations. As I pulled out of the strip mall's parking lot, I spotted a gold-colored minivan in my rearview mirror—one that was riding my bumper. I shot the driver a glare and accelerated, and the van dropped back a bit. But a moment later, I saw it in my mirror again.

It wasn't until I'd changed lanes and turned onto Sixteenth that I realized the van was still following me. I studied it in the mirror, trying to get a better look at the driver. With the van's tinted window, I couldn't tell if the person was male or female. He or she wore a ball cap and dark glasses and a dark-colored shirt. My heartbeat picked up. The newscast had said the SUV that ran Bianca off the road was gold-colored. Could a minivan be mistaken for an SUV?

My palms started sweating, but when I turned into the small parking lot of Party On, the van kept going. I let out a breath. Maybe Lexie was right. I was letting all this murder-sleuth stuff get to me.

Inside the store, I found the perfect decorations, including multicolored Mylar balloons, some confetti we could use as bread crumbs for Hansel and Gretel to follow to the storytime witch, and some cardboard trees with fold-out crepe-paper leaves. They were meant to be Thanksgiving decorations, but they would do just fine.

I made my purchase and, loaded down with goodies, went back to my truck. I kept an eye on my rearview mirror as I drove, but I didn't see the gold minivan or any other vehicle that looked suspicious.

Back at the bookstore, Lexie helped me unload the decorations and take them to the back room.

"These are great," she said, unfolding one of the trees.

"Thanks. I found a Halloween witch for the kids' section, but we'll have to wing it with Hansel and Gretel." I held up a couple of cardboard children with alphabet blocks in their hands. "I guess these are meant to be classroom decorations for teachers."

"No problem," Lexie said. "We can cover up the ABC's with books made of construction paper."

"That'll work."

We put the decorations away for the moment, opting instead to focus on completing the job of stocking the shelves. By the end of the day, we were both tired but excited.

"I can't wait for next Saturday!" I said.

"Me too." Lexie smiled. "Hey, why don't we stop by Josephine's place on our way home and take her a couple of books to read? We can invite her to the grand opening and see if she wants to help decorate. I'm sure she'd like to see what we've done with the store, since it used to be Gina's."

"Let's do it. I'm ready to call it a day." I brushed my hair back out of my eyes.

We picked out four paperback romance novels for Josephine, then headed for her place. On the way, I remembered the gold minivan, and told Lexie about it.

"That's weird," she said, frowning, "because the last time we went to Mango's, I thought I saw a car tagging along behind us. But just like with the van, it turned off a couple of blocks before we got to the club, so I didn't give it another thought."

"Maybe it's nothing," I said, "but it won't hurt to keep an eye out."

"Absolutely."

A short time later I pulled up at Josephine's, and as I put my truck in park, I spotted a familiar figure. She was wearing the same dark glasses, had the same yellow hair . . .

Oh, my God. It was the blond woman from Rafael's funeral! And she was slinking across the lawn toward a side window, keeping close to the shrubbery.

Lexie saw her too. "Hailey, look." She pointed. "Isn't that the woman we saw at the funeral?"

"Yeah. What the hell is she doing?" I started to open my truck door, but just then something flashed in the blonde's hand. A silver-plated pistol.

"Oh, my God!" I exclaimed. "She's got a gun!"

For a moment, Lexie and I sat frozen in the truck. What the heck was going on? Surely this woman wasn't after Josephine? And if she was, Josephine could be any-where in her monstrous house—in an upstairs bed-room, her private entertainment room, the roof over the pool . . .

"Oh, shit!" Lexie gasped. "She's aiming at the window!"

Well, hell! If the blonde was aiming at the window, then Josephine had to be in her sight. Or Rueben. Either way, I knew I had to act.

I laid on the horn and yelled, "Hey!" out the driver's-side window.

Lex opened the passenger door and screamed at her too. At the sound of the horn, the blonde whirled around, and I was more certain than ever that she was the woman we'd seen at the funeral. I flinched backward, thinking she was going to shoot at us, but instead, she bolted.

I scrambled from the truck and ran after her, noting she'd tucked the gun into her fanny pack. Of course, she could always pull it out again and shoot me. I hesitated, even though I didn't want her to get away. But clearly it wasn't smart to chase an armed woman when I wasn't packing my pistol. Maybe I could get her license plate number.

Ducking and dodging between parked cars, I kept her in sight. Behind me, I could hear Lexie shouting my name, but my adrenaline was pumping too hard for me to stop. The blonde climbed into a silver BMW and, peeling rubber, sped away.

But not before I saw her license plate. It was from Texas.

Unfortunately, I only caught part of the plate number. Out of breath, I turned back toward Lexie, who was running down the street at me.

"Damn, girl, you're crazy!" she exclaimed when she caught up with me. "She could've shot you!"

"I was careful." I grinned proudly. "And I got a partial plate number."

"You did? Let's call the police." Lexie took me by the

arm. "Come on, we need to get inside just in case she comes back."

I stopped at my truck long enough to grab my purse and write down the numbers of the license plate—just to be sure I didn't forget them. I snatched up the books we'd brought for Josephine, then hurried up the walkway with Lexie. Josephine answered our frantic knock, and frowned when she saw our harried appearance.

"Hey . . . what's happening, girlfriends? Hailey, you look like you've been running a marathon."

My breath was still coming in gasps. Not so much because I was winded, but because of what had happened.

"Someone just tried to shoot you," I said.

"What?" Josephine's eyes widened, and she clamped a hand to her breast.

"There was a woman outside your window with a gun!" Lexie dug in her purse for her cell phone. "I'm calling the police."

"My Lord! Get in here, quick!" Josephine yanked Lexie by the arm, propelling her over the threshold, then pulled me inside as well. Cautiously, she stuck her head out the door and looked hurriedly around, then slammed the door shut and bolted the locks.

Bling-Bling barked furiously at us. "Hush, Bling-Bling." Josephine motioned us toward the couch. "What in the world is going on?"

Quickly, I explained about the blond woman, while Lexie called 911. "I'm sure she's the same woman who was at Rafael's funeral," I finished. "She had a fancy-looking silver car too. I think it was a BMW. I wrote down part of her plate number." I handed the scrap of paper I'd scribbled on to Lexie.

"I can't believe this." Josephine's jaw gaped. "It's Louie. It's got to be him. He's after me because I ratted on Bianca."

"Wow. He sent a woman hit man? I mean a hit woman?"

Josephine's eyes rounded further. "He must have!"

"Well, don't worry. We scared her off."

I squeezed Josephine's hand as we listened to Lexie speaking to the 911 operator.

Ten minutes later, two police officers showed up on her doorstep. Bling-Bling took a snap at their heels as they came inside.

Thank God it wasn't Montoya and Schaefer. Then again, we were no longer on their Miami Beach turf. Still, I wouldn't have been surprised.

The cops questioned us—including Josephine—and I was shocked to find out I wasn't the only one who'd been followed—that is, if the gold minivan *had* been following me.

"I've been feeling like I'm being watched lately," Josephine told one of the officers—Rodriguez. "The other day by the pool, I heard something in the bushes, and so did Bling-Bling." She stroked the chihuahua's head. "When I turned around to look, I thought I saw someone. Then just yesterday I could've sworn I saw a man down by the rocks, on my private beach. I got out my binoculars to try and see what he was doing—since there's no way I was going down there alone—but by the time I got back outside, he was gone."

The policemen wrote down the information, and I tried not to imagine why Josephine would own a pair of binoculars.

"We'll see if we can bring up anything on the partial tag number," Rodriguez said. "We'll be in touch, and we'll have a unit cruise by here as often as possible to keep an eye on things. You ladies take care, now." He gave me a little smile. And I couldn't help it—I blushed.

I told myself that now wasn't the time to be checking out a cop's butt. After all, someone had just tried to shoot Josephine. But hey, he was kind of cute.

Josephine locked the door behind the officers, then sulked back into the living room and sank onto the couch. Her blue eyes were serious. "You ladies are worrying me. What if that crazy woman had shot you, Hailey?"

"I'm fine."

"Thank the Lord. But you need to stay out of this mess and let the police handle it. I think I'd better beef up my security system."

I could easily imagine Josephine's version of "beef up" including beefy guys positioned at the four corners of her property.

"I wonder how that woman got past the guard hut," Lexie pondered.

"Probably the same way you do," I told her. The woman was definitely attractive.

"I suppose." Lexie rubbed the bridge of her nose. "This whole thing is giving me a headache. I think Josephine is right. We need to take a step back, Hailey."

"I hate to," I said, "but I guess for now we should."

"Besides, we've got the grand opening of our store coming up next Saturday, which is why we came by, Josephine. We wanted to give you a personal invitation."

"How sweet." Josephine smiled.

"You're welcome to help us put up flyers," I added. "If you're up to it."

"I'd love to."

"And we brought you something to read." I handed over the sack of books that lay beside me on the couch. "On the house, of course."

"Thank you, Hailey. Lexie." Josephine's smile turned wistful. "I know Aunt Gina would be proud of what you're doing with the store. I can't wait to see it all set up again! I've missed going to the coffee bar."

"Well, come early and we'll fix you up with a Whipped Delight and some cookies," Lexie said. At home, we'd tried the recipe, and the cookies had been fabulous.

"It's a deal." Josephine pointed one long slender finger. "But you two have to promise me you're going to be more careful. Especially when you're in that bookstore alone." She shivered, and I knew she was thinking once more of Gina.

"We will," I said. I stood up. "Hey, can I use your little girl's room before we take off?"

276

"You sure can, sugar. There's one in the hallway between the living room and kitchen."

I hurried out of the living room, then stole a glance over my shoulder at Josephine. I had no intention of going to the bathroom she'd suggested. I wanted to head back into the private room and use that bathroom instead.

Creeping into the kitchen, I found that secret wall and pressed a hand to it. The door opened noiselessly.

Truth be told, I did have to pee, but not all that badly. I just wanted a chance to look around and make sure Josephine was telling the truth about not shooting up. I'm no prude, but it bothered me that she smoked weed. She was too nice a person to fry her brain cells. I believed in the mantra: Just say no. Of course, I wasn't one to talk, the way I'd slammed down tequila shooters and cosmos lately. Judge not, and all that.

I did my business, then washed my hands, and left the water running while I snooped. I looked in the cupboards above the toilet, under the sink, and in the medicine cabinet. I even checked the trash can. Nothing but a used condom.

Gross! Even though I'd only touched the edge of the waste basket, I soaped up my hands again. When I walked back into the living room, Bling-Bling barked at me as though she'd never seen me in her life.

Silly dog.

I laughed. "I don't think you need to worry too much

about security," I teased Josephine. "Bling-Bling makes enough racket to wake the dead." I cringed at my unintentional pun.

"She's a good watchdog, Mommy's poo-poo-baby-cakes, aren't you, Bling-Bling?" Josephine cooed while the little dog showered her with kisses.

When she looked up, I was glad to see her smiling. I checked her eyes, to see if she looked high, but she didn't. Maybe she was finally getting back to feeling better. It had to be rough, losing two people you loved in such a short period of time.

The thought was enough to make my mind turn right back to the blond woman and the killer—or killers. My pulse raced as Lexie and I stepped out onto the porch, and I scanned the area, looking for the blonde or anyone else who was acting suspicious.

I saw nothing out of the ordinary.

While I was excited about the opening of Nothing But Lies, that didn't stop me from wanting to keep right on playing detective. I'd just make sure to be armed and dangerous next time.

Come to think of it, being armed might just *be* dangerous—to me and to Lexie. Never mind what law enforcement preached about home owners getting shot with their own guns. I remembered the first time Travis had taught me to shoot. I'd nearly taken off my own toe. But I'd practiced since then, and I was pretty sure I could use my gun on someone if it came down to me or him—or her, if the blonde was the one literally gunning for us.

I glanced at Lexie as we drove away. "Do you think that woman is responsible for killing Rafael?"

"I don't know. You'd think she would've shot him instead of poisoning him, if that were the case."

"Not if she didn't want to be obvious at first," I said. "Maybe she's getting bolder each time. If she also killed Gina, then she could be using a more efficient and violent weapon as she progresses."

"But why would she want to kill Gina?" Lex asked. "I mean, I can possibly see another jealous woman, besides Bianca, going after Rafael if he was a player. Working at Fantasies, how could he not be tempted? But why Gina?"

"I still think this all has something to do with Louie." I smacked my palm against the steering wheel as an obvious thought hit me. "Maybe that woman is Louie's new hottie. She might think Josephine is still involved in whatever drug stuff Rafael was into!"

Lexie quirked her mouth. "Could be. I wish I'd gotten a better look at her, but I was too busy staring at that gun. I thought she was going to shoot you when you chased her!"

"Speaking of the gun," I said, "that thing was nickel-plated, with pearl handles. Not your average street weapon."

"Something else you learned on A&E?" Lex asked.

"Seriously, Lex. Maybe that was important."

"You should've told the cops."

"I was too rattled to think of it. I was thinking more about the license plate."

Lexie frowned thoughtfully. "You know what? I used to date a guy who's a Texas State Trooper. Maybe he'd be willing to run that partial plate number for me. Or look up something in the computer or whatever. You know how law enforcement is these days. They can practically run your eye color and come up with your life's history."

"Big Brother is watching," I said, only half in jest. "But that's a great idea, Lex." Then I smirked. "You didn't tell me you dated a Texas State Trooper. How'd you meet him?"

"He was in Miami on vacation." She smiled slyly. "And he has a twin."

"No kidding?" I licked my lips, my fantasies going into overdrive.

Lexie's grin widened. "Yep. A twin who is a fireman. Imagine that."

"Oh, my God, Lex—you *didn't!*"

"Why's it okay for guys to have ménage à trois fantasies, but not us?"

"Lexie!" I scolded playfully, but I couldn't help feeling a little hot at the idea of a cop and a fireman, ready to fulfill my every desire . . .

"But I didn't," she went on, then sighed as though she'd regretted playing it safe. "It's a nice fantasy, but I'm into one man at a time. Besides, Devon was hot enough for me to handle all on his own. But Derek—I think he'd be perfect palate-cleanser material for you."

"How hot is he?" I found myself asking.

"Remember that sexy firefighter calendar you used to

have? Well, he's hotter than all those guys put together."

"Stop it! You're going to make me have a wreck."

Lexie chuckled again. "I still have Devon's number. When I call him, I'll find out if he and his brother plan to come vacation here anytime soon. They can stay with us . . ."

"You're so bad," I said. "You're going to ruin my innocence." I batted my lashes.

"I thought Travis already did that," Lexie said. Then she gasped, her eyes going suddenly wide. "Shit, Hailey, look!" She pointed across the street. "Isn't that Bianca's roommate?"

My gaze flew to the opposite side of Southwest Forty-second Avenue, where a woman with spiked cherry-red hair and a gazillion piercings was casually strolling in the direction of trendy CocoWalk. I changed lanes, flipped a U-turn, and cruised back down the opposite side of the street.

When I pulled over to the curb, I hit the power button to lower Lexie's window. "Hey!" I called to her.

Startled, the girl's eyes widened as she looked at me, then narrowed into angry slits.

"Where's Bianca?" Lexie demanded.

"You two have some nerve! It's your fault Bianca was nearly killed!"

"Will you talk to us for a minute?" I asked her.

"Talk to you? Hell, no!" The girl spun around and bolted.

Eighteen

Lexie

Now it was my turn to give chase.

"I'm not letting her get away. Come on!" I reached for the door handle as Hailey parked half-ass crooked on the street.

Things were beginning to get more and more crazy, what with an armed blonde lurking in the bushes, Bianca missing, and now this. Balancing on my high-heeled sandals, I bolted down the sidewalk in hot pursuit of Miss Cherry Hair. Behind me, I heard Hailey clattering along. Still, I don't think either one of us would've caught Bianca's roommate had she not collided with an old woman carrying a Starbucks cup. The woman had to be eighty if she was a day, but this sister was stout. She raised her purse and proceeded to knock the crap out of Cherry Hair.

"Damned fool child, watch where you're goin'!" *Whack!* "What the hell's that *hair* about anyway? You a punk?" *Whack!* "A punk mugger, tryin' to snatch a poor ol' woman's purse—take her Social Security money?" *Whack!*

With each hit, her white braids bobbed, and I couldn't help but admire the spunky senior who'd managed to render Cherry Hair speechless. Plus, you've got to admire a sister who still wears braids when she's as old as Methuselah.

Bianca's roommate finally found her voice. "Hey, chill out, old woman! I'm not a mugger."

"No," I said, stepping up to grab hold of Cherry's arm. "But you are a dishonest, sneaky snake. Either come with me or I'll call the cops and report that . . . that you're a drug-using stripper!"

"What?" she asked disbelievingly.

"Not to mention that they'll haul your ass off to jail for what you did to Adam's apartment!"

The woman's eyes grew wide with worry at that statement, and I felt a bit of smug satisfaction. She disentangled herself from the angry black woman, who gave her a shove, coupled with an indignant stare, before continuing on down the sidewalk.

By now Hailey had caught up with me, and she was doing this dance-jump movement with her fists poised, like a boxer in the ring ready to fight. She glared at Cherry Hair and said, "Don't try anything stupid, or you're going down."

I raised one eyebrow as I looked at my friend, a silent, *What are you doing?*

Hailey lowered her fists and shook them out, then shook her neck too. The girl was too funny; I almost giggled. Maybe she'd been a fan of *Rocky* and all its sequels as well as Mob Week on A&E.

Hailey stared Cherry Hair down and said, "Okay, sister, let's have the facts. Where the hell is Bianca?"

"What's your name?" I demanded, ready to report her to the cops, even if they weren't exactly my and Hailey's biggest fans.

"What's it to you?" she shot back.

"What's it to me?" I gaped at her. "You're strolling around casually in Coconut Grove, where one of my good friends lives—a good friend that someone is trying to *kill*. Your former roommate was involved with this friend's lover, and very well may have poisoned the guy. So what's it to me? I don't trust you, okay? And I damn sure am not gonna let you do anything to Josephine!"

"Stop, please!" the woman cried out. "I'm not here to kill nobody!"

She sounded sincere, but still I glanced at Hailey, who read my thought—*Should I go easy on her?*—and gave me a brief nod.

"Look," I said, using a softer tone. "We just want to help. Talk to us, please. What's your name?"

For a minute I thought she wasn't going to answer.

"Roberta," she finally said, albeit begrudgingly. "But my friends call me Robbi."

"Okay, Robbi. How about you join Hailey and me for a nice, cold frappuccino? It's a hot day. I think we could all do with some cooling off."

Robbi glared at me. "Is that what it'll take to get you off my back?" She eyeballed Hailey. "Who the hell are you, anyway?"

"Friends of Rafael's," Hailey said, hands on her hips in a pose that nearly made me burst into hysterical laugher. She looked like an Old West sheriff. "That's who."

Robbi sighed warily. "Bianca was afraid of this."

"Afraid of what?"

"Afraid of getting mixed up with anyone that had anything to do with Rafael."

We marched her to Starbucks, where we sat her at a table. Robbi's eyes darted around the room as though she were afraid someone would give a rat's ass about what we were saying. "Louie's no one to screw with."

Hailey's ears literally perked. "So Louie *does* have something to do with Rafael's murder?"

Robbi stared her down, jaw jutted in a show of stubbornness. "If you think I'm dumb enough to tell you anything about Louie, you'd better think again."

"Let's just chill for a moment," I said. "I'll get the frappuccinos, then we can talk some more." I knew Robbi wasn't going to escape, not with Hailey guarding her.

I ordered the drinks and went back to the table, hoping

Robbi used the few minutes I was gone to calm down. I passed her a drink and she wrapped her hands around it as though clinging to it for dear life.

"Look," I said to Robbi, "Hailey and I are only trying to help out a friend. Whatever you tell us remains confidential."

"Right," Robbi scoffed. She took a slurp of her frappuccino. "And I'm the friggin' Easter bunny."

Her hair did look like Easter grass, but I held my tongue.

"Tell us what you know," Hailey demanded, leaning menacingly toward Robbi over the table. "Or else."

"Or else what?" Robbi's gaze didn't waver as she stared at Hailey.

Hailey narrowed her eyes. "Or else we'll take you down to the police station and let a couple of officers we know work you over."

I rolled my eyes. I really had to cut Hailey off from watching all that A&E and those late-night black-and-white detective shows.

"Ooo-oo, I'm scared," Robbi mocked. She pushed her chair back and stood up. "Louie is bad news, which is why I skipped on Bianca. And that's all I'm going to tell you."

With that, she turned and stalked away. Hailey shot to her feet, but I put a hand on her arm to keep her from going after Robbi.

"There's no point," I told her. "If she wanted to talk, she would."

I watched Robbi push the door of the coffee shop open

with enough oomph to nearly smack an incoming customer upside the head. Lucky for her, the old lady she'd met earlier on the street had already visited Starbucks.

I shrugged. "Well, so much for that. No answers about Bianca."

"Ah, but our friend left something behind." Hailey wriggled her eyebrows.

She whipped out a napkin and wrapped it around Robbi's nearly untouched frappuccino.

"Hailey, what are you doing?"

"Fingerprints!" she answered smugly. "And *DNA*!"

She looked so ecstatic, I thought she was going to spontaneously combust right then and there. Or at least pull a Meg Ryan in *When Harry Met Sally.*

Leave it to Hailey to calm my nerves. I choked out a laugh. "Babe, Robbi isn't one of our suspects."

"Better safe than sorry," Hailey said with an emphatic nod. "Hey, if she knows Bianca—Rafael's former flame and Louie's current girlfriend—then she might somehow be wrapped up in all this drug stuff as well. Whoever killed Rafael may be out to get Bianca *and* Robbi, and therefore it doesn't hurt to be careful *and* check out every lead." Smiling triumphantly, she sat back, loving this Perry Mason moment that I couldn't even begin to follow.

"Girl, I think you've finally lost your mind." I scooted out my chair and stood, holding on to my own frappuccino. "But if you want to take a used, half-full paper cup with Goth-black lipstick smears on it, be my guest."

Hailey was precariously juggling her purse, her own Starbucks cup, plus Robbi's, while trying to elbow open the door as we exited.

"Now, that's a good sign." She smiled at me as though I should be able to read her train of thought, then tossed the contents of Robbi's cup into the nearby shrubbery.

"What's a good sign?"

"That you're looking at this cup as half full rather than half empty. It's bound to be a real clue!"

I shook my head. "Hailey, you really are too much, girl. Now, if you're done playing cop, let's go home."

"Hey, I wasn't the one who raced down the street after Robbi," Hailey said defensively. I could tell by her tone that I'd hurt her feelings.

"You're right." I tucked my arm through her elbow. "It doesn't hurt to have Robbi's DNA and fingerprints—just in case." But I was beginning to have my doubts about where the investigation of this case would lead. As far as I was concerned, the cops could have half of the city of Miami's DNA on file and it wouldn't do diddly squat. Why hadn't they come up with some solid leads at this point? And would they really put much time into looking into the deaths of a stripper and a used bookstore owner when they had so many other crimes to solve?

Not wanting to dump cold water on Hailey's upbeat mood, I climbed into her truck and gingerly took the napkin-encased cup from her, setting it carefully in the cup holder. "We'll hide this in the fridge at our store," I said. "That way, if we find a reason to hand it over to the police, it'll be in tip-top shape. At home in our fridge, it's bound to get bounced around."

"Good thinking." Hailey pulled out into a break in traffic, then did a U-turn to head back toward U.S. 1. "But don't you think we should give it to the cops right now?"

"And have Montoya and Schaefer laugh at us?" I asked. "Or worse still, accuse us of being involved yet again?"

"You've got a point," she reluctantly contended. "I suppose we'll need to find more evidence before we turn everything over to them."

"That's right," I said, determined to get Hailey's mind off its one-way track. "In the meantime, let's just focus on reopening the bookstore for now."

"Sounds like a plan, Stan."

"We need to do something to relax too," I said. "How about we put up some flyers, then go for a swim on the beach?"

Hailey brightened. "God, that sounds heavenly! I haven't been to the beach since I got back home. Except when you shot that commercial, but we didn't go in the water."

"Then what are we waiting for? It's right in our backyard!"

We dropped by the bookstore, retrieved a stack of flyers we'd made on the computer, and stashed Robbi's cup in the mini fridge behind the coffee bar.

"You know, we really should stop drinking Starbucks when we've got our own coffee counter," I said.

"No way," Hailey said. "I'm addicted to their lemon pound cake. Besides, you know how that goes—nothing you make yourself tastes as good as something someone else makes."

"True."

After locking up the store, we headed home to change into our bikinis. Mine was lime green, strapless. Hailey's was slightly more conservative, but the deep blue looked good on her.

A short time later, we were strolling along the sand at South Pointe Park, a less busy beach than the world-famous one on Ocean Drive. And it was closer to our condo. We were armed with the essentials—sunglasses, tote bags, and canvas folding chairs. A light breeze stirred, kicking the water into gentle waves.

"Awww, this is heaven!" Hailey laid out her towel. "I missed the beach so much when I was in Montana."

We sat back in the low-slung chairs, and each of us pulled out a book, then laughed. We were reading the same author—Cora Robbins. Not that that was hard to do, since she had at least forty romance titles on the shelves.

"She's good," Hailey said.

"One of my favorites," I added.

We settled into companionable silence. A few minutes later, Hailey nudged my foot with hers.

"Okay, I'm about to strap myself to an anchor and jump in the water. Is that *Cedric*?"

"Where?" I craned my neck, scanning the area she'd indicated. Sure enough, there was Cedric, doing his best to look nonchalant and unobtrusive, hiding behind a magazine. He wore dark glasses and a ridiculous-looking straw hat. *Good Lord!* Any fool could see he was eyeballing Hailey.

"Do you think he followed us?" Hailey asked.

"I didn't see him there a moment ago." I pursed my lips. "He might've followed *you*. Girl, he really is your own personal stalker."

"Very funny." Hailey focused on her book. "Pretend you don't see him."

"Too late," I said. "Here he comes."

"Hailey! Lexie!" Cedric stood in front of us smiling, a beach towel draped over his arm. "What a surprise to see you here."

"Really?" With obvious reluctance, Hailey laid her book down.

"How's it going, Cedric?" I asked.

"Great. Just great. So, you girls decided to catch a little sun, huh?"

Hailey muttered a reply as I tried not to laugh. Cedric was as white as white could be, save for the lower half of his arms, which were lightly tanned. He was dressed in blue Speedos that left little to the imagination. Coupled with the ridiculous hat and the sunglasses, the excess body hair . . . well, you get the picture.

"What happened to dinner?" he asked.

"We've been busy," Hailey answered. "So busy, we had to take a break today or we were going to go mad."

"I can imagine."

Hailey's answer seemed to satisfy Cedric.

"So, next Saturday is the big day, huh?" He shook out his towel and plopped in the sand near Hailey's feet.

"That's right." She smiled sweetly. "And you're just in time to do something to help us get ready for it."

"Really?" He looked at her like a puppy dog, eager to please.

"Yep. We were going to post some flyers in a little while; maybe pass out a few to the crowds on area beaches." She reached into her canvas tote. "Want to help?"

"You bet." Cedric scrambled eagerly to his feet, reaching for the multicolored stack of paper. "And hey, since you girls obviously need a break, how about if you go to Mango's tonight with Tyrone and me? I know Tyrone misses you, Lexie." He wagged his eyebrows at Hailey. "And you can wear your cowgirl hat."

Her smile remained in place—barely. "Why, Cedric, that is just such a nice invitation, but I'm afraid we'll have to pass. Lexie and I have been working all day, and we're just going to kick back here awhile, then go home and watch a little TV."

"Great!" he said. "We could join you—bring some DVDs . . . Have you seen *Halloween Terror Part VII*? It's pretty creepy." He wriggled his eyebrows again. "You could hide your eyes on my shoulder during the scary parts, Hailey."

"Thanks, but I really don't like horror flicks."

"Well, that's okay. We can do a chick flick. I'm a man's man." He held out his arms as though to encompass the three of us. "I'm not afraid to get in touch with my feminine side."

Obviously not, since he'd danced with Josephine not so long ago.

Hailey shot me a desperate look.

"We're pretty wiped out, Cedric," I said. "Maybe another time?"

"Well, sure. Heck, yeah." He grinned, then lifted his sunglasses to give Hailey a wink. "Guess I'd better go hand out these flyers. See ya later, gorgeous."

As he walked away, Hailey groaned and leaned her head back against her chair. "Just shoot me. Please."

I couldn't help but laugh.

"Go ahead," Hailey said, gesturing. "Laugh all you want."

"I'm sorry. But on the bright side, at least he's got a nice package."

She bit her lip, then gave in and chuckled. "Yeah, it was a little hard to miss—in those blue Speedos!"

"He's into blue, you're into blue . . . I think this could be a match made in heaven," I sang.

"You are horrible! Before I know it, you'll be planning my wedding to the man."

"Cora Robbins always writes the best love stories about two people who seem like opposites falling head over heels for each other. You never know, Hailey."

"Cora Robbins has never once written about a woman falling for a guy in a pair of blue Speedos, thank you very much."

I roared with laughter. "You got me there, sweetie."

Nineteen

Hailey

The rest of the week went by fast, and by Friday night I was so fired up I couldn't fall asleep. Tomorrow was it. Our big day. The only thing marring my happiness was the fact that Gina wouldn't be there to help us celebrate. Lex and I had originally hoped Gina might stick around town long enough to see us off, so to speak, and now that wouldn't happen.

But at least we'd been able to keep Josephine occupied, something we knew Gina would have wanted. She'd come to the store on three different occasions this past week to help us put up the decorations and add some last-minute touches to the store and the coffee bar. We wouldn't be anywhere near ready for the big launch of Nothing But Lies if it weren't for Josephine's help.

The final touch had been to put up Gina's picture, and Josephine had provided us with a happy shot of her sunning on the beach with a book in her hands. Not the shot I'd expected, but it was perfect. We'd draped the memorial necklace over one corner of the frame, even though it gave us the willies.

Better there than having to wear it.

With the store's transformation complete, the three of us had chatted, and when the subject turned to the police investigation of Gina's murder, our spirits had momentarily plummeted. There'd been no new leads from the police on her death, or on Rafael's. Josephine had looked so hopeless, Lexie and I had been glad to have at least some good information to share with her. When we'd told her about Lexie's connection to the Texas State Trooper, who might possibly be able to help us gain some insight on the blonde in the silver BMW, Josephine had gotten a little misty.

"You girls are so sweet. I don't know what I would've done without you to help me through this."

"You've got a lot of people who care about you," Lexie said, rubbing her shoulder.

"I know. But you and Hailey are special."

"So are you, hon."

Determined to boost her mood once more, I'd asked her what she thought of the paint job Lex and I had done on the inside of the store. The walls, previously beige, were now a cozy shade of blue, combined with wide diagonal stripes of mauve and peach in each corner.

"Love it," Josephine said.

She'd had a little tear in her eye when we'd locked up later that night, telling us again how proud Gina would be.

Everything was set, but now I lay in bed, worrying if we'd put up enough flyers . . . wondering if people would really pay attention to the border ads we'd run in the newspapers. Lex and I had hung flyers all over South Beach, North Miami Beach, in Coral Gables, and in the Grove. And we'd hand-delivered as many as we could. We'd also given out coupons for free cookies, which we'd baked tons of over the last couple of days, using Gina's wonderful recipe. Of course, we were planning to serve punch and cookies anyway—the coupons were just a little gimmick to encourage people to come to the grand opening.

Lex and I had finished our baking marathon that night, and we'd toasted Gina with tall glasses of ice-cold milk, and white-chocolate macadamia nut cookies, hot out of the oven. Gina would've been proud, all right. But I'd eaten a few too many cookies, which was probably contributing to my inability to fall asleep. My tummy ached a little, and it was well after midnight before I finally dozed off.

The next morning, Lexie and I got up early and had a light breakfast, too nervous to eat much.

"I keep feeling like we're forgetting something," she said.

"It's just nerves," I reassured her. "We've gone over our list a hundred times."

By nine-fifteen, we were at the bookstore, scheduled to open at ten. I could hardly wait. I looked around at the colorful banners and decorations. Scrutinized, really, to see if there was anything we'd missed.

"Crud." I put my hands on my hips and wrinkled my nose.

"What?" Lexie asked. "We forgot something?"

"No," I said, despair overwhelming me. "I just realized how cheesy our cardboard decorations look. Don't they?"

Lex studied our Hansel and Gretel theme. "I don't know. Maybe a little, but it'll be all right." She touched my arm. "Remember—it's just nerves. Now come on. Let's get the money into the registers."

We took it from the little safe in the back room, and I have to say it was a lot of fun putting the various denominations of bills in their proper slots. I felt like a kid playing store, and my nerves eased into positive excitement. Just before we unlocked the doors, Lexie and I laid out the refreshments behind the coffee bar, placing several two-liter bottles of punch in containers of ice to keep them chilled. We had paper cups handy, and Saran-Wrapped cookies laid out on colorful platters.

"Ready?" Lexie grinned at me.

"Ready!" I grinned back, giving her hands a squeeze.

A tap at the front door caught our attention, and I looked over to see Josephine peering at us through the glass. I almost didn't recognize her. She was dressed as a blond bombshell, her flattering and very authentic-looking wig curled into soft waves that fell over her shoulders. One side of her bangs lay over her long-lashed, heavily made-up eyes, giving her a sultry look, like a classic movie star.

But her dress was the best of all. It was beaded—a deep hunter green—cut low front and back. Matching stilettos adorned her feet, and she had on just the right amount of accessories to ad some bling to her swing as she strutted through the door.

"Josephine, you are a knockout!" I exclaimed as Lexie flipped the CLOSED sign to OPEN.

"Thank you, sugar." Josephine struck a pose. "It's Vera Wang."

"Nice." Wow! Lex hadn't been kidding when she'd said Josephine made good money doing her shows. Not that I didn't know that by the size of her house.

And speaking of money, I sure hoped we were about to make some. I couldn't believe how many people were already waiting outside the store. They filed in behind Josephine and spread out like ants at a picnic.

Follow the bread crumbs, Hansel and Gretel . . . cha-ching!

Josephine paused to give us each a quick little hug. "Hey, girlfriends. Looks like you're going to get a pretty good draw."

"I sure hope so," Lexie said. She smiled as more customers came through the door. "I'd say things are looking good."

"I made sure to hand out plenty of flyers at the Blue Onion," Josephine told us.

"Great idea." Lexie beamed. "Thanks!"

I barely kept from squealing. "Lex." I leaned toward

her, lowering my tone. "Look! Our very first customers."

She laughed low in her throat. "Awesome, isn't it?"

We armed the cash registers, taking turns wandering through the store to make sure our prized clientele were finding the books they needed. Before I knew it, we were busy ringing up orders, chatting with longtime customers who wondered where Gina had gone, why she'd closed up. I was surprised that a number of them hadn't heard about her murder. Didn't anyone read the paper or watch the news anymore? Of course, considering how much crime was in the world today, I could see why people chose to be blissfully ignorant.

Of course, some *had* heard about Gina's murder, and had a plethora of questions for us. How did we feel doing business where Gina had been murdered? Were we afraid for our lives? What was it like to find a body? Hadn't they read that we'd also discovered the body of Gina's nephew-turned-niece's lover? What a crazy coincidence, huh?

Determined not to let anything rain on our parade, Lexie and I handled the curious as tactfully as possible, giving only brief answers while we did our best to turn their attention elsewhere—mainly on spending money in our store.

In spite of her garish getup, Josephine was a blessing. She turned out to be a whiz at making Whipped Delights and lattes, as well as handing out punch and cookies. It helped to have another hand so that Lexie and I could take care of ringing up sales, both for the store and the coffee counter. I almost felt guilty competing with my beloved Starbucks, but then I suppose their gigantic, worldwide chain wasn't exactly going to fall apart over our meager-in-comparison sales.

"I can't believe how many people are here!" I repeated excitedly.

"I know," Lexie said. "But then, Gina's customers were pretty loyal. And look—there's another one right now."

Subtly, she angled her head toward the front door as the bell on it tinkled its near-constant ring. I groaned as Cedric walked in.

"Great."

"Remember," Lexie whispered close to my ear. "He's a customer."

"Yeah, and he's going to pay for stalking me." I plastered a smile on my face as he made a beeline for the counter.

"Hailey!" He held out his arms as though expecting me to come out from behind it and embrace him.

Not.

"Hi, Cedric," I said through my frozen-in-place smile.

"We're so glad you could make it," Lexie added, just to nettle me.

"Are you kidding? I wouldn't have missed this for the world. I wish I could have come earlier, but I got tied up with something."

"Something like what?" I asked. It occurred to me that I had no clue what Cedric did. Other than stalk me, that is.

"Oh, I had to stop by the Caribbean Dreams office. Take care of some business."

"Caribbean Dreams—as in the cruise line?"

"Yep."

"You work for them?"

"Yeah, honey. I didn't tell you?"

"No, you never mentioned it," I said.

"Well, Pink Sugar, I work with Tyrone. He's a director for the cruise line, so I just figured he'd have shared that information with your good friend here. By the way, Lexie, Tyrone's comin' by a bit later. He's still got some work to do."

Cedric reached out and snatched hold of my hand, kissing the back of it before I could so much as blink. "Now, enough about work. Hailey, you look gorgeous, as usual. You too, Lexie. Anything I can do to help?"

"Spend some money," I said with a purposeful wink. "We've got a lot of good books in here."

"I'm sure you do." Cedric beamed. "Nothing like curling up with a cold beer and a good ol' detective novel."

"The mystery-suspense section is over there," Lexie said, finally taking pity on me. "Just follow the footprints and magnifying glasses."

"How clever! Thanks." Cedric practically skipped along the black construction-paper cutouts we'd made and attached to the carpet.

"Got any vodka to pour in that punch?" I asked Lexie sotto voce.

She laughed. "Hang in there. We'll get drunk tonight at Mango's on our profits."

"Mango's, hell. I want naked men."

301

"Fantasies, then." She gave me a nod, then turned to help a customer.

The day flew by, and even though my back, legs, and feet were aching something awful, I really was having fun. I hadn't even been into our condo's magnificent gym, but if I kept up this pace at the store, I wouldn't have to.

Not wanting to take time for lunch, I'd grabbed a couple of cookies around noon and wolfed them down, but by two o'clock I was starving. Lexie and Josephine had to be too.

I motioned them over and asked.

"I'd be more than happy to run over to the deli and get some sandwiches," Josephine offered.

The delicatessen was located in the strip mall, just a couple of doors down.

"Oh, would you?" I said with relief. "Thanks, Josephine."

"No problem."

I gave her some money from my purse, which I'd tucked beneath the coffee counter. "Get yourself something too," I said. "I'll take a ham and veggie. Lex?" I glanced over my shoulder at her.

She'd stepped up to the cash register to ring up a huge stack of books Cedric had piled on the counter. I bit my cheek so I wouldn't laugh. Moments ago, I'd strolled over to the suspense section, bribed him with a cookie, and pointed out several of my favorite authors, doing everything in my power to make him want to buy books.

"I'll take anything that's not moving," Lexie quipped. "I'm ravenous!"

"Okay, ladies." Josephine tucked the money inside the front of her dress, where I prayed she was wearing a bra.

I hoped she didn't bring back any change.

She started to leave, but Cedric held up his hand. "Hang on a minute, and I'll go with you. I'm buying, Josephine, so just give Hailey back her money."

"You don't need to do that," I protested.

"I insist." He beamed. "It's the least I can do."

"Well . . ." *Shit*. "All right. Thanks." Gingerly, I took back the bills Josephine fished out of her cleavage.

Lexie bagged Cedric's books, and he took them and strolled outside with Josephine.

"Whew." I blew my bangs off my forehead. "Maybe he'll go ahead and leave with his sandwich." Immediately I felt rotten. "Boy, that sounded mean, didn't it? It is nice of him to buy us lunch."

"Yeah, and he did buy all those books." Lexie put a fresh roll of receipt tape in the register. "I keep telling you, babe. He's not *that* bad."

"But he stalks me! I know he followed us to the beach last week. And he's always lurking at the clubs."

"He just likes you." Lexie shrugged. "Enjoy it. You don't have to take things any farther than you want to. But remember . . . he *is* well hung!"

I glanced around to make sure no one had heard Lexie, and satisfied that no one had, I started to chuckle. "That's why you play the field, isn't it? You get the best of being pampered without all the strings to tie you in knots."

Lex pointed a perfectly manicured French nail at me. "Now you're learning."

A short time later, Cedric and Josephine returned with our sandwiches. Josephine poured us some punch, and Lexie and I snuck tiny bites of our sandwiches in between waiting on customers. By the time seven-thirty hit, I was more than ready to close for the day.

I looked around at the few straggling customers who still lingered. They finally made their selections, and we rang them up. Josephine had stuck around, offering to help clean up, and to my chagrin, Cedric was still there too. But a few minutes later, he wished us good luck— promising to call me later—then headed out the door. I couldn't help feeling a little bad for always wanting to ditch him. He really was a nice guy, and clearly had the patience of a saint where I was concerned. Either that or he was incredibly dense.

Though we closed at seven, the last customer didn't leave till seven-thirty, when we promptly locked up. Exhausted, I slumped onto one of the stools at the coffee bar.

"Sheesh! I didn't know it was possible to be this tired."

Lexie slid onto a stool beside me. "Yeah, but it's a good kind of tired."

Josephine refilled our paper cups. "You girls did a great job. I know Aunt Gina is up there watching us, as proud as this punch." She sniffled and dabbed the corners of her eyes with a fuchsia handkerchief.

"To Gina." I raised my paper cup before tossing back the rest of my fruit punch. It was weird—the fatigue hit me all the more right then, making me light-headed, and as I stood to throw away the cup, the floor seemed to tilt beneath my feet. I stumbled sideways, reaching out to grip the counter as I bumped into Josephine.

"Lordy, sugar. Are you all right?" She peered at me, concerned, taking a gentle hold of my arm.

"I think so." I frowned. Not only were my eyelids heavy, I felt dizzy and nauseous. "I think I waited too long to eat something today—other than all those cookies. I'm feeling a little light-headed."

"You did eat a number of those cookies last night," Lexie pointed out. "It's no wonder you don't feel good."

"Thanks." I glared at her. She hadn't overindulged, but I couldn't control my sweet tooth.

"You're suffering sugar overload," she said. "And nerves. I often feel a bit woozy before an audition for a big role. Maybe that's why I don't land them," she added wryly.

"I'll get her some water," Josephine offered. She went behind the coffee counter and came back with a plastic cup.

"Maybe you ought to sit down for a minute," Lexie said. "It's been a long day. Josephine and I will clean up the last bit of this stuff."

"Okay." But as she and Josephine finished up, I didn't feel better. Instead, my stomach churned. That was it. I was gonna blow.

Cupping one hand to my mouth, the other to my stomach, I rushed for the bathroom, staggered into the doorframe, and somehow made it to the toilet. Somewhere in the distance, I heard Lexie calling my name. She appeared in the doorway as I gave it up to the porcelain gods.

"Hailey, are you all right? Damn, you *are* sick!"

She pulled my hair back out of the way as I stood shakily. I groped for the sink, rinsed out my mouth, and wiped my face with a paper towel. "I really don't feel so good."

Josephine poked her head through the open door of the small bathroom. "Is she okay?"

"I don't think so," Lexie said. "I'd better get her home."

"I'll help you get her to the car," Josephine offered.

"Thanks." Lexie draped my arm over her neck. "Come on, babe."

My stomach clenched again, and I fought not to heave. I hate throwing up, especially in front of other people. Thank God I hadn't heaved in Sid's office that day at Fantasies, in front of Cutie Casey.

Fantasies . . . the chocolates . . .

The truth hit me like a ton of bricks.

"Oh, my God!" I gripped Lexie's wrist. "I know what's wrong, and it's not the cookies!"

"Bad sandwich?" Josephine asked. "You know, now that you mention it, my tuna salad did taste a little funny."

"No, no—not the sandwich." I leaned against Josephine as she slipped her arm around my waist. "It's the mercury, Lex! It's still in my bloodstream. Oh, my God, I'm gonna die!"

Josephine's eyes flew open in alarm. "Mercury?" She drew back, gasping. "The same kind of poison that killed Rafael? Oh, Lordy, please tell me that tuna didn't have mercury in it!"

"It didn't. When we went to Fantasies," I went on with difficulty, "I ate one of Rafael's chocolates. The same chocolates the police found mercury in—the mercury that killed Rafael."

"What! Why on earth would you—"

"Hailey." Lexie cut her off. "Girl, you know that was all in your head."

"Maybe not," I said. "It's a slow-acting poison, remember? My God, it's finally getting me." I tried not to gag. "Oooh, I feel weak. You'd better get me to the hospital."

"You're making yourself sick again," Lexie said as she and Josephine guided me toward the back exit.

"I am not! Lexie, you've got to trust me on this!"

"Okay, okay." She looked guiltily into my eyes. "I'm not saying that you're not sick. Obviously you are. I just don't want you to make things worse with that wild imagination of yours."

"It's not my imagination." I pouted as Josephine took Lexie's keys to lock up the store. Lexie continued with me to the car.

My stomach lurched again, and I dry-heaved.

"Oh, God," Lexie said. "You really sound awful. I've got to get you home right away."

"Want me to ride along?" Josephine asked. "You'll need help getting her upstairs at your place."

"True." Lexie eased me into the back seat of her Lexus. "Are you sure you don't mind?"

Josephine waved her hand. "Of course not. As long as you don't mind bringing me back here later to get my car."

"No problem."

That settled, we were on our way. I leaned my head against the seat, and thought about lying down. But I was afraid that might make things worse.

The truth was, even the motion of the car made things worse. I could only hope to be safely upstairs in my bedroom before the urge to throw up again hit.

Lexie pulled up at a stoplight. "Want me to put the top down?" She glanced at me in the rearview mirror. "The fresh air might help."

"No . . . I think that much wind . . ." I let the sentence trail away as I saw something in the mirror besides Lexie's brown eyes. I moaned.

"Are you going to hurl again?" Lexie's expression changed to one of alarm, and I wasn't sure if it was caused by her compassion for me, or horror at the thought of me ralphing cookies all over the interior of her car.

"I don't think so." I turned to look over my shoulder. "But is that a purple Kia Optima behind us?"

"Where?" Lexie glanced in the mirror again, then took off as the light turned green.

Josephine craned her neck for a look.

"Two cars back," I said. "I think it's Cedric."

"How do you know what he drives?" Lexie frowned. "Hailey, did you—"

"No! God, no." My stomach whirled anew at the thought of Cedric, half naked, groping me in the back seat of his purple compact. "But thanks to you and your out-of-control libido that night we met him and Tyrone at Mango's, I had no way to get home. And Cedric was there, ready and willing to give me a ride."

"Oh," Lexie said, full of guilt.

"I'll bet it's him," I said, groaning. "That eggplant color is a little hard to miss."

"You mean Cedric the cutie?" Josephine asked. "He's such a gentleman. And hot for you, Hailey! Woo!"

Lexie squinted at the mirror again. "There *is* a purple car a couple cars back, but I can't tell who's in there. Can you see the driver, Josephine?"

Josephine looked in the side mirror. "I can't."

My vision blurred, my head felt light and fuzzy. Maybe I was hallucinating. "I think it's him, Lex. Ditch him . . . *please*." I couldn't deal with Cedric on top of feeling so nauseous.

"All right. Just calm down and lie back."

She swerved into the next lane, weaving in and out of the South Beach traffic. Her NASCAR maneuvers made me all the more queasy. "Lexie, slow down. You're making my head spin . . . not to mention my stomach."

"Well, I can't ditch Cedric and slow down too," she said.

"Pull onto Ocean Drive." Josephine gestured. "We'll

get her out of the car for a minute and walk her around. The fresh salt air might help." She looked over her shoulder at me. "Hang on, sugar."

"Okay."

Lexie turned left on Twelfth, then went to Ocean Drive. Soon we were parked along the beach. I cast a wary glance back toward the road as she and Josephine helped me out of the car. I hoped Cedric wasn't behind us, but right now my main concern was my head, which felt like it was about to float off of my shoulders. Leaning on my friends, I walked—only it was more like a stagger.

"It really is pretty here at dusk," I said, glancing all around. "Look at that huge sandcastle! With all those candles surrounding it. My, isn't it pretty?"

"Yeah, yeah, it's pretty," Lexie agreed.

"How do they do that?" I craned my neck to look over my shoulder at the people gathered around the artist who'd skillfully created the giant sandcastle masterpiece.

"Let's get her to the water," Josephine said.

"Why?" Lexie asked, frowning.

"Am I the only one who appreciates art?" I asked.

"Didn't your mama ever make you gargle with salt water when your tummy was sick?" Josephine asked.

"For a sore throat," Lexie said.

"It's baking-soda water for a sick stomach," I inserted, "but at this point, I'll try anything."

"Okay."

Lexie and Josephine led me onto the wooden path that took us from the park area onto the beach.

"Let's go left," Josephine said. "It's less crowded over there."

They steered me left, walking a diagonal line toward the ocean.

"You'll be okay, baby girl," Josephine crooned. "We'll stay on the beach awhile, then get you home to bed."

I shuddered, suddenly feeling chilled. God help me, what if there really *was* mercury in my system?

"I don't want to die out here, Lex," I said, getting wistful.

"You're not dying," she told me.

"The ocean—it's so dark. It's kinda scary, isn't it?"

"Yes, a little," Lexie agreed.

"I wish Casey were here. I could give him that kiss good-bye. And maybe something more."

"Hailey, maybe you ought to stop talking," Lexie advised.

"Do you have his number?" I asked. Then my head spun. "Oh, I need to sit down."

"Josephine, let's get her over there. The lifeguard stand."

"Breathe deep," Josephine encouraged me.

We walked a bit more, then Josephine and Lexie stopped with me at a lifeguard stand. I put out one hand to balance against one of the wooden support beams. It felt good to stop and rest.

"Thank you." Gingerly, I sat on the first wooden step. It creaked a little. "This'll do."

"Your damned right it will!" a voice called out behind us.

I turned to look in what felt like slow-motion, just as Lexie let out a shriek. Josephine gasped and clamped one hand to her chest.

Behind us stood a woman I recognized easily. The blonde from Rafael's funeral.

And she was holding a gun.

Twenty

Lexie

When I saw the woman holding the gun, my entire body froze. I opened my mouth to shout or say *something*, but I couldn't find my voice. It was as though the shriek I'd let out a moment ago had taken away my ability to speak or scream again. Not that screaming would have done much good, anyway. We'd walked a considerable ways from the crowds, and the loud music coming from various clubs on the South Beach strip would probably drown out any noise we made.

I clung to Hailey's arm, wishing she had her gun.

"Hello, *ladies.*" The blonde smirked as she emphasized the word.

"Isabel!" Josephine's jaw dropped. "W-what are you doing?"

Finally, I found my voice. I glanced at Josephine. "You—you *know* her?"

"Shut up!" Isabel motioned with the gun. "Sit down—all of you!"

Josephine and I lowered ourselves onto the step beside Hailey. Isabel advanced upon us, looking ready to fire at any minute. I didn't want to die this way—here on the beach on the steps of a lifeguard stand. And on the day of our big grand opening! Talk about sucking big-time.

I peered closely at Isabel. Her face seemed familiar, as did the pants and blouse she wore—but not from my having seen her at the funeral and again outside of Josephine's house.

"You were at the bookstore earlier," I said. "But you were . . ." My mind scrambled. "You were wearing a brunette wig!"

"I said close it, sister!" she hissed, taking yet another menacing step forward.

I shrank back, blocking Hailey's body with my own, automatically wanting to protect her.

"Oh, God, Lex. I think I'm gonna hurl."

I rubbed her back, hoping the nausea would pass. And then I remembered Hailey's words earlier. She had said for me to trust her, that she knew she'd been poisoned. What if she hadn't been poisoned from that small morsel of chocolate weeks ago, but instead had been poisoned today?

My mind raced to process the possibility. If that was true, how could it have happened?

The punch! I realized a moment later. Hailey
the fruit punch! I'd opted for the Whipped Deli
water, since I didn't want the extra calories.

Now my eyes narrowed on Isabel. "You did t
Hailey, didn't you?" Hailey and I had been so busy
wouldn't have seen if anyone had slipped anything
our unattended drinks. "Who do you think you are?"

"Isabel, I think," Hailey muttered. "That's your name
isn't it?"

"Both of you, shut up!" Isabel shouted. "I'm running
the show here, not you!"

"I've never been on the wrong end of a gun before,"
Hailey went on. Her eyes were beginning to look a little
glassy. "Where's my .44?"

"Throw your gun down!" Isabel took a policelike
stance, bracing both hands against the butt of her pearl-
handled pistol.

"She doesn't have a gun!" I cried, my heart slamming
against my rib cage. "For God's sake, she's hallucinating."

Isabel stared me down. "I swear, if you're lying, I'll put
a hole in you big enough to run a team of mules through!"
She swung the gun to point it at Josephine. "And you . . .
finally I've got you, you blood-sucking bitch! And you're
going to pay for what you did to my daddy."

"Who's your daddy?" Hailey muttered, then giggled.

"Shh!" I gave her arm a little shake.

"*Was*, not is," Isabel said. Her bottom lip trembled.
"My daddy was one of the richest oilmen in all of
Houston. J. B. Huntington the Third. But that bitch

illed him!" Again, she wagged the pistol at Josephine.

"What?" My gaze shot to Josephine.

She looked horrified. "Isabel, how can you say such a horrible thing? I loved J.B., and you know it."

"You loved his money, you twisted, filthy whore! Loved the life it could give you. The big house on the water, the fancy car, and the fancy clothes. Only you didn't want him around to share it with you." Isabel looked mad enough to catch on fire. "You murdered him. I'm sure of it."

"What's wrong with you, Isabel? Have you gone and lost your mind?" Josephine clutched one hand to her breast. "J.B. died of a heart attack. The coroner's report confirmed it."

"I don't give a doodley-ass damn what the coroner's report said!" Isabel's southern accent grew thicker as she became more infuriated. "His heart attack was caused by mercury poisoning, all right, but not from that shellfish he ate!"

"Sweet Jesus!" I let out a gasp as the dots began to connect, then stared in horror at Josephine. "*Mercury?*"

"Who drives a Mercury?" Hailey looked confused. "No, Cedric drives a Kia. It's purple. Why won't anyone listen to me?"

Josephine pointed a finger at Isabel. "Don't believe a word she says. She's out of her mind! The way I was when I lost Rafael. Grief'll do that to a person. I didn't poison anybody." She turned to glare at the woman. "What'd you do, read about Rafael's death in the paper, then add two and two and come up with five?"

"I didn't read about it," Isabel said, "but a friend of mine who lives here in Miami did. She called me right away, and I knew something was up. Knew it the way I knew it four years ago. You poisoned Daddy, and then you poisoned Rupert!"

"Rafael," Hailey corrected her. She frowned, squinting. "Did you do that, Josephine?"

"Of course not." Josephine's bottom lip trembled. "You're still as mean as a Texas rattlesnake, Isabel! You're jealous because your daddy left his money to me instead of you and your three spoiled brothers. Oh, my God!" Josephine's eyes grew as wide as saucers. "You're trying to *frame* me!"

"Not hardly," Isabel spat out. "Cut the act, Josephine. Save it for the Blue Onion. Though I doubt they'll have one in federal prison!"

"She's lying." Josephine looked frantically from me to Hailey. "She wants her father's money, money he left to me because he loved me with all his heart. She'd do anything to get it!"

"I don't give a donkey's ass about Daddy's money! It's watching you spend it that makes me sick. You—living like the queen you are! The queen you *think* you are."

"Hey, a donkey *is* an ass, you know?" Hailey said, then giggled. "Oh, Lex, I sound like Sid, don't I? 'You know.' Ha!"

"I'm glad you find this all so amusing." Isabel clenched her jaw, cocking the hammer on the pistol.

"Oh, God, please don't shoot!" I held out one hand as

though to stop the bullet. "Hailey's really out of it. She doesn't know what she's saying."

"I'm sure she is." Isabel smirked. "Seeing as how Josephine slipped something into the punch. Sleeping pills, maybe. GHB. I don't know how you're still standing if your friend's already seeing stars."

"I did not put anything in the punch!" Josephine exclaimed. "Of course I didn't. Or Lexie would be out of her mind too. Right, Lex?"

Josephine would have a point . . . if I'd had the punch.

"Cut the crap," Isabel snapped. "I saw you, Josephine."

Josephine looked aghast. "Isabel, stop lying. *Please*. And put that gun down right now!"

"Not until I shoot you, you evil witch! You're going to pay for living off my daddy's money—blood money! And you're going to pay for taking him away from me!" The gun wavered as she began to cry. "I loved Daddy with all my heart and soul! He was a good man, and you took advantage of his kindness and generosity. I want you *dead*!" She looked regretfully at me and Hailey. "Too bad you and your friend had to get in the way. You should've left well enough alone."

"Drop your weapon!"

For a moment, I didn't know what was happening. Then I realized that someone was yelling from behind us. I whirled around, but didn't see anyone.

Was I hallucinating like Hailey? Was this what stone-cold fear did to you?

And then a man appeared, moving from behind the shrubbery near the high-rise about a hundred feet away. Oh, shit. He had a gun too!

Could this day get any worse?

But as the man moved closer, Josephine said in an excited whisper, "Lexie, I think that's Cedric."

Cedric! Could it be?

"Cedric, that you?" I called.

"Don't you worry, Lexie. I'm here to save you girls." He leveled his pistol at Isabel. "Miami Beach police—drop your gun! *Now!*"

He advanced with skill, his gun trained on Isabel. Gone was the mild-mannered guy who couldn't dance. *Jesus, Mary, and Joseph! What the heck is going on?*

Isabel lowered her pistol, but made no attempt to drop it. "I'm not the criminal here," she said. "*She* is!" She pointed at Josephine.

"Drop your gun, ma'am. I won't tell you again."

This time, Isabel heeded Cedric's warning and tossed her gun onto the sand.

"Oh, thank God," I said.

"Yes, thank God," Josephine echoed.

But Cedric wasn't lowering his gun. Instead, he turned toward me and Josephine, and my heart leapt into my throat.

"All right, all right!" Hailey threw her hands up. "I'll go out with you! Sheesh. Is this what it's like to date in Miami?"

Cedric ignored Hailey, and as he moved ever closer, I realized his focus was on Josephine. "Josephine Coletti, lie down with your hands above your head."

"What?" I looked from Cedric to Josephine.

She returned my stare, eyes wide.

"Josephine, what's going on here?" I asked her.

She didn't answer me. Instead, with a look of desperation, she grabbed Hailey and hauled her off the step of the lifeguard station, throwing her hard into Isabel. Hailey went down, arms flailing, and Isabel scrambled for footing as Josephine bolted down the beach.

Cedric threw a quick look at Hailey, then charged after Josephine.

Hailey moaned. I ran to her and scooped her into my arms.

"Am I dying now?" she asked, eyelids droopy. Her face was pale and sweaty, and she grabbed me with both hands, her grip strong in spite of the sleeping pills that had sent her halfway to la-la land.

I was too consumed with concern for Hailey to pay attention to Isabel. But I looked up when I heard her yell, "Hell, no! I'm not letting that bitch get away!"

Isabel grabbed the gun from the sand, then leveled the pistol at the fleeing Josephine.

I screamed when she fired.

Surprising me, Hailey reached out with one hand and grabbed Isabel by the ankle. With one jerk, she threw her off balance. I took the opportunity to pounce on her, more pissed now than scared.

I secured both my hands around Isabel's gun hand. "Put down that gun, you southern-fried bitch, or I'll make you eat it!"

"That's telling her, Lex!"

I shot a gaze at Hailey, who gave me two thumbs up, then flopped backward onto the sand.

"Get off me!" Isabel screamed. She wriggled and fought to pull her hand free.

No way was I going to let Isabel shoot me or anybody else. I let go of her wrist with one hand so I could jab my fingernails into her eyes.

"Argh!" She screamed bloody murder. "Damn it, woman!" Isabel clamped a hand to her left eye, and I took the opportunity to wrench the pistol away from her.

I'd never held a gun before. But like Hailey, I watched *CSI: Miami* every week. As Isabel started to climb onto her knees, I fixed the gun on her. "You heard Cedric." I still couldn't believe the guy was a cop. "Stay on the ground!"

I looked up just in time to see Josephine dive into the water some distance down the beach. Cedric dove in after her, tackling Josephine in a grand show of splashing and flailing arms. I couldn't even imagine what Josephine had been hoping to accomplish by heading into the ocean, especially in the growing dark. Escape by swimming to Cuba?

Cedric dragged Josephine out of the water, threw her onto the ground, and cuffed her. Then he dragged her to her feet and shoved her in front of him. The two of them headed back toward us, Josephine limping and howling in pain.

"She shot me!" Josephine's left shoulder was bleeding. "Arrest that bitch!"

"Don't move," I warned Isabel.

I heard the sirens about thirty seconds before a team of cops descended on the beach. Cedric must've called for backup. Thank God. I didn't want Isabel trying to make a run for it.

Cedric was breathing a little heavy as he approached us, one hand on Josephine's uninjured shoulder, the other gripping her cuffed wrists behind her back.

Hailey peered at him, confused, then staggered to her feet. "Cedric? What's going on?"

"I'll fill you in later," he said, shoving Josephine toward one of the uniformed cops. He read Josephine her rights.

Cedric talked to another group of the cops, then they moved toward us. Realizing I had Isabel's gun in my hand, I quickly tossed it to the ground and threw my hands in the air. Beside me, Isabel cursed.

"That gun wasn't mine," I said quickly as the cops drew close.

"Hey, look who's here." A goofy smile erupted on Hailey's face.

I shook my head and laughed dryly. Actually, I'd have been a little disappointed if Montoya and Schaefer hadn't appeared on the scene.

I smiled brightly and said, "Hello, Officer Schaefer."

He scowled at me, but I thought I detected a little twitch at the corners of his mouth. "Muller."

Montoya patted down Isabel, then handcuffed her.

"What is it with you two?" he asked. "Always finding trouble."

"We don't have to find it," Hailey slurred. "It finds us just fine."

"Is she high?" Schaefer pointed at her, his frown deepening.

"I think someone drugged her fruit punch," I explained. "She needs to go to the hospital."

"Hey, Gibson!" Schaefer hollered, and Cedric turned. "Send down a medic!"

"I thought his last name was Jones," I said. "Oh, let me guess. He's undercover?"

Schaefer merely grunted.

"Are you arresting us again?" Hailey asked, leaning against one of the lifeguard stand's support beams.

"We never arrested you before," Montoya said. "But don't tempt me."

"Hmm, maybe he's flirting with me, Lex." Hailey held out one wrist. "Go ahead, big guy. Cuff me."

"Hailey, be quiet." I pushed her arm down, then slipped mine around her shoulders. "Lean on me. You're going for a ride in the ambulance."

"I am?" She beamed at me, then back at Schaefer. "That's awful sweet of you, Schontoya and Maefer."

Montoya smothered a laugh.

"God, is she this bad when she's drunk?" Schaefer asked.

I pursed my lips. "Worse."

"That's right. We witnessed that the first time we met

you two." Montoya eyed us. "Maybe you ought to consider joining the police academy."

Schaefer rolled his eyes. "God help us."

The officers departed, and a couple of medics came down to the beach to check Hailey over. They checked me as well, but I was fine. Cedric hurried over too.

"I've got to haul Josephine down to the station," he said.

"Why?" I asked.

"Murder. Her boyfriend, for one."

"Oh, my God." I could hardly believe my ears. "You're sure?"

"I've been watching Ms. Coletti for a long time."

"Wow." If this was true, then Josephine had certainly had me and Hailey fooled.

"Yeah, it's a seedy story, and you'll hear all about it later." Cedric looked at Hailey. "Is she all right?"

"Her vitals are good," one of the medics said. "We're taking her to the hospital as a precautionary measure."

Cedric nodded. "You going with her?" he asked me.

"You know it."

"Are you sure you're okay to drive?"

"It was Hailey who got the sleeping pills, not me." I walked with him toward my car and briefly explained how I hadn't had any of the punch. "I still can't believe you're a cop."

"And I can't believe how fast Josephine can run in this sand in high heels!" Cedric shook his head. "Holy shit, do women take lessons for that stuff?"

"Josephine's a special breed."

"Lucy—you've got some 'splaining to do!" Hailey called over her shoulder as the paramedics helped her into the ambulance.

I shook my head, trying not to laugh. *Shit*, this whole thing wasn't funny, but . . .

"You think she's gonna be all right?" Cedric asked.

I grinned at him. "Something tells me Hailey's going to be fine. See ya around, Officer."

Twenty-one

Hailey

I woke up knowing that something was wrong. I was disoriented, my head heavy and fuzzy. Blinking several times, I tried to focus. Lord, had I danced with Jose Cuervo last night? Finally, my brain connected with my eyes and I started to see colors. Pale blue walls. A myriad of colorful flowers.

Alarm gripped me. I was in a hospital.

"Welcome back," Lexie said.

My gaze flitted to the right. Lexie rose from the chair by my bed and stood beside me. "How're you feeling, Sherlock?"

"Ugh. Awful. Did you get the license number of the truck that hit me?"

"It wasn't a truck." Lexie sighed softly. "Sweetie, I don't

know how to tell you this, but it was Josephine, at our grand opening. She slipped you some sleeping pills—prescription-strength."

"Why?" I tried to lift my head, and the room spun. "What exactly happened?"

"I honestly don't know. Cedric is going to tell us everything later. All I know is he's been working undercover, and he arrested Josephine."

"I thought I was hallucinating that part." I groaned. "God, I can't get awake."

"That's okay. Just rest, babe. We've got all the time in the world."

I drifted off to sleep.

They let me go home later that day, and by that evening I felt fine. I'd had a nice big latte from Starbucks to give me the caffeine kick I needed. When Cedric called to check on me—for the third time since last night, Lexie said—I invited him to meet me and Lexie at the bookstore, which was closed, for a Whipped Delight. It would give us a quiet place to talk.

"Now, there's irony in that," Cedric said in response to my invitation.

"What do you mean?" I asked.

"I'll explain when I see you."

When Cedric arrived at the store, Lexie made Whipped Delights for the three of us, and we settled at the coffee counter with our drinks.

Seeing Cedric, I couldn't help but notice something was different about him. Actually, more than one thing. Like he was walking taller or something. And he even seemed cuter. I studied him, trying to figure out what had happened to him.

He took a sip of his drink and sighed his pleasure. "Thanks, ladies. For this, and for the opportunity to talk."

Yes, something was different, all right! As if miraculously cured, Cedric no longer sprayed spittle when he talked. And he'd had a slight overbite before, which was mysteriously gone now. So was his chronic halitosis.

"What did you do to yourself?" I asked, scrutinizing his face. Or was I still partly hallucinating because of those pills?

"You mean the mouthpiece?" He grinned, showing off a row of white, even teeth. "It was part of my disguise. Pretty good, huh?"

"Uh, yeah." *Wow.*

I gave him a slow once-over, and another lightbulb went off in my brain. For the first time, Cedric wasn't wearing a pair of awful polyester pants. Instead, he had on faded jeans that fit him nicely, and a black T-shirt that complemented his sandy blond hair.

Hmm . . .

"I was glad to get rid of it, though," Cedric said. "It made me spit when I talked, and the material it was made out of gave me bad breath."

"Really?" Lexie widened her eyes. "We hadn't noticed."

I gave her the evil eye behind Cedric's back, then smiled as he faced me once again.

"So," I said, getting to the serious business. "Josephine really killed Rafael?"

"Mmm-hmm. Josephine, AKA Joseph Coletti."

"But why?" Lexie looked as dismayed as I felt. "And what about Gina?"

"He killed her too, I'm afraid."

Lexie and I gasped. I threw a hand over my chest.

"I don't understand," I said.

"It's a long and complicated story," Cedric said. "I'll try to explain it as best I can." He paused to sip his Whipped Delight before continuing. "When Rafael met Bianca Sanchez—then broke up with her to go back to Josephine— Louie Delvecchio found out his ex had been dumped for a transsexual. Louie—who still felt proprietary over her even though they'd broken up—gave Bianca a hard time about it. I guess he got a sick kick out of the whole thing. Like it was her punishment to end up with half a man after leaving a guy like him. What Bianca tells me is that Louie then went about finding all he could about Rafael. At first she thought he was going to have Rafael offed, but when he learned about Rafael's drag queen lover, Louie thought of a better plan. He convinced Bianca to make nice with Josephine so he could use her club as a place to push crack cocaine, crystal meth, and Ecstasy.

"Apparently, Bianca wasn't crazy about the idea. In fact, she hated it. Told Louie that wasn't going to happen, because she hated Josephine, and vice versa. Louie got mad. And the man's right scary when he's mad. He's been under investigation for all sorts of crimes, but until now, nothing's been able to stick. Witnesses disappeared—that sort of thing. So Bianca had a reason to be scared. In any case, Louie went straight to Josephine and threatened her. Told her he'd kill her, Rafael, and anyone else in her family if she didn't cooperate with his plan."

"The way so many of those drug dealers or Mafia types do when they find a venue to make some cash." I shook my head. "So maybe Louie killed Gina after all."

"Hailey, let him explain." Lexie waved her hand at me. "He said it was Josephine."

"I can't believe that," I said, dismayed. "Her own aunt?"

"Sadly," Cedric began, "murder within a family happens more than you'd like to think. Anyway, it didn't take too much arm-twisting to get Josephine to cave to Louie's demands, because she got a cut of the drug money. Everything was going along just fine until Rafael found out about it."

"Josephine said Rafael did drugs." I couldn't help interrupting him.

"That wasn't exactly true," Cedric said. "He had in the past, yes. But he'd cleaned up his act after he got out of prison, and he wanted to stay clean. Rafael was pretty upset when he found out what his lover was doing. In fact, a friend of mine who worked that case against Rafael said he'd always been suspicious that Josephine had been the real culprit, but that she'd coerced Rafael to say the stash of drugs we'd found in the place was his. My friend believes that, and so do I. Josephine had Rafael right where she wanted him—desperate to maintain the life he'd become accustomed to. He took one for the team, so to speak.

"But when it came to this new scam, Rafael wanted no part of it. He begged Josephine to stop, and when she refused, he threatened to turn her in to the police. He apparently confided to Bianca that he thought Josephine was the one who'd supplied the Ecstasy to some teenagers—the ones who died a while back?"

"Oh, my God!" Lexie gasped. "Josephine tried to tell us Bianca had done that!"

"Nope. It was Josephine. She'd gotten the X from Louie as a partial payment for favors performed—if you get my drift. One of Louie's boys had a thing for drag queens."

I shivered in repulsion. It seemed there was no end to the twists and turns in this story. "Go on."

"Well, Josephine was already furious with Rafael over his affair with Bianca. She hated the fact that Bianca could give him the one thing she couldn't—a baby. Of course, Bianca ended up getting an abortion, but by then Josephine had already made up her mind. Rafael was going to pay for all the pain and trouble he'd caused her. And he certainly wasn't going to stop her lucrative arrangement with Louie. Rafael became a liability. So she started injecting his food with mercury."

"With a syringe!" I gestured triumphantly at Lexie. "Remember?"

"Hailey saw a syringe in one of Josephine's bathrooms when we were visiting her," Lex said to Cedric.

"You girls were sure making me nervous," he replied,

331

"hanging around Josephine. Especially once I got to know you." He smiled at me.

"Tell us the rest," Lexie urged with a wave of her hand.

"Josephine knew Rafael had a stomach ulcer, which would allow his body to absorb enough mercury to kill him," Cedric said. "She gradually increased the amount she put in his food, hoping to make his death look like a heart attack, since mercury poisoning can induce heart failure. She'd gotten away with it before, with J. B. Huntington. The coroner really did write his death up as a heart attack, but Mr. Huntington's body was recently exhumed. A new autopsy showed the mercury-induced heart attack was no accident, and it wasn't a case of bad seafood."

"What about Bianca?" Lexie asked. "Who ran her off the road?"

"One of Louie's boys. Louie wanted to scare her enough to make her stay away from you. Louie snuck her out of the hospital and helped her relocate. But we found her. Up in Boca Raton. She's currently under our protection as a witness in this case. This time, Big Lou is going down."

"Where did Josephine get the mercury she used on Rafael?" I asked.

"I suspect she got some of it from Louie, since she gave Rafael a gift of some soaps and skin-lightening cream that are outlawed in the United States, as well as quite a few other countries, because of the mercury content."

I remembered seeing some fancy little soaps in a dish in Josephine's bathroom. I'd almost used one. Holy crap!

"She also extracted some from some old thermometers she bought off the Internet, and from some topical medicines that are—again—outlawed."

"Wow, she was pretty creative." Lexie shook her head. "And deceptive. I just can't believe this."

"But Gina?" I asked. I still couldn't wrap my mind around that one. "Why?"

"Because Josephine started to get greedy. Saw how much money she was making at the club, and she approached Gina about using the bookstore as a front to sell even more drugs."

I sucked in a deep breath. "Please tell me you're kidding."

"I wish I was." He pursed his lips. "But Josephine gave me a complete statement over a six-and-a-half-hour interview. According to her, Gina refused to do it, but Louie started putting on the pressure, making threats again. He too wanted more cash. I know you two are going to feel betrayed by what I'm about to tell you, but the truth is, Gina already knew that Louie was making threats previously. To her as well as to Josephine, which is why she was packing up and closing the store. She needed to skip town in a hurry."

"And she needed the money to do it!" Lexie's expression grew furious. "So she sold us the store, knowing the possible harm that could come our way. I can't believe she did that to me and Hailey!"

I looked at Lexie, feeling her pain. I hated to think ill of the dead, but I could think of a few choice words for Gina, were she still here.

"I think she was just scared and made a bad choice," Cedric said. "And I know she regretted it. Like I said, Josephine spilled her guts once we had her in the interrogation room. She told us that she showed up at the store one morning—I guess Gina was waiting to meet you to give you some keys?—and she wanted to talk to Gina about business. Tried to get her to cancel the sale of the store since she didn't think you two would be down with using it as a spot to sell drugs. Gina refused. Told her off, actually. She said the sale was final, and not only that, she'd decided she couldn't leave town without you two knowing the truth. That's why she really wanted to meet you. She apparently told Josephine that she had better get Louie to back off because if not, he'd find himself in prison along with Josephine. She was prepared to go to battle for you two.

"Well, Josephine wasn't hearing it. She went into a rage, bludgeoned Gina with a steel-heeled shoe. Our guys searched her house last night and found it. Man, that thing had a stiletto heel this long!" He held up his hand, his thumb and index finger about four inches apart.

"Murdered with a designer heel." Lexie shook her head. "Only Josephine could come up with that one."

"She claims she didn't actually mean to kill Gina," Cedric said. "She just wanted to wound her enough to scare her into keeping her mouth shut. But I don't believe her. The wounds Gina suffered were pretty devastating."

"Tell me about it." Lexie shivered, and I knew that she too couldn't shake the mental image of Gina lying in our storeroom.

"What about the spiked punch she gave me?" I asked. "Was she trying to kill me too?"

"Oh, she had that planned pretty nicely. She stayed around helping you clean up so she'd be the last one there with you two. Obviously, she was hoping to drug both of you, but Lexie, you didn't drink the punch. Once she had you both in la-la land, she was going to smother you—nice and easy."

My mouth hit the floor. "Nice and easy?"

Cedric held up a hand. "I know. It's not easy to hear."

"So, when she couldn't drug me . . . ?" Lexie prompted.

"She had to come up with a new plan," Cedric explained. "Since you'd started to get groggy, Hailey, she figured the next best thing was to help Lexie get you home. Then she encouraged Lexie to head to Ocean Drive and the beach. At your place, she'd be seen on a security camera. At the beach, she hoped to carry out her murderous plan on a dark stretch of sand with no witnesses. She meant to drown both of you. You first, Lexie, while Hailey was out of it, and then Hailey."

"That conniving, murderous bitch!" Lexie's eyes flashed anew.

A quiet anger churned inside of me. And here I'd felt sorry for her. Put my life at risk trying to help her. I wished I could find Josephine and put my cowboy boot up her butt.

"I want to see her," I said.

"Josephine?" Cedric arched his brows.

"Damned right! I've got a thing or two I want to say to her!"

"Hailey, I don't know if that's such a good idea," Lexie said.

"No, maybe she should," Cedric agreed, much to my surprise. I'd expected him to try and talk me out of it. "You both need to do whatever it takes to find closure. We can hook you up with some victims' advocates to counsel you too, if you'd like."

"Thank you, Cedric." Lexie patted his arm. "You're the best."

"Yeah, you are," I said. Even Travis, who proclaimed to be a cowboy, had never heroically rescued me from an armed gunman . . . or in this case, an armed woman and a desperate transsexual.

"Does that mean you'll go out to Mango's with me on Friday?" he asked with a smile.

"Yeah. I will." I winked at Lexie. "But only if you bring a friend for Lex."

"Hey, is Tyrone an undercover cop too?" Lexie asked. She sounded a little hopeful.

"Nope. Just a good friend willing to help me out." Cedric smiled. "I was eager to go out with you, Hailey, but I also wanted to keep an eye on you and Lexie, knowing you'd been the ones to find Rafael's body."

"So that's why you conveniently kept showing up where we were," I said.

"Uh-huh."

"And is it a safe bet your last name isn't Jones?" I went on.

"Nope. It's Gibson. And I go by Eric, not Cedric."

I vaguely remembered somebody calling him Gibson. *Wow.* Cedric was a cop—named Eric.

I'd always had a thing for guys named Eric, ever since I'd started watching *The Bold and the Beautiful.*

"You know, you were stalking me," I said, folding my arms over my chest. I wasn't willing to let him completely off the hook.

Eric grinned, then shrugged. "What can I say? I couldn't help myself. Shall we write it off as police protection?"

Lexie laughed. "I told you he was all right."

"Police protection, huh?" I mulled it over for a moment. "I kind of like that."

He stood. "See you Friday, then?"

"We'll be there," Lexie said.

"Wait one second, mister."

Eric met my gaze. "Yes?"

"First—what about Isabel? What's going to happen to her?"

"Oh, her. She'll probably get off with a slap on the wrist. Some probation at the most. I think she'll make a case for temporary insanity, and considering what happened to her father, I don't even see her going to trial."

I nodded. That made sense. "And now my second question."

"Fire away," Eric said.

"I don't understand what your disguise was. Yeah, you look different, and definitely more refined now, but it's not like you had a dark wig on or anything."

"My aim was to look like I wasn't a cop, but a hopeless doofus. I'm sure you'd say I passed with flying colors."

I glanced away, smiling sheepishly.

"I'll show you the real me on Friday," Eric said, his tone full of a sexy kind of confidence. It was a bit of a turn-on.

"Don't forget to phone and tell me when I can go see Josephine," I called out as he made his way to the door.

"All right. If you're sure." He shook his head as he reached for the door handle. "I'm still amazed at how fast Josephine ran in those high heels. Damn." He chuckled. "Lends a whole new meaning to 'drag racing.'"

Lexie and I laughed, then sobered once Eric was gone.

"I'll never look at this place without remembering," Lexie said.

"I know." I wrinkled my nose. "And that sucks. But at least we know Gina meant to warn us. I guess she *was* just scared." I was still saddened by her violent death, now that my initial anger had worn off.

"We'd better lock up. Tomorrow's a workday."

Lex and I left, thinking the next day would be a slow day, since we'd had so much business on Saturday.

Boy were we wrong.

All day long—and all through the rest of the week—curious customers flocked in to browse the shelves and question us about what had happened.

338

We didn't tell them everything. After all, we had a business to run and protect, and we didn't need any old secrets spoiling our success. We merely told them Josephine had been arrested for selling drugs. Of course, most knew by now that Gina had been murdered at the store, and to our surprise, they seemed to take a morbid fascination in finding out that the bookstore was the scene of a real live murder, and of the former owner, no less.

Go figure human nature.

Personally, it was an emotional week for me. I know it was for Lexie as well. I was sick to my stomach over the fact that Josephine had chosen such a wretched life of crime. A life of crime she was willing to kill to protect. Even if that meant murdering her beloved partner, her own aunt, and two people who'd tried to be nothing but the most supportive of friends for her.

Apparently, even the money J. B. Huntington had left her hadn't been enough to satisfy her greedy need for expensive things.

By the time Eric arranged to put me and Lexie on Josephine's visitors' list at the Pre-Trial Detention Center, I'd had plenty of time to think over what I wanted to say to her. I took petty pleasure in seeing her dressed in the jailhouse orange I'd so feared. Sans wig and makeup, Josephine/Joey looked like a scared little boy.

With huge boobs.

I looked at her through the Plexiglas as I lifted the phone to speak to her. On the other side, she put her own phone receiver to her ear.

Crocodile tears welled in her eyes, as usual. "Hailey, I know I was awful to you, but I was out of my mind. I just wasn't myself. Can you find it in that gold heart of yours to ever forgive me?"

"Maybe," I lied.

Josephine's shoulders drooped with relief. "Oh, bless you! Honey, I'm so terribly sorry—"

"Hold it," I said firmly, and Josephine promptly shut up. "I want to ask you a couple of questions, and please, give me straight answers, okay?"

Josephine nodded shakily. "Okay."

"How could you go from the Joey Lexie and I knew to this?" I indicated her prison garb with my free hand.

"Well," she began softly, "I've always felt like I was a girl trapped inside a boy's body. My parents didn't understand, God bless their souls, but I grew up in a different—"

"That's not what I'm talking about and you know it."

Josephine sobbed, putting her hand against her forehead. "I know. It's just that I *don't* know. Know what I mean?"

"Cut the drama, Josephine. You're not performing anymore."

"I guess you'll never understand." With tear-filled eyes, she gave me an envious look. "You're a gorgeous woman, and you've got everything going for you."

So that's what this was about? The fact that deep down she wanted to be a woman? Was that the best she could do to explain her behavior—come up with a lame-ass excuse the way so many criminals did? The ones who blamed their horrible youths for their inability to follow the straight and narrow path as adults?

Well, I wasn't buying it. And I knew right then and there that nothing she said was ever going to make me feel better about any of this.

"Were you really going to jump off the roof of your house that day?" I asked.

"Of course not," she answered without hesitating. "You don't really think I'd leave my precious baby Bling-Bling . . ." She let the words trail off.

I hadn't thought about the little dog. "You've left her now." I stated the obvious. "What's going to happen to her?" I wondered if Lexie's condo allowed pets other than turtles.

"Rueben has her. He got her out quick, before the FBI seized my property." She shrugged. "He was my one phone call."

"I'm glad your dog is fine," I said. And I was. But I had nothing more to say to this bitch.

"Good-bye, Joey." I said this deliberately, to strip Josephine of the one thing that mattered so much to her but was beyond her control—her true sexual orientation. "Enjoy your stay here at Hotel Hell. I'm sure the boys will love ya. Oh, and say hello to Louie for us, would you?"

He'd been tracked down and arrested just days after Josephine. Eric had assured me he'd be looking at life in prison, especially since they'd made a plea-bargain deal with Bianca to testify against him—him and Joey both.

As for Joey—with two murders under his belt, he'd likely be facing the death penalty. Whenever the state got around to it in twenty years or so.

I couldn't feel sorry for Joey. He'd made his bed. And he deserved whatever he got for murdering three decent people.

I set down the phone without so much as a backward glance. Then I headed out to the small waiting area to meet Lexie, since she hadn't wanted to come in with me. Together, we walked out of the Detention Center and greeted a day that was perfect. A cloudless blue sky, no humidity clinging to us like a second skin.

We gazed up at that sky, then exchanged a glance that required no words.

We had a beautiful day, and we had each other's friendship. The rest we'd put behind us.

Epilogue

Lexie

Before Friday night came, I went on a shopping spree. For me, shopping's the kind of therapy that can cure whatever ails you.

That and chocolate, of course.

Not that I needed to be cured. The day that Hailey and I left the Detention Center, we had closed the door on Josephine and the ugly past. Now we were ready to toast a new future.

I'd gone to the upscale Bal Harbour Shops, but didn't bring Hailey, since I wanted to surprise even her with what I would wear. I'd gotten shoes at Gucci, a to-die-for dress at Fendi, and a new clutch at Louis Vuitton—in addition to what I would wear tonight. I'd also piled up on discounted stuff from Saks Fifth Avenue. I was ready—emotionally and fashionably—to turn a new page in the book of our lives with grand style.

In my bedroom, I looked at myself in the mirror. A smiled played on my lips. Hell, yeah, I was ready for tonight. I hoped Tyrone would appreciate my new outfit.

"Wanna see me now?" I called out to the living room from a small crack in my door.

"You know I've been waiting all week to see your special outfit!" Hailey called back.

With that, I exited my bedroom and strolled into the living room, an extra pep in my step.

Hailey let out a laugh. "Ohmygod! You're a cowgirl!"

I twirled around in my denim skirt, showing off my low-cut blouse, red cowboy boots, and matching hat. "Hey, don't laugh. It worked for you with Ced—with Eric." I grinned at her. "Maybe there's something to this whole cowgirl fantasy after all."

"Yee-*ha*! You look hot, girlfriend," Hailey said. "Let's go."

She looked hot too, wearing a simple tan-colored dress and her now-favorite rhinestone-studded sandals.

At the door, I scooped up her car keys off the hall table instead of mine. When she looked at me in surprise, I said, "I'm going all out with the fantasy, girl."

Downstairs, we climbed into her truck and headed for Mango's. Halfway there, Hailey's cell phone rang. I dug it out of her purse for her.

"Hello." She rolled her eyes at me, and I wondered if it was Eric.

"Hey, Bailey. No, I don't know if they're planning to televise Josephine's trial." Hailey made a face.

I could hear Bailey's rapid-fire voice buzzing away on the other end like Charlie Brown's teacher. I smothered a smile.

"Well, I doubt they'll make it into a movie." She rolled her eyes again, nearly running the red light at Fifth. "Yes, Bailey, I promise. Yes, I know you've always wanted to be an actress." More buzzing. "I can ask Lexie."

Abruptly, Hailey held the phone away from her ear, and even I could hear Bailey's shout.

"Corey! Get that snake out of here this instant! No, Connie, don't touch it!"

Hailey flipped the phone shut. "She had to go."

We laughed.

"So, what is it you're supposed to ask me?"

"If you can fix Bailey up with a good agent so she can play the part of Bianca in our movie."

"If I had a dollar for every wannabe actor I've talked to . . ."

"I can only imagine." Hailey shook her head. "You know what—I'll bet my sister wants to play Bianca so she can make out with the actor who plays the stripper! And after she gave me such a hard time about going to Fantasies!"

"You should invite her there one day. How much you wanna bet she'd become a convert?"

"You think I can sway her over to the dark side?"

"Wouldn't it be fun to try? And you could bring that little camcorder of yours—get the evidence on tape."

345

Hailey tipped her head back and laughed. "Girlfriend, I like the way you think!"

I looked toward the Mango's entrance as Hailey parked in a spot. "Well, there's Eric. And there's Tyrone. I must say, Hailey, they're both looking mighty fine."

"I know," Hailey said, a touch of something—wistfulness?—in her voice.

"Maybe this is the night you're gonna get lucky. Wipe Travis what's-his-face from your memory bank forever!"

"Maybe," Hailey agreed. And now I picked up on what was in her tone.

Lust.

I had totally expected her to reject my suggestion, and now that she hadn't, my mouth hit the floor. "Hailey . . . ?"

She opened her door. "Come on. They're waiting."

"Hailey!" I said in an urgent whisper, but she ignored me and started across the street.

This time, not only did Eric drink in the sight of her, she drank in the sight of him.

Wonders never ceased.

Inside the club, we found a table in a back corner and Tyrone ordered a bottle of champagne. When he popped the cork on the Dom Pérignon, we all erupted in applause.

"To us," Tyrone said, gesturing his glass around the table.

"To new beginnings," Eric said.

Hailey and I looked at each other, and I swear, we read

each other's minds. "To no more dead bodies," we said in unison, and then we started to laugh.

Eric held his glass high. "I'll drink to that."

He did, and so did the rest of us.

Then Eric took Hailey's hand and urged her to her feet. "And now, Pink Sugar, let me teach you how to dance."

A+

AUTHOR
INSIGHTS,
EXTRAS, &
MORE...

FROM
KAYLA PERRIN
BRENDA MOTT
AND
AVON A

The Daily Blab
Who Wants to Know?
by Lucy Gossiply

Hello, dear readers. Lucy here, with a scrumptious tidbit for you, straight from the hot chick-lit world—an interview with coauthors Kayla Perrin and Brenda Mott. These ladies are set to take the publishing world by storm! Now, I know, authors always get asked the question, "Where do you get your ideas?" and that's exactly what we want to know. So, Kayla Perrin and Brenda Mott, how did the story *How To Kill a Guy in 10 Days* come to be?

KAYLA: The idea started as a joke, actually. And it began with a turtle.

BRENDA: LOL. So true. Kayla was already a multipublished author with several BET books under her belt, and a new contract with a second major publisher. I myself had done two POD (print-on-demand) books with iUniverse and Xlibris. I asked Kayla what she thought it took to sell to the "big guys" of category, something I'd been attempting for fifteen years.

KAYLA: I told her the key would be to figure out what the next "hot" topic was likely to be . . . such as cowboys, babies, amnesia, runaway brides, etc. We began to laugh and play what-if. I'd recently told Brenda a story of a real-life hero who had saved a hapless turtle from certain death as roadkill by pulling his car over and removing the turtle from a busy Florida roadside to the safety of some grass and shade trees near a pond.

BRENDA: I jokingly said, "Now, that's a hero for me." And we began to think of appropriate titles. We came up with *The Cowboy, the Baby, and the Runaway Turtle*. From there, the brainstorming took off.

KAYLA: And the omens! Don't forget the omens.

BRENDA: Absolutely! From that moment on, Kayla and I couldn't go anywhere without running into a turtle in one form or another—I kid you not.

KAYLA: Exactly! One night shortly after our conversation, I was waiting for a table in a busy Florida restaurant, and decided to have a cocktail meanwhile. Leaning on the bar, I took a sip of my drink and turned to look around the room. Right there, just feet away from me, was a bronze sculpture of a turtle! I nearly choked on my drink.

BRENDA: Without knowing this happened to Kayla, I went to a friend's house—in Colorado, where I lived at the time—to have a look at her garden. As we strolled the path through the flowers and vegetables, I looked over at a decorative sign she had among her lawn ornaments. It read: CAUTION—TURTLE CROSSING. I chuckled to myself.

KAYLA: Next, I was gathering some old magazines to recycle, clearing away a bit of clutter. I decided to thumb through them before tossing them, and chose one at random. I flipped it open, and there on that very page was a photograph of a turtle.

BRENDA: My day job at the time was working as a bank teller, and while at the drive-up window one morning, I greeted a customer who had her little girl with her. A lot of people came through the drive-up with dogs in their cars. I noticed the little girl was holding something in her lap, and my jaw nearly dropped—literally—when I saw that it was a live turtle! A big one. I called Kayla on the phone that night, and we shared our experiences with seeing turtles everywhere.

KAYLA: I told Brenda perhaps this was an omen. That

we should write our cowboy/baby/runaway turtle book. We had a good laugh, but really didn't take things seriously. Until we kept seeing more and more turtles.

BRENDA: I'd turn on the TV and flip to a wildlife show and, of course, the topic would be turtles.

KAYLA: I went for a walk in a park near my townhouse, and there by the water, where I rarely saw anything but ducks, was a turtle.

BRENDA: I saw a boy in the grocery store wearing a T-shirt with a sea turtle on it. And on and on this went! Neither Kayla nor I had previously seen an abundance of turtles in our daily lives, yet now they were popping up everywhere.

KAYLA: We chatted by phone again and decided maybe this wasn't so funny after all. Maybe it really did mean something. We began to brainstorm in earnest.

BRENDA: You have to understand that all this happened years ago, long before the chick-lit genre even existed. So we initially started plotting out our book as a cozy whodunit. But we didn't stop there. Why one book, when we could do a series?

KAYLA: We thought it would be fun to have some sort of turtle theme in each of the books. Right away, we decided to use chocolate turtles in the first one. We even chatted about future covers—maybe a little turtle logo could appear in the corner of each one, worked into the cover art in some way.

BRENDA: Florida seemed like a good setting for the book, since the whole thing had started with the rescued Florida turtle. We chose Miami, as Kayla was living there at the time. We also thought it would be fun to have two protagonists, two women who were best friends like Kayla and me.

KAYLA: And like Bren and me, one woman would be black, the other white. Our excitement built as we thought of the possibilities of drawing in readers for a different experience. While Bren had always read BET books, we had once discussed the fact, pertaining to our romance novels, that love was not a color and that people of all races should be open to reading outside their own skin color, which is often not the case.

BRENDA: So now we had our setting and the rough beginnings of an idea, and even the names of our protagonists. But what would be our heroines' occupations? The obvious came to mind, since I'd recently traded in my teller job for one as manager of a bookstore. Lexie and Hailey would own a bookstore!

KAYLA: We gave our protagonists surnames, and plotted a little further. Brenda wrote the opening chapter and sent it to me via e-mail. I read through it, added some scenes, and the one chapter expanded into two.

BRENDA: We went back and forth this way, also doing further plotting by telephone, until we had three chapters, and the sketchy beginnings of a synopsis. Kayla and I both write by the seat of our pants . . . into the mist . . . whatever you'd like to call it.

KAYLA: We were each still working on individual projects as well, and one day a few months later, Brenda finally got "the call." She'd sold to Harlequin Superromance.

BRENDA: I couldn't believe it. After fifteen years of rejection! I began working on another project for my follow-up book. And on a personal front, my husband and I bought land in Tennessee, and, while I was on deadline, made a fifteen-hundred-mile move from Colorado with my son, Chance, and our five horses, six dogs, and four cats!

KAYLA: Shortly after Brenda's move, I had my daughter, Chloe. It seemed Bren and I were both busy with so many things. The turtle book, as we called it, got moved to the back burner.

BRENDA: More like the back closet. We totally put it

away, and didn't touch it for about four years. And then all of a sudden, chick-lit emerged as the hot new genre of the women's fiction world. Kayla and I talked about how ironic it was that our turtle book was funny and sassy and fit the tone of chick-lit like a key in a lock! Who would've known, all those years ago, when we began our idea?

KAYLA: We decided it was time for our turtle baby to be born! We plotted the synopsis in detail over the phone, and continued our method of writing material, trading it back and forth via e-mail.

BRENDA: I'll never forget how hard we laughed plotting the synopsis. Like most writers, I normally hate doing a synopsis. I'd rather go to the dentist. I told Kayla I couldn't believe how much fun this one was. She agreed.

KAYLA: And our writing voices blended together so nicely. At times, we honestly couldn't remember who had written what as we went back over each draft and polished and repolished, over and over until the book was finished.

BRENDA: We topped it off with a catchy title—*How to Kill a Guy in 10 Days*—and within just over a week, our agent sold the manuscript to Avon/HarperCollins. I can't tell you how thrilled we were! I'm so happy to be a part of the Avon family, and to finally get to write with my buddy Kayla.

KAYLA: Right back atcha, girlfriend!

And of course, dear readers, I had to ask . . . what's next for Hailey and Lexie?

BRENDA: We've already started plotting our girls' next adventure.

KAYLA: It'll be in Miami, of course.

BRENDA: And it will involve turtles in some way, of course.

KAYLA: We hope you all enjoyed *How to Kill a Guy in 10 Days*, and had as much fun reading it as we did writing it.

So, there you have it, dear readers. Until next time . . .

Hugs and kisses,
Lucy Gossiply

Kayla Perrin

Brenda Mott

KAYLA PERRIN attended the University of Toronto and York University, where she obtained a Bachelor of Arts in English and Sociology and a Bachelor of Education, respectively. As well as being a certified teacher, Kayla works in the Toronto film industry as an actress, appearing in many television shows, commercials, and movies. She is also the author of the Essence bestseller *Sisters of Theta Phi Kappa.* Kayla is also the 2002 recipient of the Romantic Times Career Achievement Award for Multicultural Romance.

Though **BRENDA MOTT** grew up in a suburb of Denver in an apartment complex, she's always had a great love of the outdoors and horses and often includes horses and other animals in her stories. "Write what you know is basically the main rule I live by." Brenda is the author of several romances.